THE IDES OF MARCH

VALERIO MASSIMO MANFREDI

THE IDES OF MARCH

Translated from the Italian by Christine Feddersen-Manfredi

McArthur & Company
Toronto

First published in Canada in 2009 by
McArthur & Company
322 King Street West, Suite 402
Toronto, Ontario
M5V 1J2
www.mcarthur-co.com

First published in English in the United Kingdom by Macmillan

First published in Italian as *Le Idi di Marzo* by
Arnoldo Mondadori Editore S.p.A., Milano

Library and Archives Canada Cataloguing in Publication

Manfredi, Valerio
        The ides of March / Valerio Massimo Manfredi ; translated
from the Italian by Christine Feddersen-Manfredi.

Translation of: Idi di marzo.
ISBN 978-1-55278-815-8

        1. Caesar, Julius--Fiction. 2. Rome--History--53-44 B.C.--
Fiction.
I. Feddersen-Manfredi, Christine II. Title.

PQ4873.A47I3413 2009   853'.914   C2009-904278-9

Typeset by SetSystems Ltd, Saffron Waldon, Essex
Cover illustration by Luca Tarlazzi © 3ntini Service

Printed in Canada by Webcom

10 9 8 7 6 5 4 3 2 1

TO JOHN AND DIANA

Those who are about to die are dead,
and the dead are nothing.

Euripides, Alcestis, 527

1

THE DAY DAWNED GREY. The winter sky was heavy, leaden, the morning a mere hint of light filtering through the vaporous mass spreading over the horizon. Sounds were muffled as well, as dull and sluggish as the clouds veiling the light. The wind came down the Vicus Jugarius in uncertain puffs, like the laboured breathing of a fugitive.

A magistrate appeared in the square at the south end of the Forum. He walked alone, but the insignia he wore made him recognizable all the same, and he was advancing at a brisk pace towards the Temple of Saturn. He slowed in front of the statue of Lucius Junius Brutus, the hero who had overthrown the monarchy nearly five centuries earlier. At the feet of the frowning bronze effigy, on the pedestal bearing his epitaph, someone had scribbled in red lead: 'Do you slumber, Brutus?'

The magistrate shook his head and continued on his way, adjusting the toga that slipped from his narrow shoulders at every flurry. He walked quickly up the temple steps, past the still-steaming altar, and disappeared into the shadows of the portico.

A WINDOW OPENED on the top floor of the House of the Vestals. The virgins who maintained the sacred fire were busy

I

with their duties, while the others were preparing to rest after their night-long vigil.

The Vestalis Maxima, wrapped all in white, had just left the inner courtyard and turned towards the statue of Vesta, which stood in the centre of the cloister, when the earth began to shake beneath her feet. The goddess's head swayed to the right and then to the left. The moulding behind the fountain cracked and a chunk broke off, falling sharply to the ground, the sound amplified by the surrounding silence.

As the Vestal raised her eyes to the wind and clouds, dull thunder could be heard in the distance. Her eyes filled with foreboding. Why was the earth trembling?

ON THE TIBER ISLAND, headquarters to the Ninth Legion, which was stationed outside the city walls under the command of Marcus Aemilius Lepidus, the last shift was going off guard duty. The soldiers and their centurion saluted the Eagle and returned in double file to their quarters. The Tiber flowed turbulently around the island, her dark, swollen waters rising to wash over the bare branches of the alders that bent at her banks.

A HIGH-PITCHED, broken scream punctured the livid silence of dawn. A scream from the residence of the Pontifex Maximus. The House of the Vestals was practically adjacent and the virgins were thrown into panic. They'd heard the scream before, but each time it was worse.

Another scream and the Vestalis Maxima went to the door. From the threshold she could see the bodyguards, two enormous Celts, flanking the door of the Domus. They were apparently impassive. Perhaps they were accustomed to the screams and knew where they came from. Could they be coming from him? From the Pontifex himself? The sound was distorted and mewling now, like the whine of an animal in pain. Hurried footsteps could be heard as a man approached the door

2

carrying a leather bag and made his way past the two Celts, solid and still as telamons. He slipped into the front hall of the ancient building.

The rumble of distant thunder still sounded from the mountains and a stiff wind bowed the tops of the ash trees on the Quirinal. Three trumpet blasts announced the new day. The Vestalis Maxima closed the door to the sanctuary and gathered herself in prayer before the goddess.

THE DOCTOR was met by Calpurnia, the wife of the Pontifex Maximus. She seemed quite frightened.

'Antistius, at last! Come this way quickly. We haven't been able to calm him down this time. Silius is with him.'

Searching through his bag as he followed her, Antistius pulled out a wooden stick covered with leather and entered the room.

Lying on an unkempt bed and dripping with sweat, his eyes staring at nothing, his mouth drooling while his teeth were clenched tight and bared in a snarl, was the Pontifex Maximus, Dictator Perpetuo, Caius Julius Caesar, in the throes of a seizure. The brawny arms of his adjutant, Silius Salvidienus, held him down.

Calpurnia lowered her eyes so that she wouldn't have to see her husband this way and turned to the wall. Meanwhile, Antistius got on to the bed and worked the wooden stick between his patient's teeth until he could force them apart.

'Keep him still!' he ordered Silius. 'Still!'

He extracted a glass phial from his bag and placed a few drops of dark liquid on Caesar's tongue. In a short while, the seizures began to let up, but Silius didn't release his hold until the doctor signalled that he could ease Caesar back down on to his back. The adjutant then gently covered him with a woollen blanket.

Calpurnia drew closer. She wiped the sweat from Caesar's brow and the drool from his mouth, then wet his lips with a piece of linen soaked in cool water. She turned to Antistius.

'What is this terrible thing?' she asked him. 'Why does it happen?'

Caesar now lay in a state of complete prostration. His eyes were closed and his breathing was laboured and heavy.

'The Greeks call it the "sacred disease", because the ancients believed it was the doing of spirits – demons or the gods. Alexander himself suffered from it, so they say, but in reality no one knows what it is. We recognize the symptoms and can only try to limit the damage. The greatest danger is that the person suffering an attack will bite off his tongue with his own teeth. Some have even been suffocated by their tongues. But I've given him his usual sedative, which fortunately seems quite effective. What worries me is the frequency of the attacks. The last one was only two weeks ago.'

'What can we do?'

'Nothing,' replied Antistius, shaking his head. 'We can't do any more than we've already done.'

Caesar opened his eyes and slowly looked around. He then turned to Silius and Calpurnia.

'Leave me alone with him,' he said, gesturing towards the doctor.

Silius shot a puzzled glance at Antistius.

'You can go,' said Antistius. 'There's no immediate danger. But don't go too far. You never know.'

Silius nodded and left the room with Calpurnia. He had always helped and supported her and was her husband's – his commander's – shadow. Centurion of the legendary Tenth Legion, a veteran with twenty years' service, he had salt and pepper hair, dark, damp eyes, as quick as a child's, and the neck of a bull. He followed Calpurnia out like a puppy.

The doctor put his ear to his patient's chest and listened. Caesar's heartbeat was returning to normal.

'Your condition is improving,' he said.

'That doesn't interest me,' replied Caesar. 'Tell me this instead: what would happen if I had such a fit in public? If I fell to the floor foaming at the mouth in the Senate or at the Rostra?'

Antistius bowed his head.

'You don't have an answer for me, do you?'

'No, Caesar, but I understand you. The fact is that these attacks don't give any warning. Or not that I know of.'

'So they depend on the whims of the gods?'

'You believe in the gods?'

'I am the Pontifex Maximus. What should I tell you?'

'The truth. I'm your doctor and if you want me to help you, I have to understand your mind as well as your body.'

'I believe that we are surrounded by mystery. There's room for anything in mystery, even the gods.'

'Hippocrates said that this illness would only be called the "sacred disease" until its causes were discovered.'

'Hippocrates was right but, unfortunately, the disease continues to be "sacred" today and will remain so, I fear, for some time to come. And yet I cannot afford to give any public display of my weaknesses. You can understand that, can't you?'

'I can. But the only one who can tell when an attack is coming on is you. They say that the sacred disease gives no warning, but that each man reacts differently to it. Have you ever had a sign, something that made you think an attack was about to take place?'

Caesar drew a long breath and remained silent, forcing himself to remember. At length, he replied, 'Perhaps. Not any clear sign, nothing that is identical from one time to the next. But occasionally it happens that I see images from other times, suddenly . . . like flashes.'

'What kind of images?'

'Massacres, fields strewn with dead bodies, clouds galloping, shrieking like Furies from hell.'

'They might be actual memories, or simply nightmares. We all have them. You more than anyone, I imagine. No one else has lived a life like yours.'

'No, they're not nightmares. When I say "images", I'm talking about something I actually see in front of me, like I am seeing you now.'

'And are these . . . visions always followed by attacks of this sort?'

'Sometimes they are and sometimes they aren't. I can't say for certain that they are connected to my disease. It's a sly enemy I've made for myself, Antistius, an enemy with no face, who pounces, strikes and slips away like a ghost. I am the most powerful man in the world and yet I'm as helpless in the face of this as the lowest of wretches.'

Antistius sighed. 'If you were anyone else, I would recommend . . .'

'What?'

'That you withdraw into private life. Leave the city, public office, political strife. Others have done so before you: Scipio Africanus, Sulla. Perhaps the disease would let go of you if you let go of your daily battles. But I don't suppose you'd ever follow my advice, would you?'

Caesar raised himself into a sitting position on the side of the bed, then swung his feet to the floor and stood up.

'No. I can't afford to. There are still too many things I must do. I'll live with the risk.'

'Then surround yourself with men you trust. Arrange things so that, if it should happen, someone is there to cover you with a toga and there is a closed litter ready to take you where no one can see you. I will be waiting there for you. When the crisis has passed you will be able to return to what you were doing as if nothing had happened. That's all I can say.'

Caesar nodded. 'It's good advice. You can go now, Antistius. I feel better.'

'I'd rather stay.'

'No. You must have other business to attend to. Send in Silius with my breakfast. I'll have something to eat.'

Antistius nodded. 'As you wish. Along with your breakfast,

Silius will bring you a potion I'll mix for you now. It will help to thin the humours of your spleen. That should provide some relief. Now, lie back and give those stiff limbs a little rest. When you feel stronger, a hot bath and a massage would be in order.'

There was no answer from Caesar and Antistius walked out with a sigh.

HE FOUND Calpurnia in the atrium, sitting in an armchair. She was still wearing her nightgown and she had not bathed or eaten. The signs of strain were evident on her face and in her posture. When she saw Antistius heading for the kitchen, she followed him.

'Well?' she asked. 'What do you think?'

'There's nothing new, but unfortunately I have the impression that the disease has taken hold. For the moment all we can do is seek to limit its effects. However, we can always hope that it will go away as suddenly as it started. Remember that Caesar is a man of great resources.'

'No man can weather so many storms of the body and spirit without suffering lasting damage. The past ten years have been as intense as ten lives and they've taken their toll. Caesar is fifty-six years old, Antistius, and yet he intends to embark on another expedition in the East. Against the Parthians.'

As the doctor was crushing seeds in a mortar and then setting them to boil on the stove, Calpurnia sat down. A maidservant began preparing her usual breakfast, an egg cooked under the embers and some toasted bread.

'And that woman is only making the situation worse.'

Antistius didn't need to ask to whom she was referring. Cleopatra VII, the Queen of Egypt, was living in Caesar's villa on the far side of the Tiber. He fell silent, knowing what would happen if he expressed any opinion at all on the subject. Cleopatra had even brought her child to the villa with her, a boy she'd dared to call Ptolemy Caesar.

'That whore,' Calpurnia continued, realizing that Antistius

was not going to pick up on her invitation to join the conversation. 'I hope she drops dead. I've even had the evil eye put on her, but who knows what antidotes she's found to protect herself, and what philtres she's given my husband to drink to keep him bound to her.'

Antistius couldn't help but speak. 'My lady, any middle-aged man would be flattered to conceive a child with a beautiful woman in the bloom of youth. It makes him feel young, vigorous . . .'

Here his voice dropped off and he bit his tongue: not exactly the most diplomatic of things to tell a woman who had never been able to have children herself.

'Forgive me,' he added hastily. 'This is really no affair of mine. What's more, Caesar doesn't need to feel vigorous. He is vigorous. I've been a doctor my whole life and I've yet to see another man of such a hardy constitution.'

'Never mind. I'm used to hearing such things,' replied Calpurnia. 'What worries me is the enormous burden he is carrying. He can't keep this up much longer and I'm sure there are many men out there who would like nothing better than to see him on his knees. Many of those who feign friendship today would turn into bloodthirsty beasts tomorrow. I trust no one, you understand? Nobody.'

'Yes, my lady, I do,' replied the doctor.

He took his potion off the flame, filtered it and poured it into a cup that he set on the tray where the cook was arranging Caesar's breakfast: fava beans, cheese and flatbread with olive oil.

Silius entered and took only the potion.

'Does he not want breakfast now?' asked Calpurnia.

'No. I've just spoken to him and he's changed his mind. He no longer wants to eat. He's gone out on to the terrace.'

'YOUR POTION, Caesar.'

Caesar had his back to Silius, his hands on the balustrade.

8

He was facing the Aventine Hill, from where a flock of starlings had risen like a dark cloud flying towards the Tiber.

He turned slowly, as if he'd only just realized that Silius was present. He took the steaming potion and set it on the parapet. After a few moments he lifted it to his lips and took a sip.

'Where is Publius Sextius?' he asked after he'd swallowed.

'Centurion Publius Sextius is in Modena, on your orders, Caesar.'

'Yes, yes, I know that, but according to my calculations he should be heading back by now. Has he sent a message?'

'No, not that I know of.'

'If a letter arrives from him, inform me immediately, at any time of day or night and no matter what I am doing.'

'You're expected shortly at the Temple of Jupiter Optimus Maximus at the Capitol to offer a sacrifice. If you're feeling strong enough, of course.'

Caesar took another sip of the potion and looked Silius in the eye.

'Of course. At times I forget I'm the High Priest of Rome and yet it should be my foremost concern . . . No bath and no massage, then.'

'That depends on you, Caesar,' replied Silius.

'Remember: wake me, even if I'm sleeping.'

'Sorry?'

'If a message from Sextius arrives.'

'Of course. Don't worry.'

'It should be the first of my concerns . . .' he repeated, as if talking to himself.

Silius looked at him with a puzzled expression, trying to follow Caesar's meandering thoughts.

'. . . my priesthood, that is. And yet I've never believed that the gods care a whit about us. Why should they?'

'It's the first time I've heard you say such a thing. What are you thinking of, commander?'

'Don't you know why we burn victims on the altar day after

9

day? It's so that the gods will see the smoke rising from our cities and remember not to trample them when they walk invisibly on the earth. Otherwise they would crush us as easily as we crush an ant.'

'What an interesting analogy, sir,' replied Silius. 'Antistius said to drink it all,' he added, pointing.

Caesar picked up the cup again and downed the potion.

'In fact, there is no smoke so black or so dense as that of scorched flesh. Believe me, I know.'

Silius knew as well. And he knew what his commander was thinking of. Silius had been at his side at Pharsalus and at Alexandria, in Africa and in Spain. Ever since Caesar had crossed the Rubicon, the bodies he'd seen burning had been those not of uncivilized enemies but of citizens like himself. The bodies of Roman citizens. Burned into Silius's memory were images of the battlefield of Pharsalus covered with the corpses of fifteen thousand fellow citizens, including knights, senators, former magistrates. From his horse, Caesar had scanned the field of slaughter with the eyes of a hawk. He had said, 'It's what they asked for,' but in a low voice, as if talking to himself, as if to clear his conscience.

It was Caesar who shook Silius from his thoughts this time, saying, 'Come now. They're waiting for us and I still have to get ready.'

They went down together and Silius helped Caesar to wash and dress.

'Shall I call for the litter?' Silius asked.

'No. We'll go on foot. The stroll will do me good.'

'Then I'll call your guard.'

'No, don't bother. Actually, I'm thinking I should get rid of them.'

'Of your personal guard? Why would you do that?'

'I don't like the idea of going around my own city with bodyguards. That's what tyrants do.'

Silius regarded him with amazement but said nothing. He blamed Caesar's strange attitude and behaviour on his illness. Could the disease be influencing the way he thought?

'After all,' Caesar continued, 'the senators have approved a *senatus consultum* in which they swear to shield me with their own bodies if my person should be threatened. What better defence could I ask for?'

Silius was dumbfounded. He couldn't believe what he was hearing and was already thinking of how to prevent Caesar from taking such a foolhardy decision. He asked to be excused, went down to the ground floor and instructed several of the servants to follow them at a distance with a litter.

THEY WALKED down the Sacred Way, passing in front of the Temple of Vesta and the basilica that Caesar was building with the spoils of his campaign against the Gauls. Although he had dedicated it two years before, driven by a sense of urgency even then, the work had not yet been completed.

It was a magnificent structure nonetheless, clad in precious marble, with a wide central nave and two aisles. The basilica was one of the gifts that Caesar had offered the city, but certainly not the last. Since his return from Alexandria, Rome no longer satisfied him. The city had grown in a disorderly, unharmonious way, building upon building, creating an impression of unseemly clutter. The imposing roads, majestic palaces and extraordinary monuments of Alexandria, which excited the admiration of visitors from every part of the world, were utterly lacking in Rome.

The Forum to their right was beginning to fill up with people, but no one noticed Caesar because he'd pulled his toga over his head and his face wasn't visible. They passed in front of the Temple of Saturn, the god who had ruled during the Age of Gold, back when men were happy with what the soil and their flocks offered them. Back when men lived in simple wooden huts, sleeping soundly after a modest meal shared around the table with their wives and children, before waking to birdsong.

Silius found himself thinking that the age destiny had reserved for him was quite different: an age of ferocity and greed, of incessant conflict, civil strife, the slaughter of Romans by other Romans, citizens banished, exiled, sentenced to death. A violent age, an age of war and betrayal. And hatred between brothers was the fiercest and most implacable hatred of all, Silius mused, as he glanced over at Caesar's face, which was carved by the shadows of the toga that fell at the sides of his head. He wondered whether this man might truly be the founder of a new age. An age in which these seemingly endless hostilities would run their course and open on to an era of peace so lasting that it would make men forget how much blood had been spilled and how tenaciously their rancour had gripped them. He raised his eyes to the grand temple which dominated the city from the top of the Capitol.

The sky was dark.

2

Romae, in via Sacra, a.d. VIII Id. Mart., hora secunda

Rome, the Sacred Way, 8 March, seven a.m.

A MASSIVE BATTLE STEED came forth from the main gate of Alesia, its proud rider dressed in gleaming armour and wearing the *phalera* he had been awarded for bravery and valour.

Caesar waited, cloaked in red, seated on the magistrate's chair outside the camp fortifications, surrounded by his officers and legionaries.

The city bastions were packed with a mute, unbelieving crowd, who watched as their supreme leader went forth to give himself up.

The great warrior rode his horse once around the man who had defeated him, then dismounted and cast off his weapons. He threw them at Caesar's feet and sat down on the bare ground. By handing himself over to the Romans, he hoped to spare the city and the people he had ruled.

AGAIN: one of those flashes of memory that struck him with such force and frightening realism that he could not distinguish it from the physical world around him. He started when he heard Silius's voice.

'Are you not feeling well, commander?'

Caesar turned towards the Tullian prison. 'Why did I have Vercingetorix killed?' he murmured.

'What are you saying, commander? It's the law, everyone knows that. A defeated enemy is paraded behind the triumphal chariot and then strangled. That's the way it's always been.'

'But it's barbaric. Traditions . . . should preserve values worth preserving, not be a throwback to archaic, primitive times and ferocious customs.'

'I wouldn't say our times were any better.'

'No, they're not.'

'Commander, only one rule holds: *"Vae victis!"* Woe to the vanquished. One must seek victory, always, as long as it is possible.'

'I just saw his ghost. Emaciated, with sunken eyes and a long beard. Madness in his eyes.'

'A man in your position should never be touched by remorse. Other men are held accountable for their actions, but you answer to no one, Caesar. You did what you felt was necessary. That's all. That's all there is to it. Remember when the battle seemed lost in Spain, at Munda? We were ready to die. Vercingetorix could have done the same and spared himself such an ignominious end. But deliberately taking your own life requires much more courage than slaying your enemies in the heat of battle.'

Without replying, Caesar continued on.

Silius hung back for a moment, watching as Caesar mounted the last ramp leading to the Capitol. His stride was energetic, resolute – a soldier's stride. He had weathered another attack and, if anything, seemed more vigorous for it. Perhaps even now he was convincing himself that he could overcome this illness, just as he had overcome everyone and everything that had ever blocked his path.

The temple was open and the statue of Jupiter was visible inside. In reality only the head could be seen at first, but as one walked up the ramp, the perspective changed and, little by little, the god revealed his chest, his arms, his groin, his knees. It was an ancient statue, its features harsh and angular, its beard stiff.

An effigy designed to be frightening, or at least to inspire awe. Jupiter was flanked, in the chambers on either side, by statues of Minerva and Juno.

The two men approached the altar, where a small crowd was waiting. Some of them were senators, including several of Caesar's friends. Others, like Antony, were missing. His duties as consul must have been occupying him elsewhere.

The second and third rows were filled with commoners, all hoping for their share of the flesh after the sacrifice. The members of the Flamen College of Pontiffs, in full ceremonial attire, filed out from the temple door.

As soon as the Pontifex Maximus, his face still hidden from sight, reached the altar, the sacrificial animal was brought forward: a calf, three or four months old, with budding horns. One of the servants accompanying the animal carried an axe, the other held a tray of *mola salsa*, a mixture of salt and emmer flour, the food of the Romans' frugal ancestors. Caesar picked up a handful and sprinkled it on the calf's head. At his signal, the heavy axe fell on its neck with a clean stroke. The head rolled to the ground and the body collapsed, blood pumping out.

Ever since his return from the last war in Spain, Silius couldn't stand the smell of blood, not even if it came from an animal. He tried to take his mind off the scene by thinking about something else, but all he could come up with was the troubling news arriving from Syria and Spain, neither of which was completely pacified yet. He glanced up at the sky, which was getting darker and darker by the minute without dissolving into rain. Meanwhile, the thunder continued its low, distant roll over the mountains that were still capped with white.

The servants turned the calf on to its back and sliced open its chest and stomach so the haruspex could examine the bowels and interpret the omens.

Caesar was just a few steps away, seemingly absorbed in the scene, while his mind followed other paths. His illness. The expedition against the Parthians. The future of the state. Enemies still living, enemies who had died, the ghosts of the martyrs of the republic who tormented him still.

All at once, his gaze chanced upon on the calf's lifeless head. He'd been careful to direct his eyes elsewhere, but that's where they'd been drawn, against his will.

Silius glanced over at him at that moment and their eyes locked. Both were thinking of the same thing: of Pompey's head, of the fixed stare of their great, defeated adversary. 'They had it coming,' was what Caesar always said, time and time again. True, he'd offered Pompey an out, more than once, and Pompey had always refused, but the thought of the decapitated head of the great Roman preserved in brine was something that would never cease to weigh heavily on his heart.

And his mind.

Gossips had even been known to suggest that the young Egyptian king Ptolemy XIII – the husband and brother of Cleopatra – had relieved Caesar of a thankless but inevitable task by killing Pompey himself, thus giving Caesar the chance to publicly spill a few tears over his former son-in-law.

The haruspex had plunged his hands into the bowels of the sacrificial calf and was searching through the steaming entrails. His confident gestures suddenly grew confused and dismay was apparent in his eyes. He seemed to be on the verge of panic and the onlookers were becoming aware that something had gone wrong. Caesar noticed as well and drew closer to the haruspex. Silius also approached, overcoming his revulsion for the blood and the stench of slaughter.

'What is it?' Caesar demanded of the haruspex. 'What do you see?'

The ashen-faced priest stammered, 'The heart . . . I can't find the heart. It's a terrible omen.'

'Not another word from you,' growled Caesar.

Setting aside his toga and rolling his tunic sleeves up past his elbows, he sank his hands resolutely into the animal's chest cavity. A dark gurgle and, for an instant, Silius thought he saw an anguished look of uncertainty in Caesar's eyes. But only for an instant.

Caesar had a basin of water brought to him so he could wash his hands and, as the water turned red, he said, 'It was covered with fat and was a bit smaller than normal. This man is incompetent and that makes him dangerous. Get rid of him. Now burn it all,' he ordered, to the consternation of the populace watching the sacrifice. 'The gods mustn't be kept waiting.'

He had another basin of water brought, finished washing and used the white linen cloth the servant held out to dry his hands.

Silius walked away and went up the steps towards the sanctuary portico. From there he could see the crowd of onlookers below, scattering and going off in different directions. A fire was lit on the altar and the animal was cut to pieces and burned in the flames. But that was of no interest to Silius; he wanted to be certain that the litter had been brought to the appointed place and that the men were alert and ready if needed.

He lingered, turning towards the interior of the temple, as if he meant to pay homage to the gods of the Triad standing straight and still in the shadows, when his attention was caught by something glittering on the purple cushion at the feet of the statue of Jupiter, so tall its head nearly touched the ceiling. It was a golden crown. A scroll carved into the wooden base proclaimed: TO JUPITER, THE ONLY KING OF THE ROMANS.

He glanced back at the altar, where Caesar was presiding over the traditional rites of purification which ended the sacrificial celebrations, then slowly walked down the steps again.

The clouds still hid the sun, parting here and there to show wisps of blue, only to close back instantly to grey. Silius waited on the south side of the steps until the Pontifex Maximus had finished saying his goodbyes and then accompanied him back to the Sacred Way. The litter followed at a respectful distance.

From the Forum they could hear the buzz of the crowd that had begun to gather for the day's business: shouting from vendors in the shops and pedlars on the street, a magistrate at the Rostra calling for people's attention.

'If you found the heart, why didn't you pull it out?' asked Silius.

'Rooting around in the bowels of a butchered animal is disgusting and there was no need for it. The animal was alive, so it must have had a heart. Do you know the story of Anaxagoras's calf?'

'I don't believe I do, Caesar.'

'Back when Pericles was just entering politics, there was a calf born in Athens with a single horn. Pericles consulted a seer, who told him that it was an omen. It meant that the people's party, which had two leaders, Pericles and Ephialtes, would soon be led by one man alone and that man would be Pericles. Anaxagoras the philosopher was immediately summoned to give his interpretation. He opened the animal's skull straight away and examined its brain, where he found gross abnormalities. He explained the true reason why the calf was born with a single horn: because of a physical deformation. There's always an explanation, Silius. And if we can't find one, it doesn't follow that we're looking at a miracle, but simply at our own ignorance and inadequacy. All it means is that we are unable to understand the reasons for whatever has happened.'

They had reached the base of the ramp, where the Sacred Way turned right towards the Temple of Saturn and the basilica. Caesar went to sit under the Ficus Ruminalis, which was just coming into leaf. Tradition had it that Romulus and Remus had been nursed by the she-wolf under this very fig tree. Caesar often chose to sit there quietly and listen to what passers-by were saying, without letting himself be recognized.

'What did you go into the temple for?' Caesar asked suddenly. 'To pray?'

'To read an inscription,' Silius replied. 'An inscription in front of a golden crown. I'd always heard about it and I was curious to see it for myself. It's the one everyone's been talking about, isn't it, commander?'

A few drops of rain thudded down and the smell of wet dust filled the air. Caesar didn't move; he knew the shower would soon end. Others ran for shelter under the portico of the basilica.

'Yes, that's the one that people couldn't stop talking about.'

'You had sent me on a mission to Capua that day, and when I got back I was never really able to piece together what had actually happened. I heard at least half a dozen different versions.'

'Which just goes to show that recovering the historical truth of an event is impossible. Not only is the power of each individual's memory different, but the very thing that draws the attention of one man will completely escape that of another. Even if we concede that an individual is acting in good faith, he will remember only what made an impression on him, not what actually happened before his eyes. So, then, which version did you believe?'

'That you were attending the Lupercalia festival. Antony offered you the king's crown twice and twice you refused it. You arranged for it to be gifted to Jupiter, the only king of the Romans.'

'False,' replied Caesar.

Silius looked up in surprise. 'Do you mean to say you accepted it?'

'No. But that's not the way it happened. If Antony had truly offered me the king's crown, do you think he would have done so without obtaining my permission first, or without me asking him to do so?'

'It's possible that you asked him in order to have the

opportunity of turning it down in front of a great number of people. To allay suspicions in a public way.'

'That's an intelligent explanation. You could dedicate yourself to politics, make a career of it, if you were a member of the senatorial or equestrian order.'

'That's not my intention, commander. I have the privilege of living next to you every day and that's enough for me.'

'Nonetheless, your hypothesis does not hit the mark. What happened was entirely unanticipated and the way events played out was governed, at least partly, by chance. I was seated at the tribune on the parade ground, the Campus Martius, watching the Lupercal priests running around with their strips of newly skinned goat hide and flicking them at women of fertile age. Antony was among them, running around half-naked . . .'

'Hmm. I can't imagine people were happy to see that.'

'You're right! You should have seen the faces of those who were around me. They were utterly scandalized. Cicero, most of all Cicero. You know, I can't blame him. Antony is my fellow consul and – from time immemorial – no one has ever seen a consul, in office, running around half-naked with a goatskin whip in his hand. In any case, it wasn't Antony who made the first move. It was Licinius, a friend of Cassius Longinus. Cassius himself was also there, along with Publius Casca.'

'Don't like any of them much,' mused Silius.

Caesar seemed not to have heard and said, 'Well, Licinius approached me and put the crown at my feet. The crowd in front of me started clapping wildly and calling for Lepidus, who was right there beside me, to place it on my head. But those who were further away – as soon as they realized what was happening – were in uproar. Believe me, it wasn't applause or enthusiasm. They were yelling out in protest and outrage. Lepidus hesitated.'

Silius didn't comment. Instead, he seemed to be watching a small group of acrobats who were entertaining passers-by and begging for coins.

Caesar continued, 'I didn't make a move. At this point Cassius approaches and puts the crown on my knees. The same reaction from the crowd – part applause and part booing. It's clear that those who were clapping had been asked, and paid, to do so. I realized that the whole scene had been staged and I was determined to find out who was behind it. I looked into the faces of those around me, so I could commit them all to memory, but most of them were my friends – officers, veterans of my military campaigns, people I'd aided and assisted in every way.'

'I wouldn't count too much on their friendship if I were you,' Silius remarked.

'The crown Cassius had set on my lap started to slip and then fell to the ground. I won't deny that I did nothing to stop it from slipping. And that was the crucial moment. I knew that the man who stooped to pick it up and offer it to me once again would be the man who was most bent on my ruin.'

Silius admired Caesar's acumen and was struck by what an extraordinary man Caesar was. The spectre of the disease had faded entirely. Or at least no traces of the episode lingered. Caesar always became animated when he was talking about a critical moment in his life. The more difficult, or deceitful, or dangerous the game was, the more it excited him.

'And?' Silius prompted.

'That was when the unforeseeable happened. Antony ran up at just that moment – panting, overheated, drenched in sweat. He saw the crown fall to the ground and he stopped. He picked it up, climbed the steps of the tribune and put it on my head. Can you believe it? He'd spoiled the whole thing! I was so furious I ripped it off my head and flung it away. But I knew I had to say something. An event of such significance could not end like that without a word from me. And so I got up, raised my hand to ask for silence and, when I had it, I said, "The Romans have no king but Jupiter and it is to him that I dedicate this crown." Then applause thundered through the parade ground, waves of applause as my words reached those who were furthest away. But I was looking carefully at the faces of the people nearest me to see which of them looked disappointed or irritated by my gesture.'

'Well? Who reacted?'

'No one. I saw nothing of the sort. But I'm sure someone there was cursing fate, exactly as I was. Antony set off at a run again without even having realized what he'd done, I believe, and so the ceremony was ended. That's the story behind the inscription you saw at the temple.'

Caesar rose to his feet then and began walking again towards the Domus. Silius was careful never to leave his side, well aware that he was Caesar's only bodyguard. He was very worried by the fact that Caesar had dismissed his Hispanic guard and could not fathom why he'd decided to make such a move. Caesar's explanation did not convince him, so he tried to imagine what might be behind such a decision. Perhaps the incident at the Lupercalia festival had influenced him: only kings – or tyrants – were accompanied by a personal guard. Perhaps, by making such a grand gesture, Caesar thought he could allay any suspicions about his ambitions. At least that explanation made sense. Silius hated to think that he'd given up on his bodyguard because of his illness. After all, Caesar was a nobleman, a man of power accustomed to risking it all, both in politics and on the battlefield. He would perceive suicide as a natural option if he felt that all was lost. But if he'd really rather die than show signs of weakness in public, he would surely use his own dagger.

There was another possibility. Caesar's intelligence was matched only by his cynicism, so perhaps he'd dismissed his official guard and established a second, invisible force who could watch over him while passing unnoticed.

There was a further unanswered question on Silius's mind: what was Publius Sextius – the centurion known as 'the Cane' – up to? Caesar himself had sent the officer north, to Cisalpine Gaul. But as Silius faithfully fulfilled his given task of maintaining contact with Publius Sextius, who was currently in Modena, and passing on any news to Caesar, he remained puzzled about the true nature of the man's mission. All he knew was that any dispatch from the north was of top priority. The messages were in code, obviously, and could be read only by the high commander himself.

Publius Sextius the war hero. The most valiant soldier of the republic. When Caesar had celebrated his Quadruple Triumph in Rome, Publius Sextius had paraded bare-chested to show off his decorations: the ghastly scars that criss-crossed his chest.

He was the senior centurion of the Twelfth Legion and had survived incredible ordeals. During the campaign in Gaul, in the battle against the Nervii tribe, he had fought on unflaggingly despite numerous wounds, barking out orders, inciting his legion to regroup and launch a counter-attack. The day finished in victory. After the battle, he was moved to a military camp where he could recover from his injuries, but when the camp came under siege, food and supplies were cut off for days on end. Nonetheless, when the enemy succeeded in breaking through the gate, there he was at the entrance to his tent in full armour. What he did next was the stuff of legends. Although he could barely stand, he convinced the others to join him in fighting off the enemy. When he was wounded again in close combat, his men managed to pull him out of the fray and drag him to safety.

Reduced to skin and bones, more dead than alive, he struggled through a long convalescence, regained his strength and returned to his place in the ranks. It was men such as Publius Sextius who had built the Roman Empire. And there were plenty more like him on both sides of the political divide, separated by their beliefs and by their allegiances during the Civil War.

Publius Sextius had earned his nickname, 'the Cane', because he never parted with the emblem of his rank: the sturdy cane of a grapevine, used to toughen up the young recruits. A man of unshakeable loyalty, he was one of the very few people Caesar knew he could trust blindly. He was indestructible, a man who didn't know the meaning of fear. The mission he was carrying out must be of exceptional importance, because Caesar asked for news of him constantly. Silius couldn't help but wonder exactly what was he doing up north. What task had the centurion been entrusted with?

As Silius followed this train of thought, he realized they'd already reached the doors to the Domus, with the litter following about twenty steps behind them.

Before entering, Caesar turned towards him and said, 'Remember, at any hour of the day or night.'

'Of course, commander.' Silius nodded. 'At any hour of the day or night.'

And while Caesar was being welcomed by the gatekeeper, Silius went to his office to check on the commander's appointments scheduled for that day.

Just then the storm that had been threatening since dawn finally broke in an explosion of roaring thunder and pelting water. The big square emptied instantly and the marble pavement became as shiny as a mirror under the pouring rain.

3

Mutinae, a.d. VIII Id. Mart., hora secunda

Modena, 8 March, seven a.m.

THE FOG THAT rose from the rivers, from the earth and from the rain-damp meadows had veiled everything: the fields and the vineyards, the farms scattered through the countryside, the stables and haylofts. Only the tips of the tallest trees emerged – the ancient oaks, elms and maples that had seen Hannibal and his elephants pass this way. Now the bare silent giants watched over the colonized land, which bore the marks of Roman centuriation: the plots were edged by long rows of poplar trees and by boundary stones identified by consecutive numbers and by direction.

Here and there farmers were at work pruning the grapevines which dripped milky tears, the sap already flowing through their veins in anticipation of the still-mute spring. Towards the west rose the walls of the city, their dank blocks made of grey hewn stone from the Apennines. To the south loomed the snow-covered peak of Mount Summano, a towering pyramid with a blunted top.

Suddenly a figure materialized in the fog – a man of sturdy build, his head and shoulders covered by a military cloak. He held a cane in one hand and wore heavy, mud-caked boots. He advanced on foot, leading his horse by the reins, down a path which led to a modest brick building whose curved clay roof tiles were adorned at the centre by a Gorgon's mask. It was a small rural sanctuary dedicated to the nearby spring, which shot out of the ground a cubit high before gurgling away into a ditch which became lost to sight as it snaked through the countryside.

The man stopped at the temple wall and looked around as if he were expecting someone. The sun appeared through the misty haze as a pale disc, casting a milky light on the scene. The fields seemed deserted.

All at once, a voice rang out behind him.

'Fog is a friend to certain encounters and in this land it is never lacking.'

'Who are you?' asked the man in the cloak, without turning.

'My code name is Nebula, my friend. No stranger to fog myself, as my name attests.'

'What news do you have for me?'

'I'll need a password before I can give you any. Better to be prudent in such times.'

'Aeneas has landed.'

'That's right. Which means I'm speaking with a living legend: front-line centurion Publius Sextius of the Twelfth Legion, known as "the Cane", hero of the Gallic War. They say that at Caesar's triumph you paraded bare-chested to show off your battle scars. It seems to be impossible to kill you.'

'Wrong. We're all mortal. You just have to strike at the right spot.'

Publius Sextius turned to face his interlocutor.

'No. Don't,' said the voice. 'This is dangerous work. The fewer people see my face the better.'

Publius Sextius turned back towards the countryside. Stretching out before him were long rows of maples, to which the grapevines were tied. Dark against the brilliant green meadows.

'Well, then?'

'Rumours.'

'That's all you have to tell me? Rumours?'

'These are quite consistent.'

'Get to the point. What rumours are you talking about?'

'One month ago someone approached the authorities of this city to obtain their support for the Cisalpine governor who will be named next year. These same authorities are in close contact with Cicero and other influential members of the Senate.'

A dog barked from a farmhouse that was wrapped in fog, making it look as if it was further away than it was in reality. He was promptly answered by more barking and then a third dog joined in. They stopped suddenly and silence fell again.

'Sounds like ordinary politicking to me. In any case, what does that have to do with my mission?'

'More than it may seem,' replied Nebula. 'The Senate have already decided who they will appoint governor. Why are they seeking the support of the local authorities for this coming year? But that's not all. You'll have noticed that there is construction work going on in the city.'

'Yes, I suppose so.'

'They are reinforcing the city walls and building emplacements on the turrets for war machines. War against whom?'

'I have no idea. Have you?'

'If they're not expecting an invasion from outside, and I don't think they are, it's likely that what they're afraid of is a new civil war. And that suggests a very specific scenario. Quite a disturbing one, I might add.'

'A scenario where Caesar is out of the picture, is that what you're trying to say?'

'Something of the sort. What else?'

'Who will the new governor be?'

'Decimus Brutus.'

'Almighty gods!'

'Decimus Brutus is, at this moment, assistant praetor and therefore, as I've said, has already been designated to take the office of governor next year. So why would he need to build up local support or reinforce the walls of Modena unless he knows that Caesar will no longer be around?'

Publius Sextius snorted and a burst of steam issued from his nose. It was still quite cold for the season.

'Sorry, but I'm still not convinced of what you're saying. Couldn't the work on the walls just be ordinary maintenance?'

'There's more,' continued Nebula.

'All right. Now we're getting somewhere. Let's hear.'

'This is information that will cost you.'

'I don't have much money with me, but I do have this,' said Publius Sextius, his hands flexing the cane that was a symbol of his rank.

'What do you suppose I care about that?' shot back Nebula. 'Don't think you can intimidate me. I've been doing this for a long time.'

'I'm not leaving here until you tell me what I need to know. I was assured that I would be getting important information from you and get it I will. You decide how.'

Nebula fell silent for a long moment, weighing his options. When he began to speak again, it was in a different voice, as if he were another person. 'Give me whatever you can, please. I need money. I spent a fortune to get this information and risked my neck as well. I've had to take out a loan and if I don't pay them back they'll slaughter me.'

'How much do you need?'

'Eight thousand.'

Publius Sextius opened one of the bags hanging from his horse's rump and handed over a satchel. 'Five thousand. It's all I have for now, but if you give me the information I need you'll get twice that.'

'Publius Sextius is known as a man of his word,' said Nebula.

'That's the truth,' replied the centurion.

'Six months ago, at Narbonne, after the Battle of Munda, while Caesar was still in Spain, someone was working on a plot to murder him.'

'I've heard the rumours.'

'We all have. But I have proof not only that the plot was put into effect but also that it may still be active.'

'Names.'

'Caius Trebonius.'

'I know him. And?'

'Cassius Longinus and Publius Casca, and maybe his brother. Those are the names I'm sure of. I also believe that Caesar himself knows something, or at least suspects something, though he's not letting on. But there's one name he doesn't know and this is the true shocker. At Narbonne, Trebonius asked Mark Antony if he wanted to join the party.'

'Watch out, Nebula. Words are stones.'

'Or daggers. In any case, Antony refused the invitation and has never made any further mention of it.'

'How can you be certain?'

'If Antony had spoken, do you suppose Trebonius would still be around?'

'All right. But how much can we conclude from that? What I'm interested in is knowing whether this plot is still active. I want proof. The rumour is out and it's impossible that Caesar hasn't heard of it. What you've told me regarding Antony disturbs me. Did you hear about what happened at the Lupercalia?'

Nebula nodded. 'Everyone knows about it.'

'Fine. In the light of what you've just told me, Antony's behaviour is suspect. He offered Caesar the king's crown in front of the people of Rome. I would call that provocation, or, worse, a trap. Caesar's reaction confirms it. Antony is no fool. He wouldn't have done such a thing without a reason. One thing is certain: if Caesar had known what Antony was planning before it happened, he would have stopped him.'

'I could learn more, but I need time.'

'There's no saying we've got the time. The situation might come to a head at any moment.'

'You may be right about that.'

'Well, then?'

'There is a solution. Don't wait here any longer. You leave now for Rome, taking a route that will allow me to reach you with messages and information.'

'That's unlikely. I'll be moving fast.'

'I have ways and means.'

'As you wish.'

'In the meantime, I'll look for more proof.'

'Do you have something specific in mind?'

'Yes. But it's still entirely hypothetical. In any case, before I take action of any sort, there's something very important that I need to know.'

'What's that?'

'Who sent you here? Who are you working for?'

Publius Sextius hesitated a moment before answering, then said, 'For him. For Caesar.'

'What is your mission? To find out if a plot exists?'

'Not as such. My immediate instructions are to contact several army officers who have informers infiltrated at the court of the Parthian king. I'm to provide Caesar's general staff with advance information regarding the routes the expedition will take, procure special maps and see that they get to Rome.'

'So then what are we talking about?'

'My task is twofold. I'm also to discover if there is a plot and who the conspirators are. First name, clan name, family name.'

'Is it Caesar who wants to know?'

'This may surprise you, but no. It's a very high-ranking person who happens to be extremely interested in Caesar's state of health. Add to that that I'm just as interested. I'd give my life for him.'

'Fine. Even if you won't tell me his name, the fact of this person's "extreme interest", as you say, is a further sign that the plot may very well be active and ready to go into effect at any moment.'

'Caesar is preparing an expedition against the Parthians. It's plausible to think that this might be the moment to act against him. If he were to win, his prestige would increase beyond measure.'

'You're right. And Decimus Brutus should be departing with him, as the second in command of the Twelfth Legion . . .'

Publius Sextius bowed his head in a pensive gesture. The screeching of birds broke through the fog before he saw their dark shapes streaking like shadows across the heavy, humid sky.

'Decimus Brutus . . . one of his best officers. One of the few friends he trusts,' he whispered. 'Who could have convinced him to . . .'

Nebula drew closer and Publius Sextius could hear the sound of three or four steps on the gravel path.

'His friend Cassius, probably, or his namesake Marcus Junius Brutus. Or both.'

Publius Sextius felt like turning round but stopped himself.

'Why, though? Caesar has never harmed either Marcus Junius Brutus or Cassius Longinus. He spared both of their lives! Why should they want him dead?'

Nebula didn't answer at once, almost as if it were difficult for him to understand what Publius Sextius was getting at. A barely perceptible breath of air made the fog quiver as it rose from the ditches and the furrows in the ploughed earth.

'You're a true soldier, Publius Sextius. A politician would never ask that question. It's precisely because he spared their lives that they may want to kill him.'

Publius Sextius shook his head incredulously. He couldn't deny that things were beginning to add up. Trebonius inviting Antony to take part in a conspiracy. Antony just a few days earlier offering Caesar the king's crown in front of a vast, excited crowd who reacted badly. Decimus Brutus acting as though there were a civil war to prepare for . . . Vague signals that were now suddenly becoming very clear.

'We must warn Caesar immediately,' Publius Sextius said suddenly. 'There's not a moment to lose.'

'It's best he be informed as soon as possible,' agreed Nebula. 'Even if it's not certain that the conspirators' plans are close to being carried out. There are further leads I need to follow up. I'll let you know when to make the next move.'

'Help me get to the bottom of this affair and you won't be sorry. I promise you it will be the best deal you ever made. You'll be able to retire and live in comfort for the rest of your life.'

There was no answer.

'Nebula?'

He turned round slowly. Nebula seemed to have melted away, leaving no trace. Or was he behind one of those trees lined up in rows, watching him? Or inside the temple, perhaps, in some hiding place only he knew about, chuckling at Publius Sextius's astonishment at such a vanishing trick? As the centurion scanned the land all around, he noticed a leather scroll tied with a string lying on the temple steps. He picked it up and opened it. It was a map of the route he was to follow to get to Rome.

At that moment the sun finally began to break through the fog and stripe the ground with shadows. Publius Sextius put a couple of fingers in his mouth and whistled, then watched as a bay horse promptly trotted up. He jumped on to its back and spurred the horse on.

'No need to break your neck, centurion!' rang out a voice. 'It won't be today, or even tomorrow.'

But Publius Sextius had already disappeared from sight.

Nebula came out from behind a stack of bundled twigs left by the men pruning the grapevines. 'Then again, maybe it will,' he said to himself.

Mutinae, in Caupona ad Scultemnam, a.d. VIII Id. Mart.,
hora tertia

Modena, the Scoltenna River Inn, 8 March, eight a.m.

THE RIVER RUSHING nearby, swollen by recent rains, was just as loud as the buzz of the regulars and the customers planning to spend the night. Nebula entered after wiping his boots on the mat at the entrance and crossed the nonetheless muddy floor of the inn, settling into a spot in a corner at the back near the kitchen. The person he was waiting for was not long in arriving.

'Well? How did it go, then?'

'There are two missions, not one. Both are vital for the man who holds supreme power in our republic.'

'Where is your man now?'

'He's racing faster than the wind along the shortest route that leads back to Rome.'

'What does that mean?'

Nebula gave a sigh, but said nothing.

'All right. How much do you want?'

'To get this information I was forced to go into debt and risk my very life.'

'What a bastard you are, Nebula. Spit it out and let's get this over with.'

'He's following a map that I made for him. I'm the only one who knows the route.'

'How much?'

'Ten thousand.'

'Forget it.'

Nebula shrugged. 'Too bad. That means I'll have to make a hasty retreat before my creditors send me to the under-world. Into Pluto's arms. But if I die, it's all over, just remember that.'

'Come outside,' growled the other man, a veteran of the

civil war who had fought on Pompey's side. His arms had more scars than the paws of a wolf caught in a trap.

Outside, they walked over to a cart under the close watch of a couple of nonchalant but clearly armed thugs.

'You can put the money on my mule,' said Nebula, handing him a copy of the map.

The man stuck it into his belt, then smiled smugly. 'Now that I think about it, it seems that two hundred ought to be enough.'

'Do you really imagine you can screw Nebula? An idiot like you?'

The smirk disappeared from the other man's face.

'You think you're so clever. You'll be giving me all of it, down to the very last penny. There's a key for reading the map and the fellow who's got it works for you lot at the Medias horse-changing station. Weasel-faced guy named Mustela. He's in with me on this, you see, and he'll open his mouth only after you've given him my receipt for payment, which you'll find in the usual place. By then I'll be long gone. Oh, and by the way, Mustela is included in the price. He'll do the walking, because you'd never manage it on your own.'

The man nodded, cursing under his breath, and transferred the money, all of it, on to the mule's packsaddle. Nebula then mounted and set off at an easy trot.

'I forgot to tell you,' he added. 'As soon as you have the receipt you'd better get a move on, because Mustela won't wait long.'

Romae, in Domo Publica, a.d. VIII Id. Mart., hora quinta

Rome, the residence of the Pontifex Maximus, 8 March, ten a.m.

THE STORM had abated and, having gathered up his papers, Silius went from his office to Caesar's.

'There are documents here to be signed, commander.'

'What are they?' asked Caesar, raising his eyes from the scroll he was writing on.

Silius couldn't help but notice that he was doing the writing himself, in contrast to his usual practice. Since the day they'd met, Silius had always seen him dictating his thoughts. During the Gallic campaign he'd even heard Caesar, on horseback, dictating two letters at the same time, for two different recipients. But since Caesar had returned from Spain he'd taken to doing his own writing, as he worked on correcting and revising his *Commentaries*.

'All acts to be submitted to the Senate for their approval: decrees, appropriations, payments for the army, special financing for paving a road in Anatolia ... the usual. And there's correspondence.'

Caesar looked up sharply with an inquisitive expression.

'Not from him, commander. Don't worry. As soon as something comes in, it will be on your table in the blink of an eye. Or it will find you wherever you are.'

Caesar continued writing, hiding his disappointment. 'Who are the letters from, then?'

'Pollio, in Cordova ...'

'Right.'

'Plancus, in Gaul ...'

'Anything marked urgent?'

'Pollio. The situation is Spain is still difficult.'

'Let me see.'

Silius handed him Pollio's letter, sent seventeen days earlier.

Caesar broke the seal and gave the missive a quick look. Silius noticed his wide brow furrowing.

'Nothing serious, I hope?'

'Everything that happens in Spain is serious. Pompey's followers are still strong and still looking for a fight, despite it all. At Munda I was ready to commit suicide.'

'Yes, commander. I was there too, but in the end we pulled through.'

'So many deaths, though ... They'll never forgive me for that. Thirty thousand Romans cut to pieces by my men.'

'They had it coming, Caesar. They asked for it.'

'I see you like reminding me of my own words.'

'It's the truth.'

'No, it's not. The phrase has a certain propaganda value, but it doesn't hold up to in-depth analysis. No one willingly chooses to die. The massacre of that many valiant warriors was an intolerable waste. Just imagine, if they were still alive, they could come with me to make war on the Parthians ... or garrison the borders of a world at peace.'

He began scribbling on a tablet with a silver stylus that Cleopatra had given him.

'You know ... lately I've been adding up a few numbers.'

'What kind of numbers, commander?'

'I've been counting the Roman soldiers killed in combat against other Romans during the civil wars. Marius against Sulla, Pompey against Sertorius, me against Pompey and then against Scipio and Cato at Tapsus, then against Pompey's sons and against Labienus at Munda ...'

'What are you thinking?'

'Nearly a hundred thousand dead. Some of the best soldiers to be found anywhere in the world. If instead of fighting among themselves they had fought united against their enemies outside, the dominion of the Roman people would stretch all the way to India and the Eastern Ocean.'

'You'll succeed where others have failed.'

Caesar angrily rubbed out the marks he'd made on the tablet using the amber ball set into the stylus before speaking.

'I don't know. I'm tired. The fact is that I can't stand being here in Rome any more. The sooner I leave the better. My departure would be opportune for a number of reasons.'

'Is that why you're waiting so anxiously for news from Publius Sextius?'

Caesar did not answer, but stared directly into the eyes of his adjutant.

Silius could not hold his gaze and lowered his head. 'Forgive me, commander. I did not want—'

'Never mind. You know I trust you. I haven't told you anything because I don't want to expose you to unnecessary risk. There's a certain tension in the air. There are . . . signs . . . clues that something is about to happen. The wait is agonizing and I can't take it any longer. Maybe that's why my illness comes upon me so suddenly, when I least expect it. I've experienced many things in my life, but I must say that there's an advantage to being on the battlefield. You know exactly where the enemy stands.'

Silius nodded and watched as Caesar turned his attention back to Pollio's letter, making notes on his tablet as he read. It seemed that months had passed since his early-morning crisis. Caesar was in perfect control of the situation, but he was tense, worried, and Silius couldn't help him because he did not know what was upsetting him.

Caesar raised his head again and looked straight into Silius's eyes. 'Did you know that last year, when I was in Spain, there were strange rumours circulating in the rear lines?'

'What rumours, commander?' asked Silius. 'What are you referring to?'

'Just rumours,' replied Caesar. 'Pass me those papers to be signed. I'll read the letters later.'

4

STRANGE RUMOURS.

The expression nagged at him and Caesar's words kept ringing in his ears. Silius tried to remember what had happened in those rear lines . . . because he had been there, in Marseilles, in Narbonne, organizing logistics, communications.

It had been a bloody campaign, perhaps the worst ever. Titus Labienus had been there then, at Munda. Labienus, who had been Caesar's right-hand man, the hero of the Gallic War, his second in command. Willing to take on any responsibility, to face any danger, never tired, never dispirited, never doubting. An old-fashioned Roman, a principled man, an officer with a formidable temperament.

He had been at the head of the enemy formation at Munda, where the fight had been to the death.

Labienus had deserted his commander when Caesar had decided to cross the Rubicon and enter the territory of the republic – a land considered sacred and inviolable – with weapons in his hand. He had gone over to the side of Pompey and his sons, to the side of those who had proclaimed themselves defenders of the republic, the Senate and the people.

At Munda the clash had been of inconceivable savagery. The combatants on both sides fought with unrelenting fury and, at a certain point, it had seemed to Silius that their adversaries (despite everything that had happened, he still couldn't force himself to think of those men as enemies) would prevail. It was then that Caesar had been prepared to take his own life. He knew that, if he lost, there could be no mercy for him, and he was convinced that, as an aristocrat, suicide was the only honourable way of ending one's life in the event of defeat.

But then the unimaginable happened. Labienus withdrew one of his units from the right wing of the formation with a view of reinforcing the left wing, which was under constant pressure, but his men had all instantly feared a retreat and panicked, abandoning their combat positions in a disorderly fashion. The battle ended in a massacre. Thirty thousand adversaries dead.

Were those the visions that ravaged Caesar's mind? Was the memory of such horror the trigger behind the seizures that were crippling him?

But Caesar's words seemed to be referring to something different: rumours circulating in the rear lines, strange rumours, obviously upsetting. What could he mean?

Who should he ask? Publius Sextius, perhaps, the man Caesar trusted most. But the centurion was far away, part of some highly sensitive mission. No one knew when he'd be back. Silius thought of another man who might be able to help, a person who had always been close to Caesar but who also maintained relations with many people in the city. Someone he could arrange to meet without difficulty. Silius walked towards the vegetable market, and from there to the Temple of Aesculapius on the Tiber Island. He knew Antistius would be there.

He found him examining a patient with a dry, irritable cough.

'Has something happened?' the doctor asked immediately.

'No,' replied Silius. 'The situation is stable. I've come to speak to you about something, if I may.'

'Are you in a hurry?'

'Not really, but I don't want to stay away for too long, given the situation.'

'Sit down in that little office there and I'll be with you soon.'

Silius entered the office and went to sit near the window. A couple of maniples of the Ninth Legion were stationed on the island and he could see the soldiers coming and going outside. They were carrying dispatches and duty orders to and from the bridges that connected the island to the mainland. Several people got out of a boat which had just docked, evidently coming from the sea.

Antistius's voice startled him: 'Here I am. What can I do for you? Is it about your health?'

'No, not mine. An hour ago I was speaking with the commander and he mentioned something strange.'

'What were you talking about?'

'I had taken him his correspondence and some administrative papers that needed signing and he came out with a phrase that had no connection at all to what we were doing. I could tell it was something that was troubling him.'

'What exactly did he say?' asked Antistius.

'Something like: "Do you remember last year, when we were in Spain, the strange rumours that were circulating in the rear lines?" As if the thought had been gnawing at him since then. It was his tone that struck me.'

'What did you answer?'

'I didn't know what to say, and anyway he changed the subject and asked me to give him the documents to be signed. But I thought that you might be aware of something. You were in the rear lines yourself back then, in Narbonne, weren't you?'

Antistius went to close the door that he'd left open and then sat down. He was silent for a few moments and, when he began talking again, his voice was low, almost a whisper. 'A doctor in the rear lines of a large military expedition finds himself meeting lots of people, listening to cries of pain, to cursings and ravings, to the confessions of dying men. Men desperate to free themselves of remorse before embarking on that great journey from which no one has ever returned.'

Silius watched him intently. So Caesar's words had real significance for him.

'It's true,' Antistius continued, 'that after Caesar's victory at Munda there was talk of a conspiracy.'

'A conspiracy? What kind of conspiracy?'

'Against Caesar. A plot to bring him down. Or worse.'

'Wait. Explain that more clearly, please,' said Silius. 'Just what are you saying?'

'Our own men, I'm afraid. Highly ranked officers, former magistrates.'

'I don't understand . . . If you knew these things, why didn't you tell him? Why didn't you give him their names? You know their names, don't you?'

Antistius sighed. 'They were just rumours . . . You can't condemn a man to death on the basis of a rumour. You can never rule out slander – perhaps lies were being circulated deliberately to ruin someone. Anyway, I'm sure he was just as aware of those rumours as I was. I've heard him say the same things he said to you today.'

'Well, then, why doesn't he crush them? Destroy them?'

'Why? Only he knows. If you want my opinion, I think it's because he believes so strongly in what he did and in what he's doing. He believes unquestioning in his – how can I say this? – his historical mission. To end the season of civil wars. Establish a period of reconciliation. Put a stop to the bloodshed.'

Silius shook his head with a dismayed expression. He'd seen too much slaughter to have faith in such ideas.

'I know what you're thinking. And yet he is sure that the only possible solution was – and still is – to destroy, on the battlefield, all those who do not realize that the times have changed, that the institutions capable of ruling a city are not capable of ruling the world. He is determined to convince them one way or another – by hook or by crook – to come round to his way of thinking. To collaborate with him in his plan. He forced them to recognize his logic and then he held out a hand to those who had survived and honoured those who hadn't. Remember the ceremony he prepared for Labienus? A hero's funeral. His coffin was borne by six legion commanders, three of ours and three of theirs, escorted by five thousand legionaries in full dress uniform, carried to the pyre up an artificial ramp five hundred feet high to the roll of drums, the sound of trumpets and bugles. The Eagles draped in black were lowered as the coffin passed. No one could hold back his tears, not even Caesar.'

'But if the very men he holds his hand out to are those who are conspiring against him, what sense does any of this make?'

'No sense at all, apparently. But he is certain that there is no way other than his own and he is set on putting his plan into operation. He wants to reconcile the factions, to extinguish the bitterness and to protect the poor, who are deeply in debt, by guaranteeing loans at a low rate of interest, while not frightening the authorities by cancelling their debts completely. On this basis he will build a new order. He will succeed or he will die trying.'

Silius shook his head. 'I just don't understand.'

'It's rather simple, actually. Civil wars have raged for the last twenty years: Marius against Sulla, Pompey against Sertorius, Caesar against Pompey, Pompey's sons against Caesar. All this can lead in just one direction: to the ruin of our world, our order, our civilization. Caesar is convinced that he is the only person on this earth who has the military might and the political intelligence to put an end to the past, once and for all, and make way for a new era. He has pursued this goal by every means available—'

There was a knock at the door and Antistius's Greek assistant, a young Ephesian slave, entered.

'Master,' he said, 'Lollius Sabinus's freedman is here waiting. He says it's about an ulcer on his left leg.'

Antistius waved him away, saying, 'Cancel all of my appointments for this morning. I'm busy.'

The slave nodded and backed out. Immediately, loud protests could be heard coming from the antechamber, followed by a door slamming and then silence.

'I can't stand the vulgarity of these freedmen,' said Antistius in an irritated tone, before continuing with his earlier train of thought: 'On the other hand, I agree with you. Certain aspects of Caesar's behaviour are disconcerting.'

'That's how I feel,' Silius said, nodding, 'but I'm only his adjutant. I can't criticize him. I don't dare.'

'No one dares, Silius. No one.'

'He places too much trust in those who fought against him. He has forgiven them. That's the problem, isn't it?'

'Yes. In part.'

'But why, in the name of the gods? Why?'

'Perhaps he feels he has no alternative. He won and therefore he must be magnanimous and pardon them, in order to break the endless round of vengeance, and retaliation. This new order has to start somewhere and this is it. Obviously there are many risks in an approach like this, some of them quite serious. But there is a certain logic, you could say, in the way he's proceeding ... if it weren't for other aspects that seem contradictory.

'The idea of this campaign against the Parthians, for example. From what I've heard, we're talking about a huge expedition, prohibitively expensive, which would involve advancing over vast distances, through deserts and over mountains, against an elusive enemy. Unconquerable, or so they say. You realize that this might be the end of Caesar, like Crassus nine years ago at Carrhae. None of his men ever returned. They say that the entire legion was deported to a distant land at the very ends of the earth. Now, it's evident that a man like Caesar, who has fought over half the world in any number of different conditions, is perfectly aware of the situation. He must know that if he is defeated or killed, everything he has worked for will be lost. His sacrifices, the battles he has fought – all will count for nothing. It almost makes you think that this Parthian expedition of his represents some sort of heroic suicide. A titanic enterprise that will consume what's left of his life. But there's no sense in any of this . . . none at all.'

Silius sighed and raised a hand to his forehead. 'I imagine you've seen the writing on the walls of Rome, on Brutus's Tribunal, on the statue of Brutus the Great?'

'I've seen it,' replied Antistius. 'And I'm not the only one.'

'Is seems that someone is inciting Brutus to emulate his ancestor who dethroned the last king of Rome.'

'Exactly.'

'Do you think Brutus may be tempted to accept the challenge and dethrone – that is, kill – Caesar?'

'It's possible, I suppose, but it seems that nothing can alter the affection Caesar feels for Brutus. Which is hard to explain in itself, although I don't believe, as so many claim, that Brutus is really his son . . . a son he supposedly conceived when he was only sixteen. Though that at least would explain such a strong, stubborn attachment. But there's another problem.'

'What's that?'

'Even if the writing on the wall seems to implicate Brutus, it puts him in the public eye and thus effectively exonerates him. If we're talking about a conspiracy, the essential thing is keeping it secret. No conspirator would dream of making his intentions public.'

'Yes, you're right, of course,' admitted Silius. 'But it's hard to believe that Caesar doesn't know or can't imagine who is behind these messages. He's well aware what his so-called "friends" are up to. What they're thinking, what they're hoping, what they're plotting . . . Right?'

'Not necessarily,' replied Antistius. 'Caesar could be thinking of an attempt to discredit Brutus in his eyes. There were others aspiring to the office of praetor, which was granted to him. But it all seems completely absurd to me.'

Silius fell silent and tried to think things through; tried to impose some sort of order on the contradictory ideas racing through his head. Antistius watched him with his clear, penetrating gaze, wearing the same intent look that his patients were accustomed to seeing.

Sounds could be heard coming from the docks: the brisk step of an honour guard rushing over from the guardhouse to pay homage to a dignitary whose boat was pulling up to the wharf. Their officer ordered them to present arms and two trumpet blasts greeted whoever it was that was disembarking. It might have been Lepidus himself, from the fuss they were making.

Silius shook off his pensive mood. 'Tell me in all honesty what you're thinking. If he was aware of a threat, would he take measures to protect himself? Would he react?'

'Quite frankly, I don't know the answer to that,' said Antistius. 'One would think so, but his behaviour leads me to fear otherwise.'

'Then I'm going to do something myself. I can't stand the thought of a threat looming over him and nothing being done to thwart it.'

'I can understand that,' replied Antistius. 'But taking action of any sort could be risky. It's best to continue investigating at this point and find out exactly what's going on, using discretion and prudence.'

'How do you propose to do that?'

'There's one person in the middle, someone who stands between Caesar and his probable enemies, who is capable of learning what's going on in both camps without alerting either of them. Servilia.'

'Brutus's mother?'

'Yes. Brutus's mother, Cato's sister, Caesar's long-time mistress. Perhaps still his mistress now.'

'Why would she talk to me?'

'There's no saying she will, but she'd have good reason to do so. She may very well want to prevent the worst from happening. Look, Servilia has already lost Cato, who preferred death over Caesar's pardon after he'd been defeated in the African campaign. If Caesar were to be killed, Servilia would lose the only man she'd genuinely loved in her whole life. If he were to be saved, she would probably lose her son, assuming Brutus is implicated in the plot. So in either case she would be interested in averting the threat, no matter where it's coming from or at whom it's directed. On the other hand, we can't imagine that she would warn Caesar personally if she did know something, because doing so would put her son's life at risk, if what we're thinking turns out to be true. There are some that say that Caesar spared Brutus after the Battle of Pharsalus because he didn't want Servilia to be hurt.'

Silius raised his hands to his temples. 'This is . . . a labyrinth! How can I hope to make my way through such a tangle of conflicting motives? I'm just a soldier.'

'You're right,' replied Antistius. 'Better not to get mixed up in it.'

'You,' continued Silius, 'how do you know so many things?'

'I don't "know". I make assumptions, reflect on them, draw my own conclusions. And then I'm a doctor, don't forget that. Any doctor who's worth the name has to strive to understand what isn't explained, to see what's hidden, to hear what hasn't been said. A doctor is accustomed to fending off death. And what I think is that Servilia – if she's privy to what's happening, that is – has only one option. To approach the person she holds dearest and point them in the right direction. And only she knows exactly what that might be.'

'But if you wanted to help Caesar, what would you do now?' asked Silius after another long pause.

'I have already taken certain initiatives,' replied Antistius enigmatically.

'So why haven't you told me? What were you waiting for?'

'For you to ask me.'

'I'm asking you now. Please. You know you can trust me.'

'I know. And I would never tell anyone else what I'm about to tell you.'

Silius leaned in closer and awaited Antistius's revelation in silence.

Eventually the doctor began, speaking slowly and clearly: 'Brutus has a Greek teacher . . .'

Silius widened his eyes.

'His name is Artemidorus. I cured him of an ugly case of vitiligo. You know how much the Greeks care about their looks . . .'

Silius smiled, thinking of all the attention Antistius devoted to his own personal appearance.

'I believe he is grateful to me. I've never told him how I do it and every once in a while he calls on me to repeat the miracle. So, you see, I have considerable power over him. I'm trying to get information from him, although I've acted very carefully. I don't want to jeopardize everything. I know what you're about to tell me: that there's no saying we have the time, but that's a risk I'm ready to take. I don't have any alternative, at least not for the moment.'

Silius thought of the centurion Caesar had sent north on a mysterious mission. Publius Sextius was the one person he would have liked to talk to at this moment of such anxiety and uncertainty. It was some consolation to think that Caesar would certainly never have allowed him to go if he had felt there was any immediate danger. Or maybe he'd sent him away because he couldn't stand the waiting any more and wanted to face his destiny. Whatever destiny that might be. There was no definite answer, no obvious solution.

At length Silius got to his feet and thanked Antistius for his time. 'I realize that it may have sounded as if I was ranting, but I needed to talk about this with someone I trust. I feel better now.'

'I'm glad you did,' replied Antistius. 'Come whenever you like. I'd rather it was here than at the Domus Publica. If I can give you some advice, don't take any initiative on your own without consulting me. And don't torture yourself. Remember that we know nothing for certain and may well be worrying for no reason. All Caesar said was that he'd heard strange rumours, after all. Such a vague expression.'

'All right,' said Silius. 'I'll do as you suggest.'

As he left, crossing the square in front of the Temple of Aesculapius, he could see the standard of the Ninth Legion flying from the island's main building. So Marcus Aemilius Lepidus was present with his soldiers. Only a madman would risk taking any kind of action with an entire cohort quartered in the heart of Rome and the rest of the legion camped just outside her gates.

Romae, in Domo Publica, a.d. VIII Id. Mart., hora octava

Rome, the residence of the Pontifex Maximus, 8 March, one p.m.

SILIUS WENT directly into the kitchen to check that Caesar's lunch was ready. The usual: flatbread with olive oil, mixed sheep's and cow's milk cheese, a few slices of Gallic ham from Cremona, the boiled eggs and crushed salt that he invariably requested, and a plate of freshly picked bitter greens. Silius lifted up the tray and took it into the study.

'Where were you?' Caesar asked as soon as Silius walked in.

'On the island, commander. Antistius wanted to know how you were feeling.'

'And what did you tell him?'

'That you were quite well and were working.'

'That's almost true. Eat something yourself,' he added. 'All this is too much for me. Have you seen my wife?'

'No. I've just come from the kitchen.'

'She left shortly after you did and hasn't returned. She's just not the same any more. She seems so . . . I don't know, restless.'

Caesar began to eat, sipping now and then from a glass of the Retico wine which one of his officers, stationed at the foot of the eastern Alps, regularly sent him. He mentioned a shooting pain that an old wound on his left side was causing: a sign that the weather wasn't quite settled and that sooner or later it would begin to rain again or worse. Silius cut the flatbread and ate some with an egg and a little salt. He agreed that the weather could certainly be better given the season, with springtime just around the corner, and it was evident to both of them that their conversation was a thousand miles away from their thoughts.

All at once Caesar wiped his lips with a napkin and said, 'While you were at the island a message from Publius Sextius arrived.'

5

Mutatio ad Medias, a.d. VIII Id. Mart., hora decima

The Medias changing station, 8 March, three p.m.

THE FIELDS STRETCHING south of the Po flew by under the hoofs of Publius Sextius's horse as he raced down the road that unwound like a grey ribbon through the green meadows at the foot of the Apennines. The fog had dissipated and the sun shone in a clear, cold sky, its light reflecting off the snow which still covered the mountain peaks.

The swift Hispanic steed, his coat shining with sweat, was showing signs of fatigue, but Publius Sextius continued to push him on nonetheless, snapping the ends of the reins against the horse's neck and urging him continually forward with words of encouragement.

The rest station, a low brick building with a red-tile roof, was coming into sight now. It stood near a little stream, surrounded by bare hawthorn bushes and flanked by two ancient pine trees. He slowed the horse to a walk and entered the main gate, a stone archway with a sculpted sun at its keystone. The small porticoed courtyard inside had a little fountain at its centre that poured water into a drinking trough carved from a boulder.

Publius Sextius jumped to the ground, took the copper ladle at the end of a chain and drank in long draughts, then let the horse slake his thirst as well, a little at a time so he wouldn't catch a chill, clammy as he was with sweat. He untied a blanket from behind the saddle and covered the horse's rump. Then he went towards a side door that led to the office of the station attendant. The man stood at the sound of his knock and let him in.

Publius Sextius opened a wooden tablet with the symbol of the Eagle and the man was quick to ask what he could do for him.

'I need a fresh horse as soon as possible and . . . something else. Does anyone else in the station have . . . this?' he asked, indicating the image carved in the wood.

The man walked to the threshold and pointed at a man intent on unloading sacks of wheat from a cart. 'Him,' he answered. 'The Wrestler.'

Publius Sextius nodded. He walked towards the workman and came straight out with what he had to say. 'I'm told I can talk to you.'

The man let go of the sack he had hauled on to his shoulders and let it drop with a thud. 'And I've been told to answer you. If I want to.'

The workman certainly had the build of a wrestler, with hair shaved close to his skull, a few days' growth of beard and thick eyebrows that joined together across his forehead. He wore a dusty work tunic and a pair of sandals worn at the heel. His hands were as big as shovels, rough and callused. There was a leather bracelet on his left wrist and he wore a studded belt at his waist. Publius Sextius sized him up, while the other man had already looked him over from head to toe.

'All right,' Publius Sextius began, 'I have a restricted message that must be taken to Rome. Extremely urgent, extremely important, very high risk.'

The wrestler wiped the sweat from his brow with the back of his hand. 'I get it. You need some runners.'

'I need them now. This instant,' pressed Publius Sextius. 'I must be certain that the message gets there . . . Or is there an alternative?'

'No, but I'll do what I can. You can go on your way, friend, no trouble.'

'No trouble?' replied the centurion as his mouth twisted into a sneer. 'There is nothing but trouble, from Cadiz to the Red Sea. I'm afraid there's a storm brewing that is about to break and it won't subside until it has swept away everything that has been accomplished so far. We have to stop it, at any cost.'

The wrestler scowled and at the same moment a cloud covered the sun, plunging the courtyard into shadow. The sky seemed to be echoing his words.

'What are you getting at, man? I can't understand what—'

Publius Sextius drew in closer. 'The message must be delivered as quickly as possible to the old guard post at the eighth milestone on the Via Cassia. The message is: "The Eagle is in danger."'

The other man grabbed his cloak to pull him closer. 'Almighty gods, what's going on? What else must I tell them?'

'Nothing more than what I've just said,' replied Publius Sextius. 'I'll take care of the rest myself. I'll be setting off at once. You get started on this as soon as possible. Good luck.'

As Publius Sextius was walking back towards the main building, he noticed a man sitting over on the ground, not far from them, behind one of the columns of the portico. He was slurping from a bowl of soup, his head low. He was wearing a grey cape and the hood covered his head but not his weaselly face. An ugly mug with a few straggly yellow hairs on his upper lip.

Publius Sextius rejoined the man in charge of the post, asked about his horse and exchanged a few words. A servant brought him something to eat with a glass of wine, while the stable hands prepared the new mount and transferred his baggage.

The man in the grey cape was still bent over his bowl of soup, but he hadn't missed a word of what had been said. He watched as Publius Sextius downed the wine in a couple of gulps, jumped on to the fresh horse and rode off at a gallop.

Then he set his bowl on the ground, got up and, with a steady step, went straight to the stables.

There he put a coin into the groom's hand and asked, 'Did you talk to that man who just rode away?'

'No,' replied the servant.

'Did you hear what he said to the attendant?'

'He asked if he'd be sure to find another horse at the next rest stop.'

'So he's in one hell of a hurry, then . . .'

'You said it. He didn't even finish eating.'

'Prepare a horse for me as well. Your best. I'll be leaving tonight, late.'

'He took the best one.'

'The best of what's left, you idiot.'

The servant obeyed at once. He prepared a sturdy-legged bay, harnessed him and took him over to the man in the grey cloak.

'If you leave late at night,' he said, 'be careful. You never know who you might meet up with.'

'Mind your own business,' the other shot back. 'And don't talk to anyone if you want more of these.'

He shook the coins in his sack before returning to the courtyard, where he slumped down in the same place, leaning against one of the columns.

A convoy of carts piled high with hay, evidently for restocking the stables, entered the courtyard. The drivers were in a jolly mood and the first thing they wanted to know was whether there was any more of the wine they'd had last time. The attendant stood at the door of his office, holding a tablet and stylus, keeping an eye on the dealings and taking note of what was being sold and what the Senate and people of Rome were spending.

'I hope this stuff isn't damp,' he grumbled, leaning over the carts. 'The last load was all mouldy. I should take off more than half of what I paid you for that last lot.'

'Blame your lazy servants, not us,' one of the drivers replied. 'They left it out all night because they were too tired to haul it under cover in the hayloft. This stuff is perfect, governor, dry as my thirsty throat.'

The attendant took his clue and had some wine brought out for the men, then returned to his office.

A little later another horseman arrived, this one just as out of breath as the first. He glanced around until he found the rat-faced man he was looking for. He gave Mustela the eye and they walked off together. He showed Mustela a receipt and handed him a scroll on which an itinerary was mapped out. Mustela took what he had been waiting for. Now he could continue.

MEANWHILE, Publius Sextius was advancing at a gallop along the dirt border that ran alongside the paved road, the Via Emilia, in the direction of Rimini, checking the milestones as he rode to calculate how far he had to go to the next station. He'd passed this way three years earlier, marching with the boys of the Twelfth. It was with them that he had most unwillingly crossed the Rubicon. He well remembered the scenario he'd been forced to invent in order to convince his men that taking that step – against their country and against the law – was necessary.

The sun had begun to set. He had at most another hour and a half of light, sufficient to reach his next stop along the left bank of the Reno. There he would decide whether to set off again or remain for the night. He slowed down when he could feel his mount straining, not wanting to wear him out. He was an infantryman and he'd learned to get to know horses and understand their needs. But he was convinced that Caesar was in great danger and that the threat was imminent. It wasn't so much Nebula's hints as his own instinct, the same feeling that, during his guard shifts on the Gallic campaigns, had allowed him to sense the enemy arrow an instant before it was let loose.

Caupona ad Salices, a.d. VIII Id. Mart., hora duodecima

The Willows Inn, 8 March, five p.m.

PUBLIUS SEXTIUS reached the banks of the Reno just short of Bologna and turned right, heading south as he followed the river upstream, according to the directions on Nebula's map. He didn't reach the inn, which acted as a changing station, until the sun had already dipped below the mountains. He entered, eager to change his horse. At the door he noticed a little statue of Isis. It wasn't particularly well crafted, but it made a certain impression nonetheless. Inside, the servants were getting ready to light the oil lamps in the rooms, taking the oil from a jar at the end of the courtyard.

He felt tired. His old wounds were bothering him, as they always did when the weather was bad. The little he'd eaten at the previous station wasn't enough to keep him going. He tied the horse's reins to a post and went to find the station attendant, who turned out to be busy playing dice with the innkeeper.

He showed the attendant his credentials and watched the man's embarrassment at being caught neglecting his duty. But Publius Sextius waved off his anxiety.

'I'm not an inspector. I'm a simple traveller and I need your advice.'

'Whatever I can help you with, centurion.'

'I'm in a hurry, but I don't know whether to continue on or stop for the night.'

'I suggest,' replied the attendant, 'that you stop and rest. You're not looking too good and in a short while it will be pitch black out there. Don't risk it.'

'How far is the next rest stop?' asked Publius Sextius.

'A little over three hours from here. It depends how fast you're going.'

'That depends on the horse you give me.'

'So you want to leave?'

'That's right. It won't be completely dark for at least an hour. Then I'll see. Before I go I'll have a hunk of bread and a little of whatever you've got. Change my horse. He's outside tied to a post. Give me the best you have and I'll remember you.'

'Of course,' said the attendant promptly, dropping his dice. 'This is our innkeeper. He'll serve you some dinner while I prepare the finest horse in the stables. Why are you in such a hurry, if I may ask?'

'No, you may not,' replied Publius Sextius curtly. 'Get moving instead.'

The attendant did as he was told and the centurion soon set off again. The temperature was falling rapidly because of the snow still covering great swathes of the mountainside, frosting the air as it swept down the icy gullies.

Publius Sextius told himself that he was worrying too much, that there was no reason to think anything was about to happen so soon. But it relieved him to know that other couriers were already on their way, making it much more probable that the message would reach its destination.

He hoped the couriers would be equal to the task. The state had been lacerated by rival factions for too long now; even the local administrations had been infiltrated by men of different and conflicting loyalties.

Any lingering reflections of the sunset had been doused and the sky, clear now and deep blue, twinkled with its brightest stars. A crescent moon took shape over the white crests of the Apennines and the horseman felt even more alone on the deserted road, his only company the pounding of the horse's hoofs and its heavy breathing.

Mutatio ad Medias, a.d. VIII Id. Mart., prima vigilia

The Medias changing station, 8 March, first guard shift, seven p.m.

As soon as darkness fell, while the others were preparing for dinner and lamps flickered on inside and outside the inn to guide in any latecomers, the man who had been unloading the sacks of wheat climbed the stairs that led to the upper balcony.

His move did not escape the grey-caped man. Under cover of the shadows that lined the portico, he stealthily reached the stairs and crept up behind him without making a sound, stopping at a door that the man had left half open.

The building was topped by a kind of tower that rose about twenty feet over the rest of the construction. Once the wrestler had reached the upstairs balcony, he walked over to this tower and used the steps built into the wall to reach its top. Out of sight now, he took wood from a readied stack and lit a fire inside a sort of cast-iron basket supported by a tripod. The wind soon whipped up the flames. The wrestler walked to a little door on the western side of the tower, opened it and retrieved a sackcloth bundle. Inside was a large, polished bronze disc. He used this to project the light of the fire towards a point high on the Apennines where someone was hopefully waiting for his signal and would understand. He made wide gestures with his arms, alternating and repeating them. The air was becoming quite chilly and the wrestler felt his chest burning so close to the flames, while his back was freezing in the cold night that was getting blacker and blacker by the moment.

The clanking of dishes and drinking jugs wafted up from below, along with the good-natured bawling of the guests, but the man didn't take his eyes off the white blanket of the mountain. Although it was surrounded by darkness, it emanated an immaculate glow all its own.

He finally made out a red spot that became bigger and

bigger until it was a pulsing red globe. The signalman up on the summit had received his message and was responding.

Down below, the man in the grey cloak didn't dare go up the tower stair: he had no desire to provoke a run-in with that animal. Even from the balcony, he could tell that the man was sending a signal, so he just flattened himself against the wall and waited for the reply.

In Monte Appennino, Lux Fidelis, a.d. VIII Id. Mart.,
prima vigilia

The Apennine Mountains, Faithful Light, 8 March,
first guard shift, seven p.m.

THE MAN AT the signal station held a canvas screen that he raised and lowered over the fire, but the wind was picking up, making his task much more difficult. The terrace at the outpost was covered with icy snow and behind the building stretched a forest of fir trees that were bent under the weight of the recently fallen snow. A hatch suddenly opened in the floor and the station commander emerged, wrapped in a coarse woollen cloak with a fur-lined hood. He was an army officer, an engineer.

'What are they sending?' he asked.

The signalman leaned the tablet on which he'd written the message close to the light of the fire. ' "The Eagle is in danger. Warn Cassia VIII." Do you know what that means? Do you know who the Eagle is, commander?'

'I do know and it means trouble. Terrible trouble. How many men have we got?'

'Three, including the one who just sent us the signal.'

'The wrestler?'

'Yes, him, plus the two we have here.'

'The wrestler will be leaving as soon as possible, if he hasn't left already. The other two will set off immediately from here. They're used to travelling at night. I'll talk to them myself.'

The light pulsing from the top of the Medias tower stopped. Transmission of the message was complete.

The commander went back down the steps, pulling the wooden hatch shut after him. Three oil lamps illuminated the passageway that led to a landing from which the living quarters of the staff on duty at the station could be accessed. The two young men inside were both about thirty. The first, clearly a local, had a Celtic build and features. He was tall, blond and brawny, with iridescent blue eyes and long, fine hair. The second was a Daunian, from Apulia in the south. He wasn't nearly as tall, his hair was sleek and dark and his black eyes sparkled. The first was called Rufus, the second Vibius. They used a strange jargon when speaking to each other, a mix of Latin and dialect from their native lands. There was probably no one else in the world who could have understood them.

They were eating bread and walnuts when their commander walked in. Jumping to their feet they swallowed quickly. They could see from the scowl on his face that the situation was serious.

'Orders to deliver a message of the highest priority,' he began. 'Naturally, you won't be alone. You know the protocol. Relying on light signals at this time of year with this bad weather is madness. If they tried it, it must mean they're trying everything. A good courier is always the safest way. The message is simple. Easy to memorize, even for a couple of chumps like yourselves. "The Eagle is in danger." '

' "The Eagle is in danger",' they repeated in unison. 'Yes, sir.'

'The concise nature of the message leads me to believe it's come from Nebula. Dirty son of a bitch, but he's rarely wrong. I can't tell you any more, but I want you to realize that the lives of a great number of men – perhaps the destinies of entire cities and even nations – depend on this message reaching its destination in time. It must be delivered orally to the old guard post at the eighth milestone on the Via Cassia. I don't care how you get there – take any damned route you please – and I don't care if you have to sweat blood to make it, but for all the demons in Hades, before you breathe your last, you must deliver this fucking message. Is that clear?'

'Perfectly clear, commander.'

'Someone is already taking care of getting your gear together. The horses will be ready as I finish speaking. You will take off in two different directions. You can decide between you which routes you're going to take. I'm not saying you have to remain on a single road the whole time, but since you'll be needing to change horses, you will have to use a road as your reference point. For the sake of security, I do not know the itineraries of any other couriers, but it's possible that they are different from your own. If necessary use your *speculator* badge to identify yourself as a scout, although it's best to complete the mission incognito if possible. The system is designed to guarantee that at least one message arrives, if the other attempts fail for any reason.'

'The reason,' said Rufus, 'being that the messenger is killed. Correct, commander?'

'That is correct,' replied his superior. 'Those are the rules of the game.'

'Who, besides us, may be aware of the operation?' asked Vibius.

'No one, as far as I understand. But that's not to say we know everything we'd like to know, and what we think most probable may be the furthest from the truth. So keep your eyes and ears open. Your order is this and only this: deliver the message at any cost.'

Taking leave of the commander, the two men went down the stairs that led to the inner courtyard, where a couple of sorrels had been kitted out for a long journey: blankets, knapsacks containing food, flasks containing watered-down wine, moneybelts. A servant helped them put on their reinforced-leather corselets, thick enough to stop an arrow from getting to the heart but light enough to permit agile movement. A Celtic dagger was the standard weapon for this type of mission. The baggage was completely covered by a coarse woollen cloak, good in the cold, good in the heat.

They walked their horses out through the main gate, where two lanterns cast a yellow halo on to snow soiled by mud and horse dung.

'What now?' asked Vibius. 'Shall we separate here or ride down to the bottom of the valley together?'

Rufus stroked the neck of his horse, who was restlessly pawing the ground and snorting big puffs of steam from his nostrils.

'That would be most logical and I'd greatly prefer it. But if they sent the signal in this direction it's because they expect at least one of us to take the short cut across the ridge in the direction of the Via Flaminia. It's tough going but will save a good half-day's journey. Sometimes half a day can make all the difference.'

'You're right,' agreed Vibius. 'So what do we use? A straw or a coin?'

'Straw burns, coins endure,' replied Rufus, and tossed a shiny Caius Marius penny into the air. It glittered like gold.

'Heads you get the short cut,' said Vibius.

Rufus clapped his hand down over the coin in his left palm, then looked.

'Horses!' he said, showing Vibius the *quadriga* that adorned the back of the coin. 'You win. I'll take the Via Flaminia Minor.'

The two friends looked each other straight in the eye for a moment, as they drew their horses close and gave each other a big punch on the right shoulder.

'Watch out for cow shit!' exclaimed Vibius, reciting his favourite charm against the evil eye.

'Same to you, you cut-throat!' shot back Rufus.

'See you when this is all over,' Vibius promised.

'If worse comes to worst,' snickered Rufus, 'there's always Pullus. His mother must have been a goat. He'll reach us wherever we get stuck.'

He touched his heels to the horse's flanks and set off along a barely visible trail that descended the mountainside, leading to the valley and the footbridge that crossed the Reno, which was glinting like a sword under the moon.

Vibius went straight up the slope instead and headed towards the ridge, where he would find the short cut through the mountains that led towards Arezzo.

6

Romae, a.d. VII Id. Mart., hora sexta

Rome, 9 March, eleven a.m.

Titus Pomponius Atticus to his Marcus Tullius, hail!
I received your letter the other day and have meditated at
length on what you've told me. The thoughts which trouble you
in this crucial moment are many and of a complex nature.
Nonetheless I feel that you cannot shun the role that the best men
of this city have ascribed to you. You must not let it worry you
that your merits in the course of past events have gone
unacknowledged in Brutus's writings, which I myself have read
recently. What he says is dictated by the love he feels for his wife,
a woman who is as wise as she is charming, but above all the
daughter of so great a father, whom she held in such high esteem.
Whoever loves his homeland and is grateful to those who defend
it certainly knows what a debt of gratitude is owed to you and
knows that you are a model to be held up to the new generations
that will one day succeed us.
If I can, I will pay you a visit shortly after you have received
this letter, entrusted to the messenger you know so well.
Take care of yourself.

MARCUS TULLIUS CICERO placed his friend's letter, which he'd
received the day before, in a drawer with others and sighed.
He hoped the promised visit would take place soon. He'd never

felt such a great need to speak to Titus Pomponius in private, to have the comfort of his opinion, his advice. He knew that his friend had long ago decided to keep out of the civil conflict and in the end he couldn't blame him. The confusion had been enormous, decisions difficult and consequences almost always unpredictable, and the situation had certainly not improved with Caesar assuming full powers.

The conqueror of Gaul had seized upon completely marginal events as a pretext for invading the metropolitan territory of the republic at the head of an army, committing an act that violated every law, tradition and sacred boundary of Rome. At first Cicero had seen Caesar's assumption of power as the lesser evil and had even gone so far as to declare, in one of the last sessions of the Senate, that if Caesar were in danger the senators themselves would be the first to defend his life. But now he understood that discontent was rife and he realized that the defence of civil liberties could not be subordinated to the desire – no matter how legitimate and understandable – for peace and tranquillity that most of Rome's citizens yearned for.

Just then his secretary walked in. Tiro had been his right hand for many years and now, at the age of fifty-nine, he enjoyed Cicero's complete and unconditional trust. Nearly bald, he walked with a limp because of arthritis in his right hip and appeared older than he was.

'Master,' he began.

'You've been a free man for a long time now, Tiro, you mustn't call me master. I've always asked you not to.'

'I wouldn't know how else to address you. The habits of a lifetime become part of us,' the secretary replied calmly.

Cicero shook his head with the hint of a smile. 'What is it, Tiro?'

'Visitors, sir. A litter is approaching from down the road. If my eyes don't deceive me, I would say it is Titus Pomponius.'

'At last! Quickly, go to meet him and bring him here to my study. Have the *triclinia* prepared. He's sure to stay for lunch.'

Tiro bowed and went towards the *atrium* and the front door. But as soon as he glanced out at the road, an expression of disappointment crossed his face. The litter, which was only about fifty paces away, had just turned on to a little road on the left and disappeared from sight. How could he tell his master that the friend he'd been anxiously awaiting had changed his mind? He paused a few minutes in the shade of an old laurel tree that stood next to the gate to reflect on what had happened, then he turned to go and tell Cicero the curious news that as Titus Pomponius's litter was nearing the gate, it vanished all at once, as if its occupant had had second thoughts.

As he was going in, one of the servants came rushing over, saying, 'Tiro, there's someone knocking at the back door! What shall I do?'

Tiro immediately realized what had happened.

'Open it right away,' he said. 'I'll be there with you.'

In a few steps the servant reached the back door and opened it without asking any questions. Tiro, who was right behind him, recognized Atticus and had him come in.

'Forgive me, Titus Pomponius, you know how foolish the servants can be. I knew it must be you. Follow me, please. My master is most anxious to see you.'

He opened the door to Cicero's study, let the man in and left them.

'I've been waiting eagerly for this visit. Has Tiro made your servants comfortable?'

'There's no need, my friend,' replied Atticus. 'By now they are accompanying my empty litter to my nephew's house. I came in on foot, from the rear courtyard. I prefer for people not to know where I'm going, even if everyone is aware of our friendship. Well, what's happening, then? Your last letter clearly led me to believe that there were more things unsaid than said.'

Cicero, who had embraced him when he walked in, now sat next to him. 'Will you stay for lunch? I've had something prepared.'

'No. I'm sorry. I won't be able to stay, but I've come because I understood you needed to talk to me.'

'Yes, you're right. Listen. Some time ago I received a letter from Cassius Longinus.'

Atticus frowned.

'An unusual letter that apparently didn't make much sense. Its true meaning was hidden.'

'What do you mean by that?'

'The letter was completely banal, speaking of the most obvious things. A useless letter, that is, unless I was meant to read it in another way.'

'That may be the case.'

'You know that Tiro, my secretary, has developed a system of stenography that he uses to transcribe my speeches when I speak in public. He's quite the expert at cryptography, so I had him interpret the text of the letter as though it were written in some sort of code.'

'And?'

'Titus, my friend, you know I've never wanted to involve you in situations that could put you in any difficulty. I know what you think and I respect your choices, so I will tell you nothing that would disturb you. What I will say is that there's something big in the air. I can feel it, even though I don't know exactly what it might be.'

'I can easily imagine what you're about to say. Tiro found another meaning in that letter?'

'Yes.'

'What?'

Cicero fell silent and looked deep into his friend's eyes. There he saw a serene spirit, touched with a certain worry and coloured by the affection that his own words confirmed.

'I came here in secret because I wanted you to be able to speak with me unreservedly. I'm not afraid and you know how important your friendship is for me. Speak freely. No one is listening and no one knows I'm here.'

'If Tiro's interpretation is correct, and I think it is, something important is in the offing. An event that will change the destiny of the republic. Someone has decided to keep me in the dark about it, but I'll be expected to step in later, if I've understood correctly.'

'You are the person who thwarted Catiline's subversive plot, even though Brutus gives his father-in-law, Cato, credit for doing so in that piece he wrote. And I'm sure Caesar wasn't happy about that. Anyone who exalts Cato offends him. Cato has already become the martyr of republican freedom, the man who preferred suicide to accepting tyranny. Am I close to the earth-shattering event you're referring to?'

'You are very close.'

'But neither you nor I have the courage to talk about it.'

Cicero bowed his head without answering and Atticus respected his silence at first. But then he began speaking again.

'If I understand correctly, you're asking yourself whether it is best for you to accept the unspoken proposal to remain outside this event and then take the reins when everything is over, or whether it might not be better to steer events yourself, as you did when Catiline attempted to overthrow the government.'

'That's exactly it,' replied Cicero. 'The thought has been tormenting me.'

Atticus drew closer, moving his chair nearer to his friend's, and looked intently into his face.

'Let's make something clear. Even if we don't want to name this event, you and I are thinking of the very same thing: the only thing that could truly mark the start of a new epoch. What troubles you is that those in charge are neither capable nor experienced enough to ensure that their "solution" won't provoke an even greater disaster. In the shadow of a great oak, only stunted saplings can grow. Am I right?'

'I fear that you are. There may nonetheless be men among them who have not displayed outstanding capabilities yet, but who may well surprise us. And that would represent an even more serious problem.'

Atticus sighed. 'When Alexander died, all of his friends became great kings. And what did they do? They dismembered his empire so each of them could have a little piece, after they'd finished tearing each other to shreds.'

'I understand what you're getting at and that's exactly why I'm worried. Brutus . . .'

'Yes . . . Brutus. You'll have heard the phrase going around about him. Something that Caesar himself came up with.'

Upon hearing that name, Cicero gave a slight but perceptible start.

Atticus continued, 'Yes, Caesar himself apparently said, "Brutus does not know what he wants, but he wants it badly."'

Atticus gave a bitter smile, then shook his head. 'Stay out of this, my friend. Thank the gods that no one has approached you with a concrete proposal. I . . .'

'What?' prompted Cicero anxiously.

'I've been told . . . well, nothing specific, mind you, but the information I've been given seems plausible. I'll try to dig a little deeper and find out whether someone has an institutional role in mind for you should this . . . event take place. I can't do much more than that. I'm no politician, my friend, all I can do is try to understand. But if I can help you I will. Don't make any move on your own. If I should learn where the danger is coming from or when the event may occur, I'll let you know. I may not be able to communicate with you in person. Most probably you'll receive a message with my seal. Inside you'll find our usual password, in code. On that day, do not set foot outside your house, for any reason.'

Atticus rose to his feet and Cicero with him. The two men exchanged a firm embrace. They were united by their anxiety in such a critical moment, by their long friendship, by their faith in the same philosophical creed and by their nostalgia for the lost traditions and values of their homeland, which had been trampled by an avidity for power and money, by partisan hatred, by resentment and by revenge.

Atticus had always remained on the sidelines, had long decided to detach himself from that decline. He had a fatalistic bent and was calmly convinced that the chaotic component of history – always predominant – had taken the whiphand. The fragile forces of humankind had no hope of prevailing.

Cicero still believed in the role of politics, but he had neither the courage nor the strength to transform his beliefs into action. He was tormented by his impotence and lived in the memory of the triumphs of his glorious consulate, when he had boldly attacked Catiline in the Senate, unmasked him and forced him to flee.

He personally accompanied his faithful friend to the rear courtyard door. Atticus stopped on the threshold before going out on to the street and pulled the hood of his cloak over his head.

'Just one more thing,' he said.

'Tell me.'

'Are you the one behind the writings that have appeared on all the walls of Rome inciting Brutus to live up to his name?'

'No,' replied Cicero.

'That's good to hear,' said Atticus, and he left.

Romae, in Campo Martis, a.d. VII Id. Mart., hora octava

Rome, Campus Martius, 9 March, one p.m.

ANTISTIUS caught up with Silius under the portico of the theatre dedicated to Pompey, which had been finished a decade earlier. Adjacent to the theatre was the Curia, where the Senate was meeting temporarily until works in the Forum were completed.

The two men sat at a table in front of an inn. The doctor ordered two cups of hot wine with honey and spices.

'Has Caesar really received a message from Publius Sextius?' asked Antistius.

'Yes, but it was written seven days ago.'

'Do you know what it says?'

'It refers to the information Caesar was expecting, regarding his expedition against the Parthians. All good news. We can count on support from Anatolia and Syria, and even Armenia, and we have a complete listing of all our forces deployed from the Danube to the Euphrates. The commander has decided to call a meeting of the general staff in order to examine the feasibility of the invasion plan.'

'So that's why he was awaiting the message so impatiently.'

'I see no other reason and he did not mention anything else himself. He seems quite determined. He means to put his plans into action.'

Antistius shook his head repeatedly. 'I don't understand. He's not well, his work here is not finished, Spain and Syria have not been entirely pacified and yet he wants to take off on an adventure with an uncertain outcome that will keep him away from Rome for years and may cost him his life. An adventure from which there may be no return.'

Silius sipped at his wine.

'Has he had any more seizures?' asked Antistius.

'No, not that I know of. I hope he never has another.'

'No one can say. Where is he now?'

'With her.'

Antistius lowered his head without speaking.

Silius put a hand on his shoulder. 'That Greek teacher . . . Artemidorus, wasn't it? Have you managed to contact him?'

'I'll be seeing him soon. I sent him word that he needed a check-up.'

'Keep me informed if you learn anything new. It's very important.'

'You'll be the first to know. Don't worry. In any case, don't leave Rome. I may need you.'

'I won't go beyond the city limits unless he orders me to do so in person.'

'Take care of yourself.'

'You too.'

The two men parted. Antistius went back to his island, while Silius remained seated, sipping his spiced wine. A stiff wind began blowing from the north and he gathered his cloak around him to ward off the chill.

Romae, in hortis Caesaris, a.d. VII Id. Mart., hora nona

Rome, Caesar's gardens, 9 March, two p.m.

'YOU'RE THE most powerful man on earth. If you don't do something it's because you don't want to do it, not because anyone or anything is standing in your way!'

The queen had raised her voice and the flush on her cheeks was visible even under the make-up smoothing her skin. Her features were too exotic for her face to be perfect, but they only added to her undeniable allure, which many felt showed the influence of her mother's native blood. Her figure was absolutely sublime, its perfection untouched by her first pregnancy.

Caesar got up abruptly from the couch she'd been reclining on when she'd received him.

'I've done what I thought was right. You should show some appreciation for the decisions I've made regarding both you and the child. I've recognized him as my son and I gave you permission to give him my name.'

'How good of you! He is your son, Caesar, what else could you have done?'

'I could have done anything. You said so yourself. But I

recognized him, not only by allowing him to take my name but by placing a golden statue of you—'

'Gold-plated,' the queen corrected him haughtily.

'In any case, a statue of you in the Temple of Venus Genetrix. Do you realize what that means? That temple is the sanctuary of my family. It means that by having borne Caesar's child, you have become part of my family and that he, your son, is of divine lineage.'

Cleopatra seemed to calm down. She rose from the couch, drew close and took his hand.

'Listen to me. Your wife is sterile and Ptolemy Caesar is your only son. I am the last heir of Alexander the Great and you are the new Alexander. In truth, you are greater than he ever was! You have conquered the West and you are about to conquer the East. No one is your equal anywhere in the world, was or will be. You will be considered a god, Caesar, and that means that two divine dynasties will be united in your son! I've heard, by the way, that in the Senate there's been a proposal to make polygamy legal – that is, a man will be permitted to take more than one wife in order to guarantee a bloodline. Is that so?'

'The initiative didn't come from me.'

'Well, it should have!' burst out Cleopatra, raising both of her hands almost to his face.

Caesar took a step back and stared into her fiery black eyes without saying a word.

'Don't you understand?' the queen continued. 'Without that law, your son will remain the bastard son of a foreign woman. You must become the king of Rome and of the world, Caesar, and your only successor will be your son, your only true son, blood of your blood. Why did you refuse the crown Antony offered you that day of the Lupercalia?'

'Because there's nothing my enemies would have liked better! They are bent on my ruin. They would do anything to make me fall out of favour with the people, to make me look like a tyrant. Can't you understand that? In Rome, being a king is detestable. Any Roman magistrate in the provinces has a queue of kings and princes waiting months on end just to be received by him. Why would Caesar aspire to a position that is inferior to that of any one of his governors?'

The queen bowed her head and turned her back to him as tears of rage and frustration flowed from her eyes.

Caesar looked at her and couldn't help but remember that night of intrigue and betrayal in Alexandria, when Cleopatra had been brought to his chambers in secret, wrapped up in a carpet. He had been under siege from every direction and was convinced there was no way out. No way out for him! The conqueror of Gaul and victor over Pompey, caught in a trap of his own making. And yet, when he had seen her standing before him dressed only in a fine, transparent linen gown, her hair pulled back in the Egyptian manner, her shiny eyes rimmed in black, framed by incredibly long lashes, her splendid breasts, everything else had vanished. The besieging armies, Pompey's beheading, the underhand manoeuvrings of those scheming Greeks . . . all faded away. Only she remained, proud and tender, so young in her body and face and so perverse in her gaze. No woman he had ever known – not even Servilia, his lifelong mistress, Brutus's mother and Cato's sister – had ever had such a dark, thrilling gleam in her eyes.

Her voice shook him from his musings: 'What will become of us? Of me and your son?'

'My son will be the king of Egypt and you will be the regent until the day he comes of age. You will be protected, honoured, respected.'

'King of Egypt?' repeated Cleopatra, in an offended tone.

'Yes, my queen,' replied Caesar. 'You should be glad of it. Only a Roman can govern Rome and only as long as he succeeds in justifying his powers.'

Caesar was plagued by the disagreeable thought that the only emotion emanating from Cleopatra was raw ambition.

Nothing else. Not that he expected love from a queen, but it made him feel very alone at that moment. He felt torn by doubt and menaced by impending threats, by his own physical ailments, by the awareness that he who climbs high has much further to fall.

'I must go now,' he said. 'I'll come back to see you, if you like, as soon as I can.'

He walked towards the door and a servant rushed over to open it for him.

'There are men who would do much more for me,' said Cleopatra.

Caesar turned.

'You'll have noticed, I imagine, how Mark Antony looks at me.'

'No, I haven't. But you may be right. That's why he is Antony and I am Caesar.'

7

Romae, in Foro Caesaris, a.d. VII Id. Mart., hora undecima

Rome, the Forum of Caesar, 9 March, four p.m.

THE EVENING SERVICE was over and Caesar was leaving, accompanied by the priests who had celebrated the rites in the Temple of Venus Genetrix. He saw Silius coming towards him from the Rostra and stopped under the portico, allowing the priests to go on their way.

'Where were you?' asked Caesar.

Silius came closer. 'I ran into some friends near the Theatre of Pompey and we had a drink together. Do you think Publius Sextius will join us here in Rome?'

'I think so. Actually, according to my calculations, he should be here within a day or two at most.'

'So he has completed his mission.'

'As far as I'm concerned, he has. But you can never say. Something unexpected might hold him up. What kills me is the waiting. Rome has a system of roads and communications like nowhere else has ever had, but still news travels slowly. Too slowly for the person waiting.'

He sat on the steps of the temple to watch the men at work in the Curia and every once in a while raised his eyes to the tattered grey clouds that flitted over the city.

'I can't wait to get away. Politics in Rome are so tiresome.'

'The expedition will not be risk-free,' remarked Silius.

'At least there I'll have my enemies opposite me, on the battlefield, and I'll be surrounded by men I can trust. Here I never know what to think about the person in front of me.'

'What you say is true. In battle you have to trust the others around you. Everyone's life depends on it.'

'See this portico? Not too long ago a delegation from the Senate came to meet me here. To inform me of all the honours they'd heaped upon me in a single session. I told them I'd rather they stop adding on new honours and appointments, and start taking them away.'

Silius smiled.

'Do you know what they answered? That I was an ingrate. That I hadn't risen to my feet as they approached, as if I considered myself a god, given the situation, or a king. Seated on my throne under the portico of a temple.'

'Yes, I heard that as well. But there's no way you can avoid such talk. Any gesture you make, even the most trifling, is amplified and suddenly assumes great significance. Major significance! It's the price you have to pay for your rise to power.'

'Well, the true reason was that even Caesar must partake in his share of human misery. Do you know why I didn't get up?' he said with an ironic smile. 'Because I had diarrhoea. The consequences might have been embarrassing.'

'No one would believe such a thing, you know that. But it is through such stories that they're trying to ruin your image with the people. Convince them that you would be their king.'

Caesar lowered his head in silence and sighed. With his arms folded across his knees he looked like a tired labourer. Then he raised his eyes and gazed at Silius with an enigmatic expression.

'Do you believe that?

'What, that you want to be king?'

'Yes. What else?'

Silius gave him a puzzled look. 'Only you can answer that, but several things you've done or said would make one believe so. Not this last thing you've told me, of course.'

'Tell me what, then.'

'The day of the Lupercalia . . .'

Caesar sighed again, shaking his head. 'We've talked about that. I told you exactly how things really went. But of course no one believes that it wasn't a scene I'd orchestrated myself. Perhaps not even you, Silius.'

'To be honest, it's difficult to believe otherwise. What's more, the presence of Cleopatra here in Rome with the child has really struck people the wrong way. Cicero for one can't stand her. It's only natural for people to think that she'd be pushing for the establishment of a hereditary monarchy, with little Ptolemy Caesar as your natural heir.'

The forum was beginning to empty out little by little. People were leaving the square and making their way back home to prepare for dinner, especially those who had guests. The priests closed the sanctuary doors and from the Capitol the smoke of a sacrifice rose and drifted into the grey clouds. Even the columns of Venus's temple had taken on the colour of the sky.

'You can't believe such a thing. Only an idiot would do something so foolish. It's sheer madness to think that the Romans would allow themselves to be governed by any king, much less a foreign one.'

'Exactly, commander. It's not about Cleopatra. It's Antony's behaviour that I can't explain. I've reflected on this at length. The question is crucial, because the answer implies a fundamental failing on the part of one of your most important supporters, a man whose loyalty you need to be able to count on.'

The look in Caesar's eye was like none Silius had ever seen there before, not even when Antistius had told him openly what he thought about his illness. A feeling of intense sadness flooded through Silius as he thought he recognized dismay and perhaps even fear in the gaze of his invincible commander.

'You know,' said Caesar, 'every so often I feel like a beer. It's been a long time since I had a beer.'

Silius was not fooled. When the commander changed the

subject so abruptly, it meant that he was bent on avoiding some particularly distressing thought.

'Beer, commander? There's a tavern at Ostia that serves excellent beer. Just the way you like it, dark and at the right temperature, straight out of the cellar. But seeing as you probably don't want to go so far, I can have an amphora brought by for lunchtime tomorrow.'

But Silius was waiting for an answer, not about the beer, and Caesar knew that.

'What do you know about Antony that I don't know?' he said eventually, scowling.

'Nothing . . . nothing that you don't know. Nonetheless I think that . . . Publius Sextius might . . .'

'Might what?'

'Might be able to learn what he's up to.'

'Have you spoken to him about this?'

'Not exactly, but I know that he has his suspicions and I'd say that he won't give up until he finds a convincing answer.'

'Are you trying to tell me that Publius Sextius is investigating Antony on his own initiative?'

'Publius Sextius would investigate anything that could possibly involve your personal safety, if I know him well. But you, commander, what do you think? What do you think of Mark Antony? Of the man who would have made you king? That gesture of his at the Lupercalia, how do you explain it? Recklessness? Mere distraction?'

Caesar was quiet for quite some time, considering all the angles of the thorny question as perhaps he never had before. In the end, he said, 'Antony may not have understood what was happening and acted instinctively. Perhaps he's been feeling overlooked lately and thought he would gain favour in my eyes with a gesture of that sort. Antony is a good soldier but he's never understood much about politics. And it's all about politics . . . knowing what your adversaries are thinking, foreseeing their moves and having your counter-moves ready.'

'In any event, you came through well, Caesar, thanks to your renowned quick thinking. The same that's made you victorious time and time again on the battlefield.'

'You say so? The fact remains that I still do not know whom I can trust.'

'Me, commander,' replied Silius, looking straight into those grey eyes – those hawk's eyes – that had dominated so many in battle but seemed bewildered now, in the convoluted labyrinths of Rome. 'You can trust Publius Sextius, "the Cane", and you can trust your soldiers, who would follow you all the way to Hades.'

'I know,' replied Caesar, 'and I'm comforted by that. And yet I do not know what awaits me.'

He stood and began to walk down the podium steps. A stiff breeze had picked up from the west, whipping his clothes around his body.

'Come,' he told Silius. 'Let's go home.'

Romae, in aedibus M. J. Bruti, a.d. VII Id. Mart., hora duodecima

Rome, the home of Marcus Junius Brutus, 9 March, five p.m.

THE SOFT BURBLING of the hydraulic clock was the only sound to be heard in the big silent house. It was an object of extraordinary refinement that had been crafted by a clockmaker from Alexandria. The hours of the day were represented in a mosaic of minute tesserae on a field of blue depicting young maidens dressed in white with golden highlights in their hair for the daytime hours, in black with silver highlights for the night.

Voices could suddenly be heard from outside, then the clanking of a gate as it slammed shut, followed immediately by quick steps. A door opened and a hissing wind invaded the house, reaching its innermost rooms. A dry leaf was carried along to the end of the corridor, where it stopped.

The woman who walked out of her bedroom upstairs was strikingly beautiful. Barefoot, she wore a light gown. She closed the door behind her without making a sound and moved down the hall to the back stairs, where the noise was coming from. She leaned over the balustrade to see what was happening below. A servant had opened the back door and was letting in a group of six or seven men, who entered one or two at a time. Each man took a quick look at the road behind him before crossing the threshold.

The servant accompanied them down the corridor towards the study of the master of the house, who was expecting them. Someone was at the door, waiting to receive them. After they had gone in the servant closed the door behind them and walked away.

The woman pulled back from the balustrade and returned to her room. She locked herself in, then went to the middle of the floor and knelt down. Using a stylus, she prised free one of the bricks. Underneath was a little wooden wedge with a cord tied at its centre. She pulled the cord and a glimmer of light shone through from the room below. She bent closer and put her eye to the crack so she could see what was going on in the study of Marcus Junius Brutus.

The first to speak was Pontius Aquila. He was tense, refusing to take a seat despite his host's invitation.

'Tell me, Brutus,' he said. 'What have you decided?'

The master of the house sat down with an apparent show of calm. 'We'll wait for Cicero's answer,' he said.

'To hell with Cicero!' burst out Tillius Cimber. 'All he does is talk. What do we need him for? We don't need any more volunteers. How many men does it take to kill just one?'

Publius Casca broke in, 'Hadn't we already decided to keep him out of this? Everyone knows he hasn't got the guts.'

Brutus tried to regain control of the situation. 'Calm down.

Haste is a notoriously poor counsellor. I want to be sure that Cicero is on our side before we make a move. I'm not asking him to take up a dagger. The fact is that Cicero enjoys great prestige in the Senate. If our plan is to be successful we have to make arrangements for what will happen afterwards. Cicero will be fundamental in managing what comes next.'

'The earth is starting to burn beneath our feet,' shot back Casca. 'We have to act now.'

'Casca's right,' said Pontius Aquila. 'I've heard that Caesar is setting his hounds on our tracks. All that it takes is one man letting his tongue slip, or one wayward look, to betray our plan. If he catches on and loses his temper, it's all over for us. Time is against us.'

'What exactly have you heard?' demanded Brutus.

'Caesar has sent his most faithful men on investigative missions to the outlying territories, so that we'll feel safe here in the capital. It's the old noose trick: pull it a little tighter each day until he strangles us. I'm telling you, we have to act now.'

Their voices were muffled and difficult to hear on the floor above, just a confused muttering with a few shrill notes here and there. The woman tried to adjust her position to find the best point from which to both hear and see.

Marcus Brutus's voice again, scornful: 'We're his most faithful men, aren't we?'

Casca had no desire for banter. 'Listen, if you don't feel up to this, say so now,' he said.

The woman in the room upstairs started, as if she'd been hit by an unseen object.

'I've always spoken the truth,' replied Brutus. 'So how dare you insinuate—'

'Enough!' shouted Casca. 'This whole situation has become intolerable. There are already too many of us. The more there are, the greater the chance that someone will lose control, get panicky.' He turned to Aquila. 'What do you mean by "outlying territories"?'

'What I've heard,' answered the other, 'is that Publius Sextius, the centurion who saved Caesar's life in Gaul, has been in Modena since the end of last month and he's going around asking strange questions. Modena, just by chance, happens to be where one of the best informers on the market is based. A man who has no qualms about selling information to just about anybody, without a thought to principle or political alliances. As long as he's well paid.

'Anyway,' continued Aquila, 'he's what I mean by faithful. Publius Sextius is incorruptible. He's not a man, he's a rock. If Caesar has decided to use him, it means he doesn't trust any of us. And Publius Sextius may not be the only one.'

A leaden silence fell over the room. Pontius Aquila's words had reminded each one of them that there were men for whom loyalty to one's principles and one's friends was a natural, unfailing quality. Men who were incapable of compromise, men who remained true to their convictions.

None of them meeting here in Brutus's home, on the other hand, had refused the favours, the help, the forgiveness of the man they were preparing to murder. And this couldn't help but give rise to an intense, grudging sense of unease – more in some than in others – and deep shame that was becoming more and more unbearable with every day that passed. Certainly, each of them could find noble reasons for the act they were preparing to carry out: stamping out tyranny, restoring faith – that word again! – in the republic. But in reality one true reason stood above all others, like a prickly weed above the prettily mowed lawn: their resentment at owing it all to him – their lives, their salvation, their possessions – after they'd lost everything, after they'd realized that they had been playing at the wrong table.

'I think it would be better to move soon. Even tomorrow. I'm ready,' said Aquila.

'So am I. The sooner the better,' added Casca, increasingly restless.

Brutus looked into their faces, one by one. 'I need to know if you are speaking on your own behalf or in the name of the others as well.'

'Let's say that most of us are in agreement,' replied Aquila.

'But I'm not,' retorted Brutus. 'Every last one of us has to agree. When a decision is made, it's necessary to stick to that decision, no matter what it costs. If there are risks, we will run those risks together.'

'What's more,' added Cimber, 'we can't predict how Antony and Lepidus will react. They might become dangerous.'

Just then Brutus noticed that a scattering of fine sawdust had settled to the floor near his feet and he instinctively raised his eyes to the ceiling, just in time to see a fleeting shadow.

The sound of footsteps was heard along the corridor, coming from the back door that led out on to the street. Cassius Longinus soon joined them, his emaciated, pale face appearing at the entrance to Brutus's study. Right behind him was Quintus Ligarius, along with Decimus Brutus and Caius Trebonius, two of Caesar's greatest generals.

'Cassius!' exclaimed Cimber. 'I was wondering where you'd got to.'

Cassius appeared no less agitated than Casca. 'As you know,' he began, a little breathlessly, 'Lepidus landed yesterday morning on the Tiber Island and has every intention of staying put. The commander's standard has been hoisted on the praetorium. That can mean only one thing: Caesar suspects something. We have to act sooner than we planned.'

'We were just saying the same thing,' said Casca, nodding approvingly at Pontius Aquila.

'No,' shot back Brutus resolutely. 'No. We will keep to the date we decided on. There will be no discussion. We need time to explore the intentions of Lepidus and Antony.'

'Lepidus and Antony are not stupid and they'll adapt,' replied Cassius. 'Smite the shepherd and the sheep will scatter.'

'Sheep?' retorted Trebonius. 'I wouldn't call Antony a sheep.

Nor Lepidus. They are fighters and they've given proof of their courage and valour on more than one occasion.'

'But,' Cassius chimed in, 'exploring their intentions would mean widening the circle of those who know even further, increasing the risk of a leak, which would be fatal. I say leave them where they are. Too dangerous.'

Brutus started to reply, but Cassius shot him a look and he stopped.

'Perhaps Brutus is right,' said Cassius after a while. 'A few days more or less won't make any difference. The situation has generated a lot of anxiety and so we're naturally tending to exaggerate, to fret about perils that in all likelihood don't exist. At least not yet. Let's maintain the date we decided on. Changing it would be complicated. I still have to see a few people and I'm hopeful these meetings will clear the air, eliminate any doubts we may still have.

'What matters is that you are still determined – that we all are. Sure of doing the right thing. Certain that what we're preparing to do is just and proper. Once this is over with, we'll be freed of a weight that has been burdening our conscience as free men. No doubt, no hesitation, no uncertainty. We have the right to do what we are doing. The law is on our side, the tradition of our fathers who made us the great, invincible people we are. Caesar triumphed in the blood of his fellow citizens, massacred at Munda. He committed a sacrilege that he must pay for with his life.'

Caius Trebonius, who had listened silently to Cassius's impassioned speech, came forward. He was a veteran of the Gallic War, had commanded the siege of Marseilles and had conducted the repression three years before in Spain against the Pompeians.

'Cut the crap, Cassius,' he said. 'Spare us your patriotic exhortations. We – all of us – have been his faithful companions or the faithful executors of his orders. We all accepted his nominations to become praetors, quaestors, tribunes of the plebs. Some of you were pardoned by him but none of you took your own lives as Cato did. Quintus Ligarius was pardoned twice: a true record. Where are you, Ligarius? Show your face.'

The man advanced, scowling. 'So what?' he said. 'I've remained loyal to my convictions. I never asked Caesar to pardon me. It was his decision to spare my life.'

'He would have spared Cato's as well had he been given the chance, but Cato preferred suicide to putting himself in that situation. Tell me, friends, is there anyone here who feels animated by the noble sentiments that Cassius has just expressed? Are those really good reasons? I think not. And yet we all want him dead. Some of you because you were faithful to Pompey and Pompey no longer exists. Not that Caesar was the one who killed him. The dirty work was done by a little Egyptian king, a puppet who wouldn't have lasted three days without our support. Others claim they want to defend republican values. But each of us has a deeper, truer reason. Each of us thinks that Caesar doesn't deserve what he has, that he owes it all to us, that without us he would have achieved nothing. He has all the glory, the love of the most fascinating woman on earth, power over the entire world, while we have to be happy with the crumbs that fall from his table. We're like dogs he tosses bones to after he's finished gnawing at them. And that's why he must die!'

No one said a word, not Casca, nominated praetor a year before, not Cassius Longinus, whom Caesar had welcomed among the officers of his army after he had opposed him at the Battle of Pharsalus, not Ligarius, twice-pardoned, not Decimus Brutus, who would soon be governor of Cisalpine Gaul and who held his tongue, frowning. Nor any of the others.

Marcus Junius Brutus, who perhaps could have spoken, said nothing because he knew he was at the centre of that eye staring down on him from the middle of the ceiling.

He knew who was watching him.

The enquiring eye, which sparkled with a light that was

almost manic, belonged to Porcia, his wife. The daughter of Cato, the republican hero who killed himself at Utica rather than accept the clemency of the tyrant. Porcia, whom he'd kept in the dark about everything. Porcia had first guessed and was now certain of what he was plotting.

He remembered what had happened just a few days before. It was the middle of the night and he was sitting in his study wide awake, tormented by his own thoughts, nightmares, doubts and fears and remorse. She'd appeared in the open doorway, a vision advancing from the other side of the *atrium*. She was barefoot and seemed to be walking on air. She moved like a ghost, white in the dim glow of a single lamp.

She'd never looked so beautiful. She wore a light nightgown, open at the sides. Her thighs, white and perfect as ivory, and her girlish, shapely knees, were bared with every step as she came closer. She was brandishing a stylus and she had that light in her eyes, fixed and trembling at the same time, the feverish light of a state not unlike madness.

'Why are you hiding your plans from me?'

'I'm not hiding anything from you, my love.'

'Don't lie. I know you're hiding something important.'

'Please, love, don't torment me.'

'I know why you won't tell me. It's because I'm a woman. You're afraid that, if I were tortured, I'd reveal the names of your comrades. Isn't that so?'

Brutus shook his head in silence, trying to hide his glistening eyes.

'But you're wrong. I'm strong, you know. I'm Cato's daughter and I have his temperament. Pain means nothing to me. No one could force me to talk if I didn't want to.'

The stylus glittered in her hand like a cursed jewel. Brutus couldn't tear his eyes away from it.

'Watch!' she exclaimed, turning the stylus against herself.

Brutus had shouted, 'No!' and run towards her, but Porcia had already stuck the stylus deep in her left thigh, digging the tip into the wound so it tore cruelly into her flesh. Blood surged out and he fell to his knees before her, ripped the iron out of her hand and covered the wound with his mouth, licked it with his tongue, weeping.

He shook when Trebonius's voice exclaimed, 'The day of the final reckoning will be the day we decided upon: the Ides of March!'

8

In Monte Appennino, Taberna ad Quercum, a.d. VI Id. Mart.,
hora duodecima

The Apennine Mountains, the Oak Tavern, 10 March, five p.m.

THE MAN IN the grey cloak arrived out of breath, his horse exhausted and wild-eyed in fright at the lightning and thunder so loud the whole mountain seemed to shake. An angry wind whistled through the bare branches of the old oak trees, each new blast tearing away the last remaining leaves and carrying them off in a spin to the bottom of the dark valley. The high snowy peaks were barely visible against the black sky.

He found himself in front of the inn unexpectedly, after a bend in the road, and had to yank at the reins to avoid crashing into the doorway, which was already bolted against the approaching storm and the dark night. Another flash lit up the figure of the rearing horse and its rider for a moment, casting their shadow on the ground that was already drinking in the first heavy drops of rain. The odour of wet dust saturated the air, mixed with the metallic scent of the lightning bolts searing the face of the sky.

The horseman jumped to the ground and pounded hard on the door, using the knocker and then the hilt of his sword. The great oak tree that gave the inn its name loomed at its side, its gnarled boughs reaching to the roof of the building.

A stable boy came to answer the door. He took the horse by his reins and covered him immediately with a blanket.

The man dressed in grey entered and pulled the door shut behind him, bolting it as if he were in his own home. He walked towards the tavern as the rain began to pour, instantly filling all the cracks in the stony courtyard.

The inside of the tavern was a smoky hole. Crookedly placed beams held up a low ceiling and a round hearth in the middle of the room shot fumes and sparks towards an opening in the roof from which the rain dripped in, sizzling on the embers. An old man with a long white beard and eyes veiled by cataracts, wooden spoon in hand, was mixing some concoction bubbling in the copper pot. The newcomer took off his soaked cape and placed it on the back of a chair near the fire.

'There's spelt-meal mush and red wine,' coughed out the old man without turning.

'I have no time to eat,' replied the other. 'I have to get to—'

'Mustela, it's you, isn't it?'

'You can't see a damned thing, old man, but your ears are holding out.'

'What do you want?'

'I have to get to the House of the Cypresses as fast as I can. Matter of life or death.'

'We've got a good horse for you, Mustela. Yours must be done in.'

'Don't make me waste time. You know another way to get there.'

'The short cut.'

'Not fast enough. Faster.'

'It'll cost you.'

'How much?'

'Two thousand.'

'I have less than a third of that, but if you tell me how to get there fast, I'll give you double what you're asking as soon as this is over.'

'Why such haste?'

'Do you want the money or don't you? I guarantee you'll get the full four thousand.'

'All right.'

Mustela reached over to his cloak and pulled out a bag. 'Shall I dump them here or should we go into the back?' he asked.

The old man left the spoon in the pot and led his guest to the larder, which was dimly lit by a smoky tallow-burning lamp. Mustela poured the contents of the bag on to the table: all silver coins, looking newly minted.

'Count them. There are five hundred, more or less. I'll keep as little as possible for myself, but let's get moving, damn it!'

The old man returned to the room with the fireplace, followed by Mustela. He called the stable boy as his guest retrieved his cloak, which was no less drenched than before but a little warmer. They walked into the courtyard and were greeted by a thunderclap that seemed to announce the collapse of the heavenly vault above them.

'You won't need your horse,' said the old man, ignoring the storm. 'I'll keep him here as part payment of what you still owe me.'

'What do you need all that money for?' grumbled Mustela between one roll of thunder and the next.

'I like to touch it,' answered the old man.

The servant led the way, holding his lantern high enough to light up a tortuous path full of rain-soaked dead leaves. The red light cast a bloody glow on the trunks and branches of the big oaks and twisted chestnuts. The old man moved with a sure step over the slippery ground, as if he knew its every bump and hollow. He gave the impression of moving onward with eyes closed, guided more by the hooked toes of his feet than by the dim haze of his vision.

They ended up in front of a rock covered with moss and

tangled thorn bushes. The servant pushed away a creeping bramble with his hands and uncovered a crevice in the rock.

The two men entered.

They found themselves in a narrow underground tunnel ending in a rough stairway cut into the stone, worn by time and dripping water. They groped their way down with their hands on the walls, step after step. The stairs became steeper and more irregular, but the difficulty of their descent was offset now by a rope that had been threaded through holes made in the jutting rocks. From deep below they could hear the sound of rushing water and the tunnel soon widened into a sandy-bottomed cave crossed by an underground torrent that bubbled up ferociously between the bare rocks and big limestone boulders.

'This leads to a tributary of the Arno,' said the old man pointing to the coursing stream.

Mustela looked at him in shock.

'Isn't this what you wanted?' asked the old man. 'The secret way?'

'How long?' asked Mustela with terror in his gaze.

'That depends on you.'

'What are you saying? Isn't there a boat?'

'There will be when you surface. You'll find it hidden among the willows on the left bank.'

Mustela couldn't tear his eyes away from the water, which in the dim light of the lantern seemed as violent and threatening as the surging Styx. The old man's sunken, wrinkled face, framed by a stringy beard, was Charon's.

He looked back at the water foaming between the sharp rocks and said with horror in his voice, 'This is madness.'

'You're not obliged to take this way,' said the old man. 'I can understand your uncertainty. We'll go back, if you like. I'll give you a strong, experienced horse who will take you down the short cut.'

Mustela's eyes hadn't left the swirling current, as though he had been bewitched by it. 'I'll end up smashed against the rocks,' he whispered, 'it's so dark down here . . . or I'll die of the cold.'

'Half make it,' muttered the old man.

'And half don't,' Mustela replied.

The old man shrugged, as if to say, 'So what?', and Mustela realized with a rush how stupid he'd been to pay so much for a passage to Hades. But evidently his terror conflicted with the even greater fear of being required to explain why he had failed.

In the end, with a deep sigh, he lowered himself into the torrent, holding on to the river rocks in an attempt to steady himself. He fought against the current briefly, then slowly let himself go and was sucked into the darkness, swallowed up by the swirling waters.

In Monte Appennino, Caupona ad Silvam, a.d. VI Id. Mart.,
prima vigilia

The Apennine Mountains, the Woodland Inn, 10 March,
first guard shift, eight p.m.

PUBLIUS SEXTIUS galloped along the track that wound down into the valley and then ascended again towards the summit. He was following Nebula's map along a route that left Aemilia and cut through the mountains heading south, towards Etruria.

He rode mostly under the cover of the twisted boughs, his path lit up now and then by flashes of lightning. When the road started ascending, he slowed his pace so he wouldn't exhaust his horse, letting him walk once in a while to allow him to catch his breath. He was a generous animal and it pained the centurion to oblige him to undergo such strain, to put his life at risk in such a desperate race against time. The rain began falling and the storm broke as he came into sight of the *mansio*. Just in time, as the horse was about to collapse beneath him. It seemed that one of the soldiers on guard had recognized him.

'Something wrong, soldier?' he asked as he dismounted and led the horse towards the stables.

'No,' said the legionary. 'I was just thinking I'd seen you somewhere before.'

'You're right. Weren't you with the Thirteenth?'

'Ye gods!' exclaimed the guard. 'But you are—'

'Front-line centurion Publius Sextius,' replied the officer, turning to face the soldier.

The guard saluted him. 'Can I be of help, centurion? It's an honour to serve you. There's no one who fought in Gaul who hasn't heard about your deeds.'

'Yes, you can, son,' replied Publius Sextius. 'I need to rest for a couple of hours while they change my horse and bring me something to eat. Keep your eyes open and, if anyone else arrives, inform me immediately, especially if it's someone asking questions. You understand?'

'Count on me, centurion. Not even the air can get by here without our permission. Rest easy. I'll have something to tell my grandchildren about when I'm an old man. Great gods, Publius Sextius in person. "The Cane" himself! I can't believe it.'

'Thank you. You won't regret it. You're doing me a great service and I'll remember this. What's your name, boy?'

'It's Baebius Carbo,' replied the soldier, standing stiffly at attention.

'Very good. Keep your eyes open, then, Baebius Carbo. It's a bad night.'

Another soldier took the horse and led him into the stables. Publius Sextius pulled his cloak up over his head to protect himself from the rain, walked to the door of the inn and entered. He was dead on his feet, but a couple of hours' sleep would do the job and he'd be ready to resume his journey. At least he hoped so.

The innkeeper came up to him. 'You must be in one hell of a hurry to be out on a night like this, my friend. But you're in our hands now and you can take it easy.'

'I'm afraid not. Prepare me something for dinner, but give me a couple of hours' sleep first. Then I'll eat and be on my way.'

The tone of his voice was peremptory, while the look in his eye and his bearing commanded fear and respect. The innkeeper didn't say another word. He had the guest accompanied upstairs and went into the kitchen to prepare something for his dinner. The wind was getting stronger outside and it was pouring, but as the temperature dropped the rain mixed with sleet and covered the ground in white slush. When Publius Sextius awoke it had stopped raining completely and the snow had begun falling.

The centurion opened the window and looked outside. The two lanterns out in the courtyard lit up the big white flakes whirling about on the north wind. The tree trunks and branches were fast being blanketed by a layer of pure white which was getting thicker and thicker by the moment. The room was warm, thanks to the braziers and to the fire blazing in the fireplace downstairs, which warmed the walls and ceiling as well. Publius Sextius sighed at the idea of going out in the cold to travel down a road covered with snow in the middle of the night.

The innkeeper arrived to wake him and to tell him that dinner was ready. Having found the centurion already on his feet, he couldn't resist warning the man against his plan.

'You can't really mean to resume your journey now. You can't be so mad, my friend! Setting off at night, in such foul weather ... Who could blame you for staying? Listen to me. Forget about leaving now. Eat, drink a glass of good wine and go back to bed while it's still warm. Tomorrow I'll call you early, as soon as it's light enough to see, and you'll go wherever it is you need to go. Consider that you're likely to get lost in the dark, in this snowstorm, and then any time you'd gained would go wasted.'

'You're right,' replied Publius Sextius. 'I need a guide.'

'A guide? But . . . I don't know, I don't have any—'

'Listen, friend, I don't enjoy travelling under these conditions and I have no time to lose. Is that clear? Find me a guide or you'll be sorry. I have written orders of absolute priority. Do you understand what I'm saying?'

'Yes, yes, I understand. I'll try to find someone who can take you to the next rest stop. But if you end up down in a gully, you'll have only yourself to blame.'

'That I already know. I'll eat whatever you've got prepared. You worry about arranging the rest.'

The innkeeper accompanied him downstairs, grumbling and holding his lantern high. He sat his guest down in front of a plate of lamb with lentils and went off, still muttering.

Publius Sextius began to eat. The meat was good, the lentils tasty and, as for the wine, he'd drunk worse. A hot meal was just what he needed to get himself moving again. As he ate, he calculated and recalculated how he might make his route any quicker. He began to wonder whether the innkeeper wasn't right after all about waiting until morning, but when he'd swallowed the last mouthful of food and downed the last of his wine, he was more convinced than ever that he'd made the right decision. He threw his cloak over his shoulders and went outside.

The courtyard was completely white. A stable hand brought out a horse with his baggage strapped on to its back. Nearby stood another horse and, beside him, the man Publius Sextius assumed would be his guide: a fellow of about fifty wearing a waxcloth over his shoulders and a hood pulled up over his head. His face was stony, completely impassive, and he held a lit torch in his left hand to light their way. Another three or four spare torches were tied to the horse's side.

There were only two legionaries on guard now. Neither one of them was Baebius Carbo.

'I'm sorry to put you to this trouble, friend,' said Publius Sextius to the guide, 'but I'm in a hurry and I can't afford to waste any time. Do your duty well and you'll be amply rewarded. Just take me to the next rest station and after that you can turn back.'

The man nodded his head and then, without saying a word, got on his horse. Publius Sextius mounted as well, touched his heels to the horse's flanks and rode him out the gate. The two legionaries saluted him and the other rider gave them a quick salute back. They let the two horsemen pass before closing the gate behind them.

As soon as they were outside, they were struck by a blast of cold wind and blowing snow, which was beginning to fall faster and faster.

Publius Sextius drew closer to his companion, who still hadn't opened his mouth. 'What's your name, friend?' he asked.

'Sura.'

'I'm Publius. We can go.'

Sura started down the road, setting a slow, steady pace and lighting the way with his torch. Publius Sextius rode behind him, staying to the centre of the path. He couldn't shake the impression that they were being followed, and kept turning to scan the forest around them. The road was winding and sloped steeply upwards through the oak and chestnut trees green with moss and white with snow. There were no signs of human presence, but the light cast by Sura's smoky torch was weak, so he couldn't be sure.

Publius Sextius had realized immediately that his guide was not a man of many words and he didn't try to make conversation. He asked questions only when necessary, obtaining grunts of assent or refusal in response. He tried to keep his mind occupied with thoughts, reflections, plans. His intention was to reach Caesar in time to depart with him on his expedition to the east, about which he'd heard great things. Caesar's objectives were, as always, formidable.

He had been with Caesar in Gaul and in Spain, and would gladly follow him to Mesopotamia, to Hyrcania, to Sarmatia if necessary. He would follow him to the ends of the earth.

Publius Sextius believed that Caesar was the only man who could save the world.

Caesar had ended the civil wars and had achieved reconciliation with all his adversaries. He was firmly convinced that the only civilization capable of governing humankind was the one that had its fulcrum and force in Rome. He believed that Rome was the world and the world was Rome. He understood his enemies, the peoples who had fought against him to save their independence, he even admired their bravery, but he knew that his victory over them was already destined, written in stone.

Whenever Publius Sextius had had the opportunity to speak with him, he'd been impressed by the expression in Caesar's eyes and by the sense of determination and command that emanated from him. A predator, yes, but not bloodthirsty. He was quite sure that Caesar felt repugnance at the sight of blood.

How often he had marched at his side, watching as the commander rode by, as he spoke with his officers and with his soldiers. When Caesar recognized someone who had distinguished himself on a day of pitched battle, he would always get off his horse to talk with him, make a joke or two. But his most vivid memory of Caesar went back to the night after the battle against the Nervii, after he, Publius Sextius, commander of the Twelfth, had returned to camp on a stretcher, a bloody mess, more dead than alive, but victorious. He had seized the standard that day and carried it forward towards the enemy himself. He had regrouped the fighting units, instilling courage into his men, and had been the first to set an example.

Caesar had come to visit him, alone, in the tent where the surgeons were trying to stitch him up by the dim light of a few tallow lamps. Leaning close, Caesar had said:

'Publius Sextius.'

The centurion could barely form a word but he recognized his commander.

'You saved your comrades today. Thousands of them would have been massacred and years of work would have been lost in a single moment. You saved me, too, along with the honour of the republic, the people and the Senate. There's no reward that equals such an act, but if it means anything to you, you should know that you will always be the man I rely on, even if everyone else abandons me.'

Then he'd lowered his gaze to look at the centurion's body, covered with cuts and gashes.

'So many wounds,' he whispered with dismay in his voice, 'so many wounds . . .'

Publius Sextius wondered why, in this moment of total solitude, in the middle of a night-long journey through the deserted forests of the Apennines, with a snowstorm raging all around, he should remember those words.

In front of him, the inscrutable Sura plodded on at a steady pace, holding the torch high, staining the immaculate snow with its ruddy reflection, leaving behind him the prints of a good, strong, patient horse who continued, one step after another, further and further up the twisting path, under the skeletal branches of the beeches and oaks.

It occurred to Publius Sextius that someone might have gone ahead and be setting a trap. Maybe Sura was leading him into an ambush from which he wouldn't escape. Maybe the message would never arrive at its destination in time. But then he remembered how the innkeeper had insisted that he spend the night in the *mansio*, safe inside under the watchful eye of four legionaries, including Baebius Carbo of the Thirteenth. No one knew where dawn would find him tomorrow.

Sura lit the second torch and threw the first stub into the snow. It glowed for an instant, then died in the darkness of the night. A bird surprised by the sudden light of the torch took to the sky with a shriek that sounded like despair before disappearing far away in the valley.

The wind died down. There wasn't a sound now, or traces of life of any sort. Even the rare milestones along the road were buried in the snowdrifts. All Publius Sextius could hear were Caesar's words, repeated endlessly in his lonely, empty mind: 'So many wounds . . . so many wounds.'

9

In Monte Appennino, per flumen secretum, a.d. VI Id. Mart.,
secunda vigilia

The Apennine Mountains, the secret river, 10 March,
second guard shift, ten p.m.

MUSTELA FLOUNDERED helplessly in the swirling waters of the underground torrent, dragged along by the current. The whirlpools would suck him under the surface, where he tried to hold his breath for as long as he could in a struggle to survive until he was tossed up further along, where he would spit out the water he'd swallowed, gulp at the air and then disappear under the waves again.

He stifled his cries when the current smashed him against the rocks and he could feel blood oozing from his cuts. More than once he thought he would lose his senses as he hit his head hard or took such a pounding from the waves that he didn't think he would survive.

Suddenly he felt something grazing his belly. Gravel and sand. He grabbed at an outcrop of rock and managed to stop and to catch his breath as he lay in a small bend of the river where the water was shallow.

Panting uncontrollably, he tried to work out whether he had any broken bones and to ascertain what was pouring from his side. He touched his hand to his mouth and could tell from the sweetish metallic taste that it was blood. He stuck his fingertips into the wound and discovered that the skin was torn from his hip to his ribcage on the left side. However, the gash had not penetrated too deep and so he hoped that no serious damage had been done.

He could hear the sounds of the waterfall he'd already gone through coming from upstream. Further downstream there was a different noise, deeper and gurgling, but the utter darkness filled him with an anxious uncertainty verging on panic. He had no idea where he was, how far he had come and how much further he had to go. He'd lost all sense of time since the moment when he'd lowered himself into the icy river and let go of the last handhold along the water's edge.

His teeth were chattering and his limbs were completely numb. His feet hung like dead weights and jolts of pain shot up from his side and one of his shoulders. He backed into a craggy area that turned out to be a small, dry cave. It was warmer there and big enough for him to crouch in. He even managed to stop the bleeding by tying a strip of fabric ripped from his clothing around the wound as a bandage. He let himself fall back and drowsed, more out of exhaustion than any desire to sleep. When he came to, he couldn't have said how long he'd been there, but he knew that he had to continue his journey through the bowels of the mountain. He invoked the gods of Hades, promising to make a generous sacrifice if he managed to get out of their underground realm alive. Then he dragged himself back towards the water, lowered himself into the freezing river and let the current carry him away.

For a long time he was tossed around, battered, knocked under and thrown back up, as if he were in the throat of a monster, a sensation that felt more real to his terrified mind than being in the river.

Then, little by little, the speed of the current began to lessen and the channel became wider and less precipitous. Even the crashing noise of the waves died away. Perhaps the worst was past, but he couldn't be sure. He had no way of knowing what new dangers the river might have in store for him.

But he was so exhausted from the cold, his endless struggle and his constant gagging as he coughed up the water he had swallowed that he merely let himself go, abandoning himself like a man would to death. A long time passed, how long he couldn't tell.

The darkness had been so enveloping and so dense until then that he couldn't believe it when the faintest glimmer of light came into view in the distance. Could he have reached the end? Would he see the world of the living again? Hope instilled a surge of energy and he dived into the middle of the river and began swimming. The vault of the tunnel within which the water flowed seemed to lighten imperceptibly, so that he was no longer in pitch blackness. This was the promise of light more than light itself, but with the passage of time it grew stronger until he became aware of the pale glow of the moon brightening the night sky.

Utterly exhausted by the enormous strain on his body and frozen half to death, Mustela fell to the ground, finally outside, finally under the vault of the sky, on a low, sandy bank. He laboriously dragged himself towards dry land and collapsed, without a single drop of strength left in his body.

In Monte Appennino, ad fontes Arni, a.d. VI Id. Mart.,
ad finem secundae vigiliae

The Apennine Mountains, at the source of the Arno, 10 March,
end of the second guard shift, midnight

THEY CONTINUED on the ever narrowing road, one closely following the other, black figures in the reddish glow of the torch, moving over the snowy stretches. Publius Sextius forced himself to count the milestones, when they weren't completely covered, and to keep a lookout for signs of animals that might attack them.

Oppressed by his solitude and worries, he turned to his companion.

'Don't you ever talk?' he asked.

'Only when I have something to say,' replied Sura without turning, adding nothing further.

Publius Sextius went back to his thoughts, brooding over the revelation that had upset him most: that Mark Antony had been asked to participate in a plot against Caesar and, even though he hadn't accepted, hadn't told Caesar either. That could only mean one thing: he was on no one's side but his own. Quite a dangerous quality in a man. Antony must have reasoned that, if the plot was successful, the conspirators would be grateful to him for his silence, and if it failed, he would have lost nothing. But how, then, to explain that gesture of his at the Lupercalia festival? If he was really so smart and so cynical, how could he have committed such a huge error? He had chosen to stand out by making such a blatant move at such a sensitive moment. Perhaps he'd always deliberately acted the part of the simple soldier, who knows nothing of politics, in order to hide his bigger ambitions. But even if that were so, what sense did it make to attempt to crown Caesar king in public? Evidently Antony had known, or had thought he knew, how the crowd would react, so why didn't he worry about Caesar's reaction? Even if he thought he could continue to hide behind his pretended ingenuousness, Antony couldn't ignore the fact that – if a conspiracy was being planned – his gesture would contribute to making Caesar more vulnerable and more alone.

So why had Antony chosen to do such a thing? What could the reason possibly be?

Publius Sextius continued turning it over in his mind, again and again, but it was like beating his head against a wall. Finally, he gave up and instead watched the snow descending silently in huge flakes in the light of Sura's torchlight as they proceeded slowly, ever more slowly, while he would have preferred to race like the wind, to devour the road, to reach his destination before it was too late. Maybe it was already too late. Perhaps all his efforts would prove to be in vain.

There had to be a reason. Fleetingly, when the vice loosened and the cold air let him breathe, he felt he was close to finding a solution. The answer must lie with several key people, not many, perhaps three or four. With the balance of power or interests among them. He forced himself to consider every possibility, the likely motives of each individual and how they might overlap or conflict. He would have liked to jump to the ground and use the tip of his knife to sketch out the complicated connections on the immaculate snow, in the way that he would use the hard ground of an army camp to plan the action for his unit during a battle. But then he would lose track and his thoughts would dissolve into thousands of small, confused fragments, at which point he would realize he was no closer to a solution than he had been at the start and his gaze would drift again to the spinning white flakes.

Now and then he even suspected that the map Nebula had given him in Modena, before disappearing into the morning fog, was leading him straight into a trap. But even if that were so, he convinced himself, he had no choice and had to run this risk. The alternative was arriving too late to pass on his message.

Sura now broke one of his interminable silences to announce that they were close to the source of the Arno river and were on an ancient Etruscan road. He said nothing more.

Publius Sextius rode on, torturing himself with his thoughts all night long.

In Monte Appennino, a.d. V Id. Mart., tertia vigilia

The Apennine Mountains, 11 March, third guard shift,
after midnight

ONLY RUFUS was suffering as much pain as he struggled to
reach the Via Flaminia Minor in as little time as possible, which
meant cutting straight across the mountainside. At first he
followed the barely visible path that wound down the slope
forming the western embankment of the Reno valley to get to
the river. He managed this with considerable difficulty, often
having to dismount and lead his horse by the reins, until he
arrived at the riverbank. The weather had taken a turn for
the worse. The falling snow was now mixed with a fine, relent-
less drizzle that trickled down his cloak and dripped on to the
ground from the hem.

He found the ford by following the sound of the water
rushing between the rocks and urged his horse into the river.
The water deepened at the centre, rising to the horse's chest,
but they were soon treading on a bed of fine gravel and sand,
having reached the opposite bank.

The path on that side ascended steeply, but when Rufus
met up with the snow again the low glimmer of the white
blanket helped him to get his bearings, enabling him to set
forth on the path he had used so many times before. He soon
reached the hut of a shepherd he knew well and he stopped
there to drink a cup of warm milk and eat a chunk of bread
and cheese. The cabin was lit inside by the flames in the hearth.
Its walls, plastered with dried mud, were completely blackened
by the smoke. The whole place stank of sheep, from his host to
the hulking Molossian hound lying on the ash that circled the
hearth, a hairy beast that everyone called by a different name.
Rufus scratched him behind his flea-ridden ears by way of
greeting.

'What are you doing out here at this hour?' asked the shepherd, in a mix of Latin and his Ligurian dialect that not everyone could decipher.

'I have an urgent message to deliver,' replied Rufus between one mouthful and the next. 'What's it like on the summit?'

'You'll be able to make it over, but be careful. I've seen a pack of wolves up there: an old male, two or three young ones and four or five females. They might get brave in the dark and latch on to your horse's hocks. You'd best take a brand from the fire and make sure it doesn't go out until you've reached the top.'

'Thanks for the warning,' said Rufus.

He left a couple of pennies for what he'd eaten and drunk, then, with firebrand in fist, he went back out into the open. At least here he felt that he could draw breath again, clearing the foul stench that had saturated the hut and filled his nostrils.

He took his horse by the reins and started to make his way up on foot, lighting his path with the brand he held high in his left hand. He wondered from what distance the light could be seen. Perhaps at that very moment his commander was standing on the upper terrace at *Lux fidelis* and looking his way. He could almost hear him cry out, 'There he is! I'll bet a month's pay that that bastard has already made it to the crest!'

He didn't have far to go, in fact. Up ahead, less than half a mile away, a group of towering firs marked the ridge.

His horse was the first to sense the wolves and Rufus saw them himself an instant later, the flaming brand reflected in their eyes with a sinister gleam. He didn't even have a stone to throw at them and they didn't look likely to retreat. He shouted and waved the brand. The wolves ran, but stopped just a few paces further away.

Rufus shouted again, but this time the wolves did not retreat. In fact, they began to circle around him, growling. This did not bode well. They were carrying out the pack's strategy for isolating prey and attacking. And he was their prey, or the horse, or both of them.

His horse was bucking and becoming difficult to control. If he panicked and fled, it would be all over for Rufus. He tied the reins to a tree branch so he could move more freely, then clutching his knife in one hand, he continued to wield the brand, which had burned right down to a stub, with the other.

Wolves had never been a problem before. It had always been easy to scare them off. Why were these ones so tenacious and aggressive? He thought of the legend about how his ancestors first arrived in Italy, guided by a wolf. But these were different, ravenous beasts with the worst of intentions. He backed up against a big fir tree and felt the lowest branches crackle, dry and brittle against his cloak. The gods had sent him help. He snapped them off and tossed them on what remained of the brand. The flame sparked up thanks to the resin in the wood and he thrust it forward.

The sudden flare repelled the wolves, but drove them back only just beyond the circle of light. The horse was kicking and whinnying and tugging wildly at the reins. If he hadn't been wearing a bit, he would already have run off. Rufus wondered whether his commander could see this fire as well from the terrace of *Lux fidelis*. Someone was seeing it for sure, but they would never abandon the base without a good reason.

The duel between hunger and flames was about to end with the fire going out. Rufus then did the last possible thing he could, although it was deeply repugnant to him. He begged the gods of his forefathers to forgive him before he piled all the dry branches which remained around the base of the trunk. The fir tree caught fire and in just minutes had turned into a huge blazing torch. His Celtic soul was horrified by the screams he could hear from the spirit of the great fir racked by the flames, but his Roman soul justified the act because he was following the orders of his superiors.

The wolves fled. Rufus picked up one of the fallen branches that was still burning, mounted his horse and continued on his way, crossing a wide clearing and finally reaching the grey slate slabs of the Via Flaminia Minor.

In Monte Appennino, Lux fidelis, a.d. V Id. Mart., tertia vigilia

The Apennine Mountains, Faithful Light, 11 March,
third guard shift, one a.m.

THE STATION COMMANDER had just fallen into a deep sleep when a servant shook him awake.

'What in Hades is going on?' he demanded.

'Master, come immediately – you must see this!'

The commander threw a cloak over his shoulders and, dressed as he was, made his way to the upper terrace. It was snowing and the vision that greeted him was like nothing he'd ever seen before. Directly to the south, at a distance that was difficult to assess, and at an altitude that made the scene look as if it was playing out in mid-air, he could see a globe of intense light surrounded by a reddish halo that trailed off in the direction of the wind in a kind of luminescent tail.

'Ye gods! What is it?'

'I don't know, commander,' replied the sentry. 'I have no idea. I sent the boy to wake you as soon as it started.'

'A comet ... with a tail of blood ... powerful gods! Something terrible is about to happen. Comets bring misfortune. This is a cursed night, lads,' he added. 'Keep your eyes wide open.'

He pulled the cloak tight, as if warding off any evil influence, then hurried back down the stairs and locked himself in his room.

Outside, on the terrace, the servant could not take his eyes off the strange phenomenon, and it surprised him when the light became much brighter for a few instants and then faded until it was swallowed up by the darkness.

The servant turned towards the sentry. 'It's gone,' he said.

'Right,' replied the sentry.

'What does that mean?'

'Nothing. It means nothing. The commander said it was a comet. Didn't you hear him?'

'What's a comet?'

'How am I supposed to know? Go and ask him. And while you're downstairs get me some hot wine. I'm freezing out here.'

The servant ducked down through the hatch, leaving the sentry alone to keep watch over the night.

Ad flumen secretum, a.d. V Id. Mart., tertia vigilia

The secret river, 11 March, third guard shift, one a.m.

MUSTELA AWOKE feeling groggy and numb. He had no idea how long he'd been lying there, curled up in the damp grass. He was completely soaked through. There was no part of his body that didn't hurt and his chest shook with a dry, hacking cough. It was dark and all he could see was the water of the torrent flowing at a short distance. Where was the boat the old man had promised him? He looked around and immediately noticed a clump of trees a little further along the bank. He staggered in that direction. Could those be willows?

A break in the clouds revealed a sliver of moon and for a few seconds Mustela could see that they were indeed, and, sure enough, there was a boat tied to a stake in the river. The dark outline stood out clearly against the silvery moonlit water.

He was close now to the end of his mission. The worst was over, as long as he didn't pass out first. He touched the bandage on his side and his hand came back sticky. So he hadn't managed to stop the bleeding. He fastened the bandage tighter, then walked over to the boat and got in. He pushed off from the bank using one of the oars, then rowed his way into the middle of the current.

All he had to do was let the water carry him, so that's what he did, and little by little, as the river made its way to the plain, the temperature became milder. A light, warm breeze from the south dried him off. The sky behind him was dark and streaked with lightning bolts, but it was slowly growing lighter in front of him. Every now and then, Mustela sunk down to the bottom of the boat and drifted into a light sleep, just for long enough to clear his head.

At the slightest bump his eyes would jerk open and he would take to watching the scenery, the villages and isolated farms gliding past, dark objects standing out against the pale light of dawn. He could hear sounds, but they were largely unintelligible. Once there was someone calling, another time he thought he heard a wail of despair, but for the most part it was just the mournful hiccuping of the screech owls and the insistent, syncopated hooting of other night birds.

It was full daylight and the countryside had begun to come to life when he finally saw it: the Arno!

The torrent he was travelling on flowed into the great Etruscan river that wound lazily down the hillside in great loops, heading towards the plain. The current was becoming much slower, but Mustela was sure that he had been carried many miles downstream.

Although it was hidden by the clouds, he calculated that the sun was high by the time he reached the landing pier at a little river harbour where goods from the mountains were stocked before being sent on to Arezzo, still a considerable distance away. With what little strength he had left, Mustela used the oars to bring him towards the pier and managed to draw up alongside it. The owner of one of the storehouses rented him a mule and gave him a piece of clean fabric so he could change the bandage on his wound, then Mustela continued his journey to the house of the cypresses, hidden inland.

Of all the messengers who had left the Mutatio ad Medias, he had to be the one who had arrived furthest south. Who else could have got as far as he had by travelling downstream on a rushing underground torrent?

Every jolt, at just about every step the mule took on the cobblestoned street, produced a stabbing pain in his side. His muscles, stiff from exertion, numb with cold and cramping with hunger, had long ceased to respond, and tough old Mustela – who'd been through thick and thin in his long life as an informer – could think of nothing other than crawling into a clean bed, in a warm, sheltered place.

The villa appeared on his left after a crossroads and a shrine dedicated to Trivia Hecate, which he took in with a fleeting glance. He turned away from the main road here and set off down the path which led up the hill to the spot where the villa stood, surrounded by black cypress trees.

He was greeted by the furious barking of dogs and by the sound of footsteps on the gravel courtyard. He tried to dismount from his mule so he could announce himself and ask to be received, but as soon as his feet touched the ground he felt his head begin to spin. He realized that he was deathly tired and at the same instant lost consciousness, collapsing like a rag. The last thing he heard was excited shouting and a voice saying, 'Call the boss, fast. This bloke's dying!'

Everything was muddled. He thought he felt the snout of a dog or maybe two poking at him, felt their breath. One was growling, while the other licked at his side where the blood was.

More agitated footsteps. A booming voice: 'Throw him into the cesspool. Who knows who the hell he is!'

He was being lifted by his arms and feet, and suddenly he knew that he had to find enough energy to speak up, at any cost.

'Tell the master that Mustela has to talk to him, now,' he managed, turning to the man who was holding his arm.

'What did he say?' asked the overseer, who was walking alongside them with the dogs.

'He says he has to talk to the master and that his name is Mustela.'

'Move it, you son of a bitch,' Mustela snarled, 'if you don't want to end up in the grinder. Your master will skin you alive if he finds out you didn't give him my message.'

The overseer stopped the little convoy and took a good look at the man they were about to toss in with the excrement. He saw the wound, noticed the hilt of an expensive dagger sticking out from under the ragged tunic and had a moment of doubt.

'Stop,' he said.

10

Romae, in insula Tiberis, a.d. V Id. Mart., hora tertia

Rome, the Tiber Island, 11 March, eight a.m.

ANTISTIUS HAD arrived early, by boat, from Ostia, and was already at the Temple of Aesculapius preparing for the day's work. He belonged to the Hippocratic school and set great store by symptomatology. He kept a register for each and every patient, with a detailed description of his illness, the diet he'd recommended, the remedies applied and the results obtained. He also believed strongly in cleanliness, beating his servants with a rod if he found dust anywhere, or any other sort of filth in the more remote and less visible corners of his office.

This morning he was even more scrupulous than usual, since he was expecting a client for whom he had the highest regard: Artemidorus. He wanted to check on the state of the Greek teacher's vitiligo.

One of Antistius's secrets, and one of the reasons for his success, was his reliance on empirical medicine. But this was something he could ill afford to confess and would never do so, not even under torture.

In the course of his long practice as a physician, he had become convinced that women were the true repositories of medical wisdom, their knowledge being far superior to that of men. He based this conviction on a simple observation: women had cared for their own children since the beginning of time, and since their children's survival was more important to them than their own lives, they had built up a store of remedies whose effectiveness had actually been tested. In other words, they weren't interested in what had caused the illness, what balance or imbalance of humours and elements was at the root of it. They were interested only in stopping the illness from killing their children, and finding reliable strategies to fight it off.

Men were much more adept in the field of surgery: cutting, sawing, cauterizing, amputating, stitching. These were all arts in which men excelled, both because they were more brutal by nature and because they had had ample practice in the rear lines of the field of battle, where – since the beginning of time – thousands upon thousands of men had been sent out to massacre each other, for reasons that had never been adequately studied, much less explained.

This was how Antistius had become the personal physician of Caius Julius Caesar: by demonstrating his imperturbable skill in recomposing the mangled limbs of battlefield survivors. Later, he had also proved that he could take on the elusive symptoms of stealthy diseases by applying remedies known only to him, whose composition he would reveal to no one.

When his assistant announced that Artemidorus had arrived for his check-up, Antistius said that he would see him immediately. He peeked outside and saw no litters. So, Artemidorus had arrived on foot.

'How's it going, then?' asked Antistius as soon as his patient stepped in.

'What can I say? These Romans try hard, you can't deny them that, but what a travesty! Their accent is horrible when applied to the masters of our poetry. But if you were referring to my condition, it's here, look, on the nape of my neck, that I think something is coming out again.'

'Let's take a look,' said Antistius solicitously.

He moved aside the Greek's hair and found the area he was

complaining about. It was just slightly reddened. With a worried clucking, he diligently examined the spot, then went to his locked medicine cabinet. From there he extracted an ointment which he applied with a gentle touch to his patient's neck, which was soon showing signs of improvement.

'This remedy is so effective!' Artemidorus exclaimed gratefully. 'I don't know how to thank you. How much do I owe you?'

'No, nothing at all. Not this time. It's just a little relapse; it's only right that I treat it without asking for a further fee.'

'No, I absolutely won't accept that,' replied Artemidorus, insisting that he must pay, but Antistius was adamant.

'To think,' said the Greek, 'on top of everything, that I'm being treated by the personal physician of Julius Caesar!'

'Our perpetual dictator does honour me with his trust, that's true,' replied Antistius, 'and I'm quite proud of that. In all frankness, I do believe I'm the person best suited to curing his ailments, at least those I have a hand in. The rest . . . is in the laps of the gods,' he concluded with an eloquent sigh.

Artemidorus was puzzled. It was clear that the doctor's words, in particular their tone and the sigh at the end, concealed some kind of message. He might have ignored this and pretended not to understand, but his curiosity and the sensation that something big was in the offing led him to take the bait.

'What do you mean by that?' he asked.

'There are rumours circulating to the effect that Caesar's . . . health may be at risk,' replied Antistius. 'If not much worse.'

'Much worse . . . than his health?' prompted Artemidorus.

Antistius gave a slow nod, accompanying the movement of his head with a long sigh.

Artemidorus leaned in closer until he was practically whispering into the doctor's ear. 'Is it something to do with Brutus?'

Antistius's answering expression needed no words.

'I see,' said Artemidorus.

'You've heard the rumours?' asked Antistius, adding, 'You

know, I do realize that I'm asking a lot of you, perhaps too much, but I swear to you that whatever you tell me will remain within these walls. I will never reveal the source of any information you give me. I must say that I'm honoured to have one of the most eminent proponents of Hellenic culture in the entire city in my care.'

Artemidorus was struck by the doctor's praises. He pondered at length before answering.

'Brutus treats me like a servant,' he finally confessed. 'With arrogance. He humiliates my dignity, for the sole reason that my livelihood here depends on the meagre salary he pays me. You have taken care of me, and you continue to treat me for a repugnant disease that would have disfigured me and made me a laughing stock, without worrying about how much I can pay you. You've expressed more appreciation for my modest talents than I deserve. If I have to make a choice, I would prefer to be on your side, whatever that may involve.'

'I'm infinitely grateful to you,' replied Antistius, trying to hide his excitement. 'When the moment comes, I promise you won't be sorry about this.'

'Tell me what I can do for you.'

'Brutus's name has recently appeared on the city walls and even on the courthouse door, accompanied by an instigation to emulate the distant forefather who drove the last king out of Rome. The implication is clear. It means there's someone out there who wants Brutus to take matters into his own hands and bring down Caesar, the very man who spared his life.'

Artemidorus did not answer and Antistius hurried to reinforce his words.

'Brutus acts in a way that is difficult to understand. Some time ago, he sided with Pompey, despite the fact he was behind his father's death, and now it seems he's plotting against Caesar, to whom he owes his life. Caesar, who pardoned him after the Battle of Pharsalus and allowed him to take up his seat in the Senate and continue his political career . . .

'You Greeks hold liberty and democracy in great regard, and I can imagine that you do not think well of Caesar. But remember that he refused the king's crown when it was offered to him and has used the powers granted to him only to end civil strife. Don't forget that Caesar has no legitimate son. Why would he aspire to a monarchy that would die with him?'

'I'm convinced of what you say. There's no need for you to justify Caesar to me.'

'I'm sorry to hear that Brutus treats you unfairly, even as far as your salary is concerned. I want you to know that if you help us, your troubles will be over for ever. Caesar's generosity knows no limits.'

'I'm willing to help you without any recompense,' replied Artemidorus firmly. 'What do you need to know?'

'Forgive me! I did not mean to imply that I was offering you money in exchange for your help, although we're both well aware that in this corrupt city money is often the only solution. The truth is that I'm very worried about Caesar. I've heard disturbing rumours and the writing on the walls speaks clearly. I'm afraid that Brutus might be persuaded to act rashly, to make a move that would have dramatic consequences.'

'Do you mean . . . a conspiracy?'

Antistius nodded with an enquiring expression on his face. 'Do you know anything that could help me?'

'Nothing certain, mind you. It's really no more than a fleeting . . . sensation. People coming in and going out of the house at odd hours.'

'What do you mean by odd?'

'In the middle of the night, before dawn. Why would any-one receive friends so late at night unless he was hiding something?'

'You're absolutely right. Do you know who these friends are?'

'No. It's always been after dark and the meetings are always held behind closed doors, in Brutus's study. Once I was awakened by the dog barking and then I heard Brutus's voice greeting a group of people coming in through the rear gate.'

'How many people, would you say?'

'I couldn't be sure, but quite a few. Six or seven, maybe more.'

'Can you think of any reason besides a conspiracy for such meetings?' asked Antistius.

'Yes, of course there could be other reasons . . . a political alliance, for example. There are elections coming up. Maybe they are putting together some electoral strategy that they want to keep secret.'

'Possibly, but I'm suspicious nonetheless, and worried. I'd ask you to remain watchful. I want to know who is visiting the house, how many of them there are and why they are meeting. Are there others involved, perhaps, who never show up in person? Keep your eyes open and inform me of anything new immediately.'

'It won't be easy,' replied Artemidorus, 'but I'll do my best. If I learn anything, I'll be sure to let you know.'

'Come here when you have news. If I'm not around, my assistant will know where I am and how to find me at any time. Farewell, Artemidorus. Be careful.'

Artemidorus promised he would and took his leave.

Antistius reflected on the meeting in silence and didn't move until the servant knocked to say that a new patient had arrived.

Romae, Taberna ad Oleastrum, a.d. V Id. Mart., hora octava

Rome, the Wild Olive tavern, 11 March, one p.m.

SITTING UNDER the olive tree, Silius looked at the sun and then at the shadow cast by the pole holding up a skeletal grapevine.

He called the tavern boy over and said, 'Bring me a glass of Tuscolano Rosso and some toasted bread.'

His order was promptly filled. Silius dipped the toasted bread into the wine and began to eat. There weren't many people on the road at this time of day. A sausage vendor had set up a cart at the other end of the square and a group of rowdy youths was swarming around him. Two or three of them distracted him while the others were busy stealing sausages and passing them behind their backs to the last in line. At this point, they exchanged a signal and scampered off laughing. The vendor ran after them with a whip, while others popped out of a narrow alleyway and made off with another three or four sausages.

'The pack at work,' mused Silius, 'drawing the victim away from safety.'

He raised his eyes to the sky for a moment to watch the flight of a couple of gulls. There was no sign of the person he was waiting for. He finished eating and waited some more, ordering another glass of wine now and then.

The owner of the tavern passed by with a bowl of dormouse stew for some other customers and Silius stopped him.

'Are you sure no one has asked for me?'

'I've already told you,' replied the man, 'not a living soul. I know everyone around here. If a stranger showed up I would spot him immediately. Don't you know what this bloke looks like? Tall, short, fat, thin . . .'

'No,' said Silius, looking down. 'I have no idea.'

The tavern owner shrugged and widened his hands as if to say, 'So what do you want from me?'

Silius swallowed another mouthful of wine, wiped his lips with the back of his hand and made to leave. But as he was getting to his feet, he saw a person at the corner of the house on his left making an odd gesture. Could it be him?

Silius took a quick look around and, trying not to attract any attention, walked towards the individual who was beckoning to him. Now he could see the person well. It was a woman of modest appearance, probably a servant or a freedwoman, wearing work clothes, with a rope belt around her waist. She looked about forty, and had the callused hands of a woman accustomed to working in the fields.

'Come this way,' she called as Silius approached. 'I'm the person you've been waiting for.'

'Good. Well, then?'

'The person who sends me says they can't meet with you. They don't know you well enough and can't receive you.'

Silius was clearly irritated. 'Damn it all! But why? Don't they know how important this is? That it's a matter of life or death?'

'I know nothing,' replied the woman. 'I've never even seen the person who sent me here before. I don't even know who it is.'

Silius grabbed her arm. 'Listen to me! I must – whatever the cost – meet with the person who sent you. If you do as I say, I'm willing to pay you well. Say that I have very important information that directly regards the person – and that person's son. You're a slave, aren't you? Am I right?'

'You are,' she replied.

'Well, I promise you here and now that I'll give you enough money to buy your freedom. Just do what I'm asking, by all the gods!'

The woman lightly touched the hand that was gripping her sleeve so Silius would let go, then responded without looking at him, 'Do you really imagine that a woman of my condition can speak to a high-ranking person? I received an order and I learned the words I told you by heart. Tomorrow I'll be on some farm or other tying up bundles of twigs. I'm sorry. I would have helped you willingly.'

She hurried away.

Silius leaned his elbow against the wall, his head on his arm, and didn't move from that position for a long time, torn between anger and frustration, not knowing what to do.

A hand fell on his shoulder. Silius spun around, his fingers round the hilt of the dagger he wore in his belt. He found the innkeeper in front of him.

'That person you were looking for came.'

'What are you saying? I just—'

'A tall bloke, skinny, black circles around his eyes. He left a message for you.'

Silius didn't say another word, but followed the man back to the tavern. The people sitting at the other table were just mopping up the remains of their tasty dormouse stew with some bread. A dog waited hopefully for the bones, which were not forthcoming. The wine jug and empty glass still occupied the table where Silius had been sitting.

The owner took him to the back of the shop and handed him a small sealed scroll. Silius reached for his moneybag and handed over a couple of *denarii* for his trouble, which the man pocketed happily.

Silius moved away until he was safely out of sight in the shade of a portico, then opened the message:

To Silius Salvidienus, hail!

Although your words were veiled, what you are asking is sufficiently clear. I cannot meet you for reasons you can easily imagine. There's not much I can accomplish because I've been kept out of everything.

A chasm lies on either side of the road that will be taken. I shall do whatever is in my power to do, however small that may be.

This letter begins without my signature. My name is in the person you met a short time ago.

Farewell.

Silius at on the base of a column and reflected upon each word of the letter he'd been given. The response to his request was thorough, but difficult to interpret. If the person writing to him had been kept out of everything, what could be done? What was this road between two chasms?

As he pondered the puzzling message, the words fell into place.

A person who was torn between two powerful, contrasting emotions.

A person who could do little but who promised to act.

The signature was there. The name lay in the messenger who had been sent: a servant.

This confirmed that the person writing to him was Servilia.

He had to conclude that she was being kept under strict surveillance, so someone must be afraid that she might reveal something. Who, if not her son? What, if not a plot against Caesar's life?

She couldn't say anything specific because she evidently feared, despite her precautions, that her letter might be intercepted. That was why she signed the letter so cryptically, so that only the designated receiver could identify the sender. Perfect. At this point he had sufficient evidence to warn Antistius first and then Caesar. He would force his commander to defend himself! Perhaps Publius Sextius would arrive soon and could be consulted about organizing a proper defence.

He destroyed the letter and scattered the pieces as he walked swiftly down the long stretch of road that led towards Antistius's hospital on the Tiber Island.

He arrived as the sun was beginning to set. The legionaries of the Ninth, guarding the Fabricius Bridge, lowered their spears as a sign of respect for his rank, since they knew him well. He entered Antistius's office. Each had important news for the other.

Antistius went first: 'Artemidorus says he'll collaborate. He has reason to detest Brutus.'

'What does he know?'

'Not much, to tell the truth. Strange meetings at odd times – in the middle of the night, just before dawn.'

'Names?'

'Not a single one. He couldn't see them in the dark and they went straight to Brutus's study. But I've asked him to investigate and to report back anything he learns. He's said he will and I believe him. And you? Any news?'

'I got a message through to Servilia. It wasn't explicit, but she understood and answered. She can't meet me but she says that she will do whatever she can.'

'Can I see the letter?' asked Antistius.

'I destroyed it as soon as I'd read it, but I remember it very well. It wasn't very long.' He recited it word by word.

'Yes,' agreed Antistius. 'Your interpretation is correct, I'd say.'

'Good. I'll go and tell Caesar.'

Antistius didn't answer at first and Silius watched him, perplexed by his silence. Finally, the doctor said, 'Are you sure that's a wise decision?'

'Of course. Without a doubt.'

'What can you tell him that he doesn't already know? Do you really think he hasn't picked up on the rumours, felt conspiracy in the air, if not already in making? It's clear to me that he doesn't intend to quash any uprising on the basis of hearsay alone. He doesn't want blood. Not now, at least.'

'But Servilia is under surveillance, isn't that sufficient evidence?'

'No, it's not. It means that Brutus might – just might, mind you – be involved. If a conspiracy exists, that is.'

'But don't you understand her words, "a chasm lies on either side of the road"?'

'It depends on how you interpret them. The expression she's chosen is anything but clear. Listen. Imagine that Caesar takes your word on this and unleashes a wide-scale repression. What would he have to do then, exactly? Capture Brutus and put him to death? On the basis of what accusation? Or hire some assassin to take him out? His murder would be instantly attributed to Caesar by those who seek to destroy him. He would be held up to public scorn as a bloody tyrant whose true, vindictive nature had finally been unmasked. That's exactly what Caesar wants to avoid. Telling him would just put him in a worse dilemma.'

'So what should we do?'

'I'm counting on Artemidorus. Imagine that he manages to discover that there truly is a conspiracy and to identify who is in on it. At that point it will be easier for Caesar to lay a trap, expose their plan and then decide what should happen to them. What's more, Servilia has said that she will do something and I think that something may prove to be important. She'll find a way to save her son and the man she loves, even if that seems impossible. We must give her that chance.'

'How can she accomplish such a thing?'

Antistius was creating elaborate doodles on a wax tablet with the tip of his scalpel, as though he were mapping out complex thoughts. He raised his head slightly and looked up at Silius.

'By letting Caesar know the day they've chosen.'

11

Ad fundum Quintilianum, a.d. V Id. Mart., hora duodecima

Villa Quintiliana, 11 March, five p.m.

'YOU'RE FINALLY AWAKE! I thought you'd never open your eyes.'

Mustela turned in the direction the voice was coming from and met the eyes of a heavy-set man with a vigorous, no-nonsense look. A soldier at first glance. An officer.

'It was careless of you to reveal your code name to a servant and even more so to ask to meet me in my home,' he said.

Mustela tried to bolster himself up on his elbows but the effort made him grimace in pain.

'What time is it?' he asked.

'Forget about the time and answer me.'

'I had no choice,' said Mustela. 'Look at me. Your men were about to throw me into the cesspool. Wouldn't have been a nice death, not even for a bloke like me.'

'It's dangerous for you to be here. The sooner you go the better. What do you want?'

Mustela looked out of the window, then said, 'It's late.'

'The twelfth hour, more or less.'

'Oh, gods, I risked my life for nothing. You should have woken me. Why didn't you wake me?'

'Have you lost your mind, man? They had to stitch you up, in case you haven't noticed, with needle and thread. You were more dead than alive when you got here. They had no choice.'

'Listen to me. Two men, three or four at the most, are trying to reach Rome on different roads in order to prevent justice being done. I intercepted a few words at a *mutatio* on the Via Emilia and I recognized one of the two: Publius Sextius, known as "the Cane". Do you know who he is?'

The man's face flushed with sudden anger. 'You bet I know that son of a bitch. He's a damned bastard. I'd like to see him dead.'

'Then stop him, and stop the others.'

'All right. Let's pretend that this is possible, that it's not already too late. How in the name of Hades can I stop the others? You don't even know who they are, do you? Or how many of them are out there. You're asking for a miracle.'

Mustela had finally struggled to a sitting position on the edge of the bed.

'The fact that Publius Sextius left in such haste and that he sent out other messengers as well means that he's determined to stop what's going to happen. It's a fight against time. If we get there first, we'll live. If we get there second, we'll die, and with us the freedom of the republic.'

The officer shook his head. 'Don't feed me that line about the freedom of the republic. I know your kind too well. Follow me, if you can manage it.'

He left the room and walked towards the peristyle. Mustela stumbled after him, groping his way along the wall. They entered a room on the other side of the courtyard. This was the study of Mustela's reluctant host, the master of the villa, who opened a cabinet and removed a scroll. He spread it out on the table. It was a rough map of all the roads between Cisalpine Gaul and Rome.

'If they're in such a hurry, they'll use the easiest roads to travel, so it shouldn't be impossible to intercept them . . .' His finger traced the black lines that represented the consular roads.

'The Via Cassia . . . or the Via Flaminia. What's more, I've been told that it's stormy up on the mountains and that certain passes have been blocked by snow. The couriers I'd been expecting showed up here almost a full day late. Your men won't have an easy time crossing.'

He lifted his eyes and looked directly at Mustela. 'Besides Publius Sextius, who did you see?'

'A stocky man, not very tall, grey beard, hands as huge as a bear's paws, eyebrows joined up over his nose.'

'All right. And then? What did they say to each other? Give me a clue.'

Mustela shook his head. 'How can I do that? I don't have the slightest idea, but I saw this bloke send a signal, so I'm thinking that other messengers may have been sent out as well. Anyway, if we're willing to wager that they'll use the main roads, at least for the last stage of their journey, they'll have to carry considerable sums of money with them or make big promises with the innkeepers on the way if they want to keep changing their horses.'

'But they won't be the only ones. We risk killing off someone who is just going about his business. A merchant, for instance.'

'That's a risk we'll have to take. Anyway, there is something that sets them apart.'

'What's that?'

'The hurry they're in. A damned great hurry. No one will be trying to move as fast as they are. That's how we'll recognize them.'

'I could send light signals . . .'

'No. You can't include enough information, and anyway, they can read them too. They're professionals, remember, and probably well organized. And if I'm here, that means they're probably still crossing the mountains, and will be able to see them easily.'

'You may be right. Let's split up, then.'

'I'll take the old Etruscan trail,' said Mustela.

'We'll cover the other roads.'

Mustela realized that the man hadn't revealed his name. But that was part of the game. From what he'd seen of the mementoes on the walls and the suit of armour in the corner, he was willing to bet that the master of the villa was one of Pompey's veterans. Had probably fought with him at Pharsalus. He was one of those who had held out, the tough ones who had never surrendered and never asked anyone to pardon them. He was surely in touch with the other supporters of Pompey who were still in hiding. He would do anything in his power to stop those couriers from reaching Rome.

'I need a horse,' said Mustela.

'Ready and waiting. But are you sure you want to go on? You've lost a lot of blood. You're in bad shape. The stitches might not hold.'

'I have a contract to fulfil. And if I make it to the end this time, I just might be ready to leave this line of work. I'm too old to run myself ragged like this. But you're right. If I get on a horse, I'm done for. Give me a light vehicle with a couple of horses, some supplies and a blanket or two.'

'As you wish,' replied the officer.

He took Mustela to the stables, where he picked out a couple of sturdy animals and had them hitched up to a wagon. Mustela got on board as a servant was loading the supplies he'd asked for.

'Which way will you go?' asked the officer.

'I'll head down the Etruscan road towards the Via Cassia, but I might decide along the way to follow my nose,' replied the informer. 'That's why they call me Mustela, the weasel.'

As soon as he was ready, he called out to the horses and flicked the reins on their backs. As he was riding off, he said, 'Tell me, commander, why do they call him "the Cane"?'

'Publius Sextius?' shot back the veteran with a smirk. 'I hope you don't find out on your own hide.'

'Get the others moving fast,' said Mustela as he set off. 'There's not a moment to lose.'

He rode off down the path that led from the villa towards the open plain.

A nasty north wind had picked up, fresh from the frosty Apennine ridges, the kind that chills your flesh and gets into your bones. Mustela was still weak and light-headed, but he felt refreshed by the medical treatment he'd received and food he'd been given. He was starting out well rested and he knew he had a vehicle he could put to good use when he felt weary or sleepy. As he ventured into the countryside heading south, he thought that, after all, this wasn't the first time he'd been in such a fix; in fact, he'd been in worse, but if things went as they should, this would be the last time.

INSIDE THE VILLA, the officer mustered his men. A couple of them were his bodyguards and came from the gladiators' school in Ravenna, another couple had served in his unit during the war in Africa and a fifth, Decius Scaurus, was the most experienced of his veterans and had also served in Gaul under Caesar. He rallied them in the peristyle and addressed them.

'Listen closely. Your task is to intercept a certain number of men who are moving along the roads that lead to Rome from Cisalpine Gaul. The most dangerous of them has a name and a nickname. Publius Sextius, known as "the Cane". He's a centurion from the Twelfth, a bastard who has nine lives, like a cat. Have any of you ever met him? He enjoys great fame in certain circles.'

Decius Scaurus raised his hand. 'I served in the Twelfth before going to Africa with you, commander. I know him.'

'Good. Then you'll go with them,' he said, indicating the other two veterans. 'The man who left a few moments ago will probably be travelling the same road, but I wouldn't lay money on his succeeding. The most important thing is stopping the messengers. As for you two,' he continued, turning towards the gladiators, 'you'll recognize him easily even if you've never seen him. He's five feet and a palm tall, neck like a bull's, features carved by a hatchet. He's covered in scars and he's always got that damned cane in his hand. Don't do anything stupid. If you find him, grab him from behind before he sees you, or while he's sleeping. If you take him on face to face, you haven't got a chance in Hades. He'll kill as many of you as are there.'

'We'll see about that,' replied one of the gladiators.

'Shut up, you idiot,' his commander hissed at him. 'You'll do as I say! You two take the Via Flaminia going through the mountains, the rest of you,' he said, turning to the veterans, 'use the Flaminia Minor and then turn on to the Via Cassia. Mustela prefers to work alone, but if you meet up with him and he asks you to follow him, do as he says. The other men you're looking for are from the Information Service. One of them will be easy to identify – a big, burly guy with hands like a bear's paws and eyebrows joined up over his nose. What I told you holds for him as well. He's tough and probably an officer. There's something else that will help you identify them. They're all in a hurry. They won't sit down to eat or stop to sleep. Maybe you'll find them sleeping on their feet, like horses, an hour at a time, then off again. They are determined to get to Rome at any cost. If you succeed in this mission you'll be amply rewarded. You'll earn more than your miserable lives are worth. Now get a move on.'

The men split up, hurrying to prepare their mounts and assemble supplies. The first to set off were Decius and the two veterans. They galloped away down the little path and, once they reached the end, took off to the left, disappearing in a cloud of dust. The others headed in the opposite direction.

The man who owned the villa stood at the doorway watching them until they had all vanished from sight. He signalled for his servants to close up and went back to his study, where he could ponder what had happened in these few hours.

His name was Sergius Quintilianus and he had fought against

Caesar at Pharsalus, where he had lost a son in battle. From there, he had followed Pompey to Egypt. He had been on the ship that fated day, had seen Pompey get into the boat that had been sent from shore. Pompey had been led to believe that he would meet King Ptolemy, from whom he hoped to receive aid, but instead he met his death. Quintilianus had watched help-lessly as the commander of Ptolemy's army, Achillas, pulled out his sword and drove it into Pompey's side: a terrible scene that continued to haunt his dreams. How many times he'd woken himself up, shouting, 'Watch out!' only to realize bitterly that there was no one left to warn. His ears were still full of the screams of despair of the women on board the ship as the sails were immediately raised so they could flee that land of traitors!

After that, Quintilianus went to Africa, where he joined the republican troops of Cato and Scipio Nasica, who had fought and failed against Caesar at Thapsus. He had even taken up arms under Titus Labienus at Munda.

The final outcome of all those battles was that he had lost his son and seen his own men massacred.

He had always fought against other Romans. In defence of political ideals at first, then later consumed by hatred and a thirst for revenge. Always with infinite, piercing bitterness, a feeling that had eaten away at his soul and hardened him against himself and against the world.

Finally, once there was nothing left to hope for and nothing left to believe in, he had retreated to the villa enclosed by ancient cypress trees. He had surrounded himself with armed guards, gladiators and cut-throats, and now and then he indulged in the pleasure of attacking one of his political adversaries. They lived such tranquil lives now, smug in their victory and certain that they were shielded from all danger. He paid well and his mercenaries never failed. Many knew who he was and realized what he was doing, but no one dared react. Their protectors were far away, while he was close.

And merciless.

Mustela had given him reason to hope. Perhaps all was not lost. If he could stop the message from reaching Rome, then everything would fall into place, just as it should.

As he was brooding over his thoughts, he wondered whether he shouldn't have gone out on his own, got into the game personally. Why not defy fate himself, run the risk of dying on a mission fraught with such danger? But he hadn't gone in the end. He hadn't saddled his Pannonian steed, black as the cypresses that loomed over his villa. There was no specific reason, just a kind of paralysis. He was so full of bile he was powerless to make any decision, much less take any action. All he could do was pace back and forth like a lion in a cage, in a house whose decorations spoke only of defeat and humiliation.

Among his mementoes was a portrait of Cato, who, after being defeated at Thapsus, took his own life at Utica rather than live under a tyrant. He was portrayed dressed in a toga as he harangued the Senate. Quintilianus had been there, at that session, and he had been able to instruct the artist in such detail about the bearing of that great orator and patriot that the image was incredibly lifelike and very powerful.

Sergius Quintilianus was a superstitious man as well. In a corner of the room, on a carved wooden pedestal, stood a wax statue of Caius Julius Caesar decked out in full triumphal garb, his decorations a testament to his victories over other Romans, his booty for having spilt the blood of his fellow citizens. The statue was pierced by a number of long pins that Quintilianus scalded in the lamp flame before driving into the wax. It felt like sinking iron into flesh.

Now all he had to do was wait until his men intercepted those messengers. He had no doubt about the reason for such haste, even if Mustela had not explicitly confirmed it. The conspirators had finally decided on the day of reckoning. So it would be happening soon, even though the date remained a secret. Caesar's murder.

Could that be true? The death . . . of Caesar!

The thought took root in his turbulent thoughts.

In front of his eyes was a small door that was closed.

Suddenly he got up and opened it. He found himself inside the little domestic sanctuary that he had dedicated to his fallen son, run through from front to back before his father's eyes on the bloody field of Pharsalus.

He had had a statue crafted, at the base of which was an urn containing the boy's ashes. Every now and then he entered that place of pain and spent some time there. He felt as though he could speak to his son and hear his voice answering him.

He said aloud, 'I will go myself this time. I will be the one to avenge you, son. And if I fail, at least I'll join you in Hades. I'll have put an end to this unbearable life.'

It had become quite dark. Sergius Quintilianus went to the armoury and donned the armour in which he had fought all his battles. He went to the stable, put a bridle and bit on the black stallion and, having mounted, spurred him on.

After a while he had melted into the night, black as his own grief and hatred.

In Monte Appennino, Caupona ad Silvam, a.d. V Id. Mart.,
hora duodecima

The Apennine Mountains, the Woodland Inn, 11 March, five p.m.

IT WAS STILL coming down. Not quite as heavily and without the wind, but the steadily falling flakes continued to thicken the blanket of snow on the ground. In the inn's courtyard, the servants were shovelling the snow into a pile, trying to clear as much of the paved area as possible. The sentry on guard up on the walkway was struck by a dark figure advancing on horseback, coming towards the station. He called his comrade on guard at the main gate, Baebius Carbo.

'Hey, someone's coming!'

'Who is it?' asked Carbo.

'I don't know. A big, heavy-set man on a fine horse. He's heading this way. This place is funny all right. Not a living soul for days and days, then two in a row.'

'All right. I'll open up.'

Carbo pulled back the gate and the horseman entered.

'I'm exhausted and hungry,' he said. 'Is there anything to eat?'

'There's a tavern inside,' replied Carbo. 'If you've got the money.'

The man nodded. He handed his horse over to a servant with orders to dry him off, cover him with a blanket and give him some hay. He turned to Carbo then.

'Terrible weather. Must be tough being on guard duty all night.'

'We're used to it,' replied Carbo.

'Many people come by here?'

'Depends.'

'A man of few words, I see.'

'In my line of work we're free with our fists, not with our tongues. But inside, if you're interested, there's a whore who does the exact opposite,' replied Carbo.

'Not tonight, I'm afraid. I'm in a hurry. I'll get something to eat then. See you later.'

He entered and Carbo watched him until he disappeared behind the door.

The legionary turned to his comrade. 'That lout asks too many questions for my liking.'

'He wanted to know if a lot of people had come by. He asked one question. What's wrong with that?'

'Well, I say he's asked one too many.'

The other guard shrugged and went back to his post on the walkway.

The traveller came out an hour later, claimed his horse and

went towards the gate. Before mounting, he called out to Carbo, 'Valiant soldier! Listen, have you seen anything strange out this way lately?'

'What do you mean?' asked Carbo, thinking to himself, I was right about this bloke! The centurion would be proud of me.

'Well, have you seen anyone whose behaviour struck you as being odd? Someone who was journeying in a great hurry, for example.'

Carbo drew his sword and pressed its point to the man's throat. 'Stop where you are!' he shouted. 'Spread your arms. If you make a move, you're dead.'

'What in Hades is wrong with you, you idiot?'

'One more word, half a word, and I'll slash you open from top to bottom like a billy goat.'

The man obeyed, snorting, and let himself be searched.

A moment later Carbo triumphantly pulled out a Celtic knife. 'Look at this!' he said to his comrade. 'I told you I didn't like this bloke and look at this. He's armed.'

'A lot of people are armed these days,' said his friend sceptically.

'Listen, boy, put down that sword and I'll explain everything.'

Carbo called up loudly to the other guard, 'Come down here. We have to interrogate him. This man is suspicious and I've been ordered to stop anyone who seems suspicious.'

'You've been ordered? By whom?' asked the other, but Carbo was unyielding.

'Get over here, by Hercules!'

The prisoner was held at knifepoint, bound and taken to the guardhouse. Carbo lit a couple of lamps and diligently set about his task.

'What's your name?' he asked.

'My name is Rufus.'

'Rufus what?'

'Just Rufus. Isn't that enough?'

'Don't try and be clever with me. Why were you armed?'

'Because I'm on a mission for the Information Service. So will you untie me now? I do exactly what you're doing: I obey orders given to me by the state and this is a matter of the utmost urgency.'

'Why should I believe you?'

'Listen, I have to get moving. Wasting a single hour could be fatal. I've been racing through the mountains like a madman, trying to gain time, and now you have me trapped here. Hey, if you untie me right now I promise I won't report you.'

'You are in no condition to negotiate. I'm the one who decides here,' replied Carbo without batting an eye.

The soldier who had been on guard duty with him broke in, 'Listen, my friend, this fellow has me convinced. Why don't we let him go? Interference with a state messenger in the line of duty can get you into real trouble.'

'I want proof,' insisted Carbo.

Rufus was furious with himself for having fallen so stupidly into the hands of an inexperienced recruit seeking to get himself promoted, but he tried to stay calm.

'I have a badge but I'm not authorized to display it with my hands bound. If I lose it to anyone, I'll be expelled from the service. Untie me and I'll show it to you.'

Carbo muttered under his breath for a while, then said to his comrade, 'All right, then. Untie him. I'm curious to see where he's hiding this badge of his. I searched him and I didn't find a thing.'

The other soldier obeyed and released the prisoner's hands. Without missing a beat, the gigantic Celt landed a lethal punch and sent Carbo falling to the ground. He simultaneously grabbed his knife in a lightning-swift move and wheeled about to send its point straight at the other soldier's throat before he had even realized what was happening.

'Do you have questions to ask too?' he said.

'No,' replied the soldier. 'No, I don't think I do.'

'Good,' said Rufus. 'If you don't need me here any longer, I'll be on my way.'

With that, he jumped on his horse and rode off in the flurrying snow.

Carbo got up slowly, rubbing his swollen jaw. His opportunity for glory had ended ignominiously.

12

CAESAR LEFT the bath chamber and went for his massage in the small thermal room that had been set aside for him in the home of his brother Lucius, on the Via Aventinus. Antistius sat opposite him with a linen towel around his loins and a tablet resting on his knees.

The masseur, a powerfully built man from Thrace, grabbed his shoulderblades and pulled them back, causing Caesar to utter a stifled moan of pain.

'Ah! My back isn't getting any better! I don't know how I'll be able to ride when I'm leading my troops in the East.'

Antistius looked up from his notes. 'It's riding too much on all your previous campaigns that got you into this fix. That's why your back hurts.'

'It was the Egyptian campaign that really did him in!' snickered the masseur. 'They say that the filly you rode there really put you to the test!' He loosened his hold and let his patient fall back on to the bed.

'Don't talk rubbish, you idiot. Just shut up and worry about doing your job if you can,' said Caesar.

The Thracian began massaging the muscles in his shoulders, then worked his way along the spinal column, dipping his hands now and then in a bowl of scented oil. The room was thick with steam and Antistius was sweating profusely, but he continued to make notes on his tablet.

Caesar raised his head and looked at him upside down. 'What are you writing, Antistius?' he asked.

'Names.'

Caesar gestured to his masseur, who picked up his tools and left the room.

'Names? What names?'

Antistius hesitated for a moment, then said, 'Names of my patients. I write down their illnesses, the progress made in therapy, any worsening of the symptoms . . .'

'What you say is credible,' replied Caesar. 'But something tells me you're lying.'

Antistius started slightly, but continued writing on the tablet. 'Want to take a look?'

Caesar sat up on the bed and stared at him with his grey falcon's eyes without managing to meet his gaze.

'It's like playing at dice, isn't it? You're inviting me to call you, to see your throw. But to see one has to raise the bet. What do you want, Antistius, to raise the cup? To show me your dice?'

'Nothing, Caesar. It makes no sense to raise the bet. There's nothing important to see.'

'Well, then . . . I pass,' said Caesar, turning his gaze to a fresco faded by the dampness on the wall. It depicted Theban king Pentheus being torn apart by the maenads.

A long silence followed, pierced by the loud squawks of a seagull fishing in the river.

Silius walked in and approached Caesar.

'The guests will all be present,' he said. 'And there's a message for you.'

'News about my . . . cane?' asked Caesar.

Silius shook his head as Antistius was saying, 'You may have an aching back, Caesar, but you don't need a cane. Not yet. And if you follow my advice you won't be needing one for quite some time.'

Caesar got up, put on his military fatigue tunic and followed Silius out, under the perplexed, pensive gaze of his doctor. They walked towards the Domus Publica.

'Unfortunately we haven't heard anything further from Publius Sextius. Why are you so worried, if I may ask? You have already got the news you were waiting for. What more do you require from him?'

There was the slightest hint of jealousy in his tone.

'You're right, Silius, but I've been feeling the need to surround myself with people I trust completely and Publius Sextius is one of them. I want him here, now. When that first message came, I thought he'd be following soon after. It's strange that he hasn't arrived yet.'

They had reached the Domus, and Silius led the way to Caesar's study. There, sitting on a silver tray, was the minuscule cylinder of leather, bearing a seal, that had just been delivered. It had a worn look. Caesar smiled.

Words rang in his mind: 'Have it back, you villain!'

Obsessively: 'Have it back, you villain!'

'Have it back, you villain!'

It was Cato's voice, ringing in his mind. Cato, who would kill himself at Utica. Caesar's nightmare, the implacable ghost that haunted him like a Fury. And yet those words had brought to mind a situation more comic than tragic. It had happened twenty years ago, in the Senate. Cato had accused him of colluding with Catiline and his rebels in trying to overthrow the state, and as he was still speaking Caesar received a scroll in a leather case just like the one sitting now on his table. Cato had noticed the slave delivering it and he thundered, 'Here is your proof! This villain is receiving instructions from his accomplices before our eyes, in this very hall!'

Without batting an eye, Caesar had passed the missive directly to the outraged orator, who, upon opening it, realized it was a torrid letter of love from his sister Servilia, inviting Caesar to come to her house in her husband's absence. In very explicit terms that left nothing to the imagination. Cato had thrown it at him, shouting, 'Have it back, you villain!'

When he saw the stupefied expression on Silius's face, Caesar realized that he had actually pronounced those words out loud.

'Don't worry about me,' he said gently. 'It's just my condition. Sometimes the past becomes the present and the present vanishes like a distant memory. I live in uncertainty, Silius. And I still have so much to accomplish. So much needs to be done. But leave me now, please.'

Silius walked away reluctantly.

Caesar broke the seal with the tip of a stylus and opened the case that contained a tiny parchment scroll with a few words written in a hand he knew well. He smiled again and put the message into a drawer, which he locked.

He walked through his bedroom into the dressing room, took off his fatigue tunic and dressed carefully, taking fresh clothing from a chest.

Calpurnia walked in just then. A slanting sunbeam lit up her dark eyes. She was thirty-three but still had the fresh grace of a country girl.

'What are you doing? Why is no one helping you?'

'I don't need help, Calpurnia. I'm used to dressing myself.'

'What's wrong?'

'I'm worried. Normal for a statesman, wouldn't you say?'

Calpurnia looked into his eyes. 'Are you going out?'

'Yes, but I'm not going far. I'll be back for dinner.'

Caesar felt touched by a wave of affection for the woman he had married for reasons of state. She was meant to give him a child and she wanted to do so. He could feel her humble melancholy and it weighed on his heart. Calpurnia had been an excellent wife, above any and all suspicions, as Caesar's wife should be, and he had grown quite fond of her. Perhaps he even loved her.

'Who's going with you?'

'Silius. Silius will come with me. Tell him to wait for me in the *atrium.*'

Calpurnia walked off with a sigh.

Caesar finished dressing, adjusted his toga on his shoulder as he was accustomed to wearing it, then walked down the stairs.

'Where are we going, commander?' asked Silius.

'To the Temple of Diana in the Campus Martius. But you stay here at the Domus. Everyone will assume that I'm here as well. If Calpurnia sees you and asks you what you're doing here, tell her that I changed my mind. It's a nice walk. It'll do me good after the massage.'

'Does this walk have something to do with the message I brought you?'

'Yes.'

Caesar said nothing else and Silius asked no further questions.

He walked to the temple, immersed in thought. He reached the sanctuary, entered the silent, empty building through a side door and went to sit on a bench set against the perimeter wall to the left of the statue of the goddess. It wasn't long before the silhouette of a female figure with her head veiled appeared in the entrance. The woman walked straight to the image of Diana: a lovely Greek marble statue that portrayed the goddess in a short tunic, carrying a bow and quiver. The woman placed a few grains of incense in the perfume brazier.

Caesar emerged from the shadows and stood behind a column.

'Servilia . . .'

The woman uncovered her head. She was still stunning, even though she was nearly fifty. Her hips swelled below her high-waisted gown and its low neckline revealed firm, full breasts. Only her face revealed the signs of all the emotions of a troubled life.

'Who but me?' she replied. 'It's been so long . . . I wanted to see you.'

'Is there something you have to tell me?'

They drew nearer until their faces were so close that their breath mingled.

Servilia hesitated before answering. 'I wanted to say goodbye, because I didn't know if I'd see you again. Rumour has it that you've drawn up your forces for your expedition to the East. I didn't know whether I'd see you before you left. You have so many responsibilities . . . so many duties, pressing upon you . . . so your old friend just wanted to see you, to say farewell.'

Caesar took her hand and stood that way for long moments, as if unwilling to let go. Then he raised his eyes to hers.

'I've stayed away for a long time before and you never felt the need to say goodbye. Why now?'

'I don't know. This huge enterprise that you're taking on, it may keep you away from Rome for many years. Who knows? I'm no longer a young girl. I might not be here when you come back.'

'Servilia . . . why say such a thing? It's much more likely that something will happen to me than to you. I try to look to the future with serenity, but I'm tormented by such frightful visions . . . I feel cold . . . and I'm afraid sometimes.'

Servilia drew so close that he could feel her nipples touching his chest.

'I would like so much to warm you, as I used to do, when you loved me, when you couldn't stand to be without me, when I was . . . your obsession. I'm worried to hear that you're afraid of leaving for the war. You've never felt that way before.'

'I'm not afraid of leaving . . . I'm afraid of not leaving.'

'I don't understand.'

'Don't you, truly?'

Servilia dropped her gaze and fell silent. Caesar's fingers

brushed the big black pearl set between her breasts. A fabulously precious gift that he had given her, worn proudly whenever she was in public, like a soldier flaunting his decorations. He had sent it to her the day he married Calpurnia, to let her know that his passion for her was as strong as ever.

'I want to go, to leave this city. Rome is against me. She is my enemy.'

Servilia's eyes were bright with the promise of tears.

'The greater your power, the more you are envied. The greater your courage, the more you are hated. It's inevitable. You've always won through, Caesar. You'll win through this time as well.'

She brushed his lips with a kiss and walked towards the door.

'Wait . . .' The word seemed to escape his lips.

Servilia turned.

'Is there nothing else you want to tell me?' asked Caesar.

'Yes, that I love you. As I always have and as I always will. Good luck, Caesar.'

As she walked away, he leaned his head against a column and let out a deep sigh.

Servilia crossed the threshold into the bright sunlight, tinted golden in the doorway. Her figure was about to dissolve in the rosy glow of the setting sun but she stopped, without turning.

'Heed the warnings of the gods. Do not ignore them. That's all I can tell you. Farewell.'

She vanished.

Caesar stood pondering over those words, which sounded so mysterious on Servilia's lips. She knew how little stock he placed in the gods and in their warnings. What was she trying to tell him?

He left the temple as he had come in, through the side door, and walked towards the Tiber. Servilia had disappeared completely. He couldn't catch sight of her anywhere. A couple of beggars asked for alms without recognizing him. A dog chased after him for a little while, wagging its tail, then stopped, panting, weak from hunger.

Further up the road on the right, near the banks of the Tiber, stood a *sacellum*, an old shrine displaying the image of an Etruscan demon, worn with age. As if by magic, as Caesar was approaching a man cloaked in grey emerged from behind the little shrine. He was neither young nor old, his hair was straggly and matted, his sandals unstitched. Jangling metallic discs hung from the cane he held tight in his hand. Caesar recognized him. He was an Etruscan augur, from an ancient, noble family, the Spurinna line. He led a lowly life, scraping by thanks to the offerings of the faithful and those who came to him to learn what the future would bring. Caesar had often seen him attending the ceremonies at which he officiated, when the augur had sometimes been allowed to examine the entrails of the animals killed in sacrifice and to interpret the will of the gods.

He meant to approach him and to greet him, but the man stopped short. He stared at Caesar, his eyes rolling, and hissed, 'Beware the Ides of March!'

Caesar blurted out, 'What on earth . . .' but he never finished his question, for Titus Spurinna had already vanished, like a ghost.

Upset by the soothsayer's words, Caesar wandered the city streets for some time, seeking to understand their meaning, while Silius, troubled by his long absence, was at the Domus Publica, preparing a search party. If anything had happened to Caesar he could never forgive himself.

When he was close to the Tiber Island, Caesar was startled by the blast of a bugle that called him back to the real world: the signal that the first shift was mounting guard at Ninth Legion headquarters. He quickened his pace and soon met up with Silius at the Temple of Saturn, just as his adjutant was about to unleash a thousand men to turn the city upside down.

Calpurnia, who had been told of his return, ran towards him weeping.

Caesar looked around in amazement. 'What is happening here?' he said with a tinge of irritation.

'We feared for your life, commander,' replied Silius. 'You were gone too long.'

Caesar did not answer.

In via Flaminia Minore, Caupona ad sandalum Herculis,
a.d. IV Id. Mart., ad initium tertiae vigiliae

The Via Flaminia Minor, the Hercules's Sandal tavern, 12 March, start of the third guard shift, after midnight

THE HORSEMAN rode up at a brisk pace from the snowy road. He was numb with the cold. There was a vast clearing at the side of the road where a stone house stood, covered with slate roof tiles. A squared-off stone wall enclosed the courtyard and a wooden shed with a lean-to on the right offered shelter for horses and pack animals, on a nice bed of straw. A sign hung over the main entrance with a drawing of the sandal that gave the inn its name. The place seemed deserted. The man dismounted and passed under the torch that lit the entrance, revealing the gaunt face and prickly beard of Publius Sextius, 'the Cane'. He strained his ears and heard the faint sound of voices and other noises coming from the courtyard.

He tied his horse to an iron ring hanging from the wall and knocked three times on the door with the hilt of his sword. There was no answer, but the door swung open and inside he could see a knot of people gathered around something near the stable. As he got closer he noticed a trickle of clotted blood at their feet, staining the snow that covered the ground.

Publius Sextius pushed his way into their midst and found the object of their attention: the body of a man, lying with his face in the dung, with a large wound at the nape of his neck from which dark, steaming blood was still flowing. He was wearing a grey wool cloak, torn in several places and stained with dried blood as well. Cuts on his arms and hands showed how hard he'd fought off his assailants.

Filled with foreboding, Sextius got down to his knees in front of the stiff body. He signalled for one of the bystanders to shine his lantern closer and turned the man over.

It was the workman he'd met at the changing station. How could he have made it so far, so soon? Certainly by way of short cuts that he'd kept secret, but that had ensured he'd arrive just in time for an appointment with death.

His hands were as big as shovels, his palms covered with calluses. The eyebrows meeting at the centre of his forehead, the bristly beard and the wide wrestler's shoulders left no doubt as to his identity.

Now he was only a poor lifeless thing.

Publius Sextius felt a wave of fury swelling the veins in his neck and accelerating the beating of his heart. He turned to the bystanders and got to his feet, a man of imposing bulk, gripping his shiny, knotty cane in his hand.

'Who did it?' he growled.

A timid, stout man with watery eyes stepped forward – surely the innkeeper.

'Two blokes showed up three hours ago, from the south. We had already tended to their horses and they were about to leave when this man arrived. He watered his horse and asked for fodder and barley. He said he'd eat something in the stable, because he had to set off again immediately. I thought I saw the other two exchanging a look . . .'

Publius Sextius loomed over the little man. 'Continue,' he ordered.

'They must have gone after him. We didn't hear anything. It was the stable boy who found him when he went to change the bedding for the animals and he ran in to get me. When we arrived he was already dead. Then you showed up.'

Publius Sextius glared at them as if deciding which of them to assault with his cane, but he saw only bewildered expressions, faces frozen with cold and fear.

'We had nothing to do with it, centurion,' swore the innkeeper, who had noticed the knotty symbol of Publius's rank. 'I promise you. I'll make a written report and you can give it to the judge in town.'

'There's no time for that,' replied Publius Sextius brusquely. 'Tell me what the two of them looked like.'

'Oh, they were riding fine horses, they were well dressed and equipped, they wore boots of good leather. But they were as ugly as could be, jailbirds if you ask me. Hired assassins, most probably. This man had nothing valuable with him. And it doesn't look like they stole anything from the satchel he was carrying, although it was clear they searched through it. They were looking for something, that's for sure.'

'Was there anything peculiar about their features?'

'One of them had a slash across his right cheek, ten or twelve stitches wide, an old scar. The other was hairy as a bear and his bottom teeth protruded over the top ones. Really ugly, like I said. Looked like gladiators.'

'You're quite observant,' noted Publius Sextius.

'You have to be, doing the job I do.'

'How far is it to the Arno river ferry?'

'It's over that way,' said the innkeeper, pointing towards a path that headed down into the valley. 'It won't take more than two hours. You might even make it across in that time if you manage to wake up the ferryman and convince him to take you.'

'Can you change my horse?' asked Publius Sextius. 'This one is done in. But he's a fine animal. In a couple of days you'll be able to use him again.'

'All right,' said the innkeeper. 'Can you pay the fee?'

'Yes, if it's not too high. And I'll leave you something to bury this poor wretch.'

Publius Sextius quickly settled his negotiations with the innkeeper for changing his horse, adding enough for a modest funeral. He was deathly tired, the muscles in his arms and legs were seizing up with cramp and he had blisters on his inner thighs from riding so long. Still, he gritted his teeth; he'd known worse.

He rode off, and after a while realized that the road had begun to descend. Well before dawn he heard the voice of the river flowing down below.

In Monte Appennino, ad rivum vetus, a.d. IV Id. Mart.,
tertia vigilia

The Apennine Mountains, at the old river, 12 March,
third guard shift, one a.m.

RUFUS, who had managed to escape the clutches of the over-zealous guard, was trying to make up for lost time by travelling as fast as he could along a short cut through the chestnut wood. The ride wasn't too difficult, since the earth had been beaten flat by the passage of innumerable flocks of sheep and he was able to keep up a good pace. Every now and then he'd run into a tree trunk and a pile of snow would come crashing down on to his head or on to the horse's neck, but that didn't slow him down. The freshly fallen snow still reflected enough light and, if his calculations were right, the moon would be rising soon. He thought of Vibius, who was travelling just as fast as he was, towards the Via Flaminia, cutting straight across Italy to get there. He'd always arrived sooner than his comrade and he wasn't going to be beaten this time either.

A night bird, maybe a tawny owl, let out a hoot in the silent immensity of the surrounding mountains and Rufus muttered a magic spell under his breath.

13

Romae, in aedibus Bruti, a.d. IV Id. Mart., hora secunda

Rome, the home of Brutus, 12 March, seven a.m.

ARTEMIDORUS'S ROOM was worthy of a master of rhetoric who thrived on literature and Stoic philosophy. His *capsa* was filled to the brim with scrolls, each of which was classified and labelled. They were his wealth and well-being, and he would never dream of parting with them. He sat on a wooden chair with a dark leather seat and back. On his work table were a pitcher of water and a trayful of his favourite sweets prepared by one of the girls in the kitchen, a hedonistic weakness that he would swiftly spirit away whenever anyone knocked at his door.

His relationship with the master of the house was based mainly on his imparting instruction in the technical skills required for speaking the Greek language, such as grammar and syntax, the correct pitch required for public discourse, the ability to cite the great authors with due emphasis. Brutus had never sought other knowledge from Artemidorus, had never asked for a lesson in the art of living or in philosophical meditation, and this made the Greek feel belittled, his intellectual status disparaged. Whenever he had attempted to introduce a loftier topic, Brutus had cut him off, making it clear that he didn't consider him equal to the task. This was the true reason Artemidorus despised his student and was willing to betray him. He couldn't stand feeling excluded, his status as a philosopher going unrecognized.

Brutus's stoic faith ran deep; he was nearly a fanatic. His idol, as everyone knew, was the uncle who had died at Utica. Cato, the patriot – the man who had preferred to die rather than to plead for his life, to give up his freedom.

Brutus had joined Pompey's cause before the Battle of Pharsalus and was proud of his choice. Although he held Pompey responsible for his father's death, at that moment he was the defender of the republic, and Brutus had been ready to set personal resentment aside and fight at his side.

ARTEMIDORUS's bedchamber communicated directly with his study and that morning, at dawn, as he was still half sleeping, he had heard noises. He went from his bed to his study and from there, standing at a slight distance from the window, he could see the little portico of the inner courtyard, where a group of people had gathered. It was almost impossible to recognize them, however, from that vantage point. He left his study, moving stealthily down a narrow corridor and into a tiny service yard. From there it was just a few steps to the latrine, which was separated from the courtyard where they'd chosen to meet by a flimsy wall that Artemidorus realized he could easily perforate with a stylus. There were areas where the urine fumes had eaten away the whitewash, leaving it paper thin. He could see, and hear, what was taking place on the other side.

He put his eye to the hole he'd made in the wall, but his view was mostly blocked by the grey tunic of whoever was standing closest to it. He could clearly hear, on the other hand, the unmistakable timbre of Cassius's voice addressing a man he called Rubius, then naming Trebonius and Petronius.

This last man asked, 'Where's Antony?'

'Antony,' replied the man who had answered to the name of Trebonius, 'must stay out of this. I've always said he shouldn't be involved.'

Another man, whom Artemidorus could not see, said, 'Right. Which means we'll leave him with a free hand to play whatever game he pleases. The old man says—'

'Hold your tongue,' ordered Brutus's distinct voice. 'We all know what the old man thinks. But I'm convinced he's wrong. There will be no discussion. Antony has nothing to do with this.'

'No?' shot back the man Brutus had hushed. 'Antony is closer to him than anyone else. He is the consul in office, and he may well take the situation in hand once our man is eliminated.'

'He won't make a move,' replied Brutus. 'I'm sure of it. What do you think, Quintus?'

'Quintus,' reflected Artemidorus inside the latrine. 'That must be Quintus Ligarius. Yes. The man who was accused of high treason before Caesar, who was defended by Cicero and absolved of his crime.' He was becoming more certain with every passing moment that these were conspirators and they were plotting against Caesar. They meant to kill him.

Quintus's reply was muffled as the group moved off through the garden, probably heading for Brutus's study. He recognized again, at a distance, the voice of Cassius, who had visited the house countless times. He was thinking of going back to his room when he heard the crunch of approaching footsteps on the gravel in the courtyard. He realized he was trapped. One of the men was coming to use the latrine and he would be caught in an embarrassing, and highly suspicious, position. He tried to act like a man who'd had an urgent call of nature so they wouldn't imagine he was there for other reasons, but the footsteps suddenly stopped. Another step and then that one stopped as well.

Voices.

One belonged to Quintus Ligarius. 'Do you want to know what I think, Cassius? I think the old man's right.'

'Yes, so do I. Antony is too dangerous. He must be eliminated as well. His first reaction will be to seek revenge and then to take our man's place. Or vice versa. It won't matter, will it?'

Quintus had called this man Cassius, but his voice was quite different from the Cassius Artemidorus knew so well. So there must be two Cassiuses. This one must be . . . Of course, he'd met the man himself right there in Brutus's house. They'd spoken about the theatre on an evening that Cicero had been present as well. So it must be Cassius Parmensis, then. Imagine that! The tragic poet meant to move from fiction to reality, to stain his hands with blood just as his characters dipped into the red lead oxide on stage.

'Unfortunately,' added Quintus Ligarius, 'Brutus won't hear of it and I don't understand why.'

'I think it has something to do with Caius Trebonius. I've heard that they met last year in Gaul after Caesar had won at Munda. Something happened then, but Trebonius has never wanted to talk about it. At least not with me. Perhaps a mutual pact of non-belligerence, or some other kind of alliance. I'm not sure.'

'What does Brutus have to do with it?' asked Cassius Parmensis.

'That I don't know. But he refuses to be reasonable about Antony. Not even the old man could convince him, even though he's always said, "If you don't kill him as well you'll regret it!" And maybe the old man's right.'

'We'd better go back to the others,' said Ligarius. 'We've had more than enough time to take a couple of pisses.'

As they walked away, Artemidorus had his heart in his mouth and tears in his eyes from breathing in the urine fumes. He finally let out a sigh of relief. He waited until the footsteps crossed the gravel, then echoed on the pavement of the peristyle, before slipping out of the latrine. Unfortunately for him, he didn't realize that he'd left his hiding place too soon and had been seen by one of the two men.

Having reached the safety of his study, Artemidorus sat

down and took several long breaths, wiping the sweat from his brow with the sleeve of his tunic. When he felt calm enough he went to a cabinet from which he took a jar full of salt. He dipped his hand into the white crystals and fished out a small roll of parchment paper on which he'd written a few names. He took his pen and added a few more:

> *Cassius Parmensis*
> *Quintus Ligarius*
> *Rubrius . . .*
> *Caius Trebonius*
> *Petronius . . .*

He made a note at the side of his list: 'The one they refer to as the "old man" must be Marcus Tullius Cicero. But he's never been present. He must not be in on it.'

He sprinkled some ashes on the fresh ink, rolled up the parchment and hid it in the salt jar.

Romae, in aedibus Bruti, a.d. IV Id. Mart., hora quarta

Rome, the home of Brutus, 12 March, nine a.m.

'YOUR MOTHER has been out.'

Porcia pronounced this very brief phrase with the tone of one proclaiming a death sentence. Brutus was sitting in his chair with his head between his hands. He was scowling and deep wrinkles were furrowing his brow, as usual of late. He got up slowly and placed both palms on his desktop.

'What does that mean?'

'It means that she escaped our watch and left the house.'

'When?'

'Yesterday evening, towards sunset.'

'So where did she go?' asked Brutus in a monotone.

'I don't know. Do you, perhaps?'

'How could I know? I have other things on my mind.'

'Tell me that you don't realize the seriousness of what I'm telling you! Your mother, for years, was Caesar's mistress!'

'That's enough!' burst out Brutus.

'I'm sorry,' said Porcia, bowing her head and softening her tone of voice. 'But I'm not saying anything you don't already know. Your mother may have met with Caesar and put him on his guard. Maybe she even told him about the conspiracy!'

'My mother knows nothing.'

'Your mother knows everything! Nothing escapes her, not the smallest detail. She has eyes and ears everywhere. By putting her under surveillance all you did was confirm her suspicions.'

'If what you're saying was true, the tyrant's cut-throats would already be at our door.'

'There's still time. That may yet happen.'

'No, it's impossible. My mother would never betray me.'

Porcia drew close and took one of his hands in hers. 'Marcus Junius,' she began, 'do you really know so little about the heart of a woman? Don't you know that a woman will stop at nothing to save the man she loves?'

'Even having her son murdered?'

'She knows that won't happen. Why do you think Caesar spared your life after Pharsalus? Why has he always protected you so stubbornly whenever any of his men have demanded your head?'

'Enough, I said!' he repeated, furious.

'For love of your mother. Last night she may have revealed the entire plan to him, asking him to spare you. Caesar would have assented. There's nothing she could ask for that he wouldn't give her.'

'Please, that's enough now,' said Brutus again, trying to control his rage.

'If you insist,' replied Porcia. 'But shutting me up won't

change anything. I will now tell you what I know. You are free to act as you feel best.'

Brutus said nothing and Porcia started speaking again.

'Your mother went out yesterday evening, towards sunset, with her head veiled. She left via the back door of the laundry, sending one of her serving maids to take her place in her chambers. She walked all the way to the Temple of Diana and she remained there for some time, an hour at least. Then she returned to the house, coming in the same way she'd gone out.'

'How can you say she met Caesar?'

'Who but him? Why else would she set up such an elaborate ruse? Your mother does not believe in the gods, so she certainly didn't go to the temple to pray. The only plausible reason for her slipping out like that is that she wanted to see Caesar. And if she did, we are all in serious danger. I am ready to sacrifice myself, you know that. I'm not afraid. But if your plan fails, the republic will remain in the grips of a tyrant for years. Rome will be humiliated and will not be able to rise from the state of degradation she has fallen into. Brutus, forget that she is your mother. Think of her as a potential enemy of the state. I'll go now and leave you to decide. There's another person outside who wants to speak with you.'

'Who is it?'

'Quintus Ligarius.'

'Tell him to come in.'

Porcia walked out, leaving behind the slightest hint of lavender, the only outward sign of her femininity.

Quintus Ligarius walked in. 'Please pardon this intrusion,' he said before even taking a seat. 'I was already halfway home when a thought and an image came to me, and I felt I must share them with you.'

'Go on. I'm listening.'

'When we were meeting early this morning, Cassius Parmensis and I saw a man leaving the latrine in great haste, a person we've often seen here in your home. Your Greek teacher, Arte-midorus.'

Brutus gave a wry smile. 'Everyone needs the latrine now and then.'

'Yes, but Cassius and I had been speaking in the courtyard and he may have heard something. The latrine door is quite thin.'

'Were you speaking of something . . . important?'

'We speak of nothing else these days, as you well know.'

Brutus frowned. 'I understand, but I certainly can't—'

'I'm not talking about taking drastic measures, obviously,' replied Ligarius. 'But I would increase surveillance until the day we've agreed upon, as a precaution. In other words, I would not allow him to leave this house for any reason. Your servants can take care of getting him anything he needs, for the moment.'

Brutus nodded. 'You're right. We mustn't run any further risks.'

'Any further risks? Why, has something else happened?' asked Quintus Ligarius in alarm.

'No, not that I know of,' lied Brutus.

'Thank goodness for that. With every passing hour, things are becoming more dangerous for us. I'll leave you, then. I'll wait for your signal when the time comes.'

'I'm seeing Cassius Longinus this afternoon. It seems he has important news. We may need to see each other again soon.'

'You know where to find me,' replied Ligarius as he left.

As soon as he had gone, Brutus called in the head servant, a man named Canidius who had always been loyal to his father-in-law and was just as devoted now to his wife, Porcia. Brutus asked him to sit down and said that he had reason to be suspicious of Artemidorus and that the Greek mustn't be allowed to leave the house for several days. He would inform them when this restriction on the man's liberty was no longer necessary.

'How far must I go in enforcing this?' asked Canidius.

'You must physically prevent him from leaving the house, if words do not suffice. But don't irritate him any more than necessary. Do not humiliate him and, above all, don't arouse his suspicions.'

'What reasons shall I give for restricting his freedom?'

Brutus reflected for a few moments. 'Perhaps you won't need to. Artemidorus goes out very little as a rule. I'll assign him an urgent task that will keep him busy for as long as necessary. If he insists on going out, tell him that it's a temporary measure of discretion that the family is adopting for a limited amount of time. Or simply have him followed if he does leave the house.'

Canidius nodded and withdrew without asking further questions.

ARTEMIDORUS, in the meantime, was strolling along the peristyle of the indoor garden with an air of nonchalance until he found himself at the spot in which he'd made the hole in the wall that separated the latrine from the garden. He plugged it up with a little plaster mixed with water from the fountain. He wasn't worried, but he did want to finish up the little investigation he was carrying out for his doctor, Antistius. He was convinced that there were still just a few names missing. One of the young slave boys who went to bed with him in exchange for a few coins had a friend who had lived since her birth in the home of Tillius Cimber, another person who had frequently visited the house at odd hours, and he was hopeful that his list would soon be complete.

When he was summoned by Brutus a couple of hours later, he felt a bit uneasy. Brutus was a man who respected schedules and it wasn't lesson time.

Brutus told him that he was expecting visitors from Greece, a philosopher with his disciple, in a few days' time. The Greek library was in disarray and must be put in absolutely perfect order before the guests arrived. He wanted to make a good impression and so he expected Artemidorus to personally – with a certain emphasis on the word – take care of the matter.

Artemidorus agreed to do so immediately. In truth, it didn't seem to him that the Greek library needed much tidying up. He'd consulted a text by Aratus of Soli just the day before and everything had looked more or less in place. At the worst, it might take him a couple of hours to sort through the scrolls. He walked to the west side of the house where the library was located, but even before he crossed the threshold he stopped dead in his tracks. It looked as though an entire horde of barbarians had ransacked the place, or that someone had been searching for something hidden among the scrolls that were lying here and there in utter confusion, either piled up in huge mounds or scattered all over without reason or logic.

The sight of that disaster left him perplexed at first, but then a certain doubt wormed its way into his mind and fear replaced surprise. He set to work grudgingly, brooding over any number of the thoughts that were crowding his head, none of them reassuring.

Romae, in aedibus M. T. Ciceronis, a.d. IV Id. Mart., hora nona

Rome, the home of Marcus Tullius Cicero, 12 March, two p.m.

A MESSENGER had appeared at the door, announcing that Caius Cassius Longinus was in the vicinity and asked to be received. Tiro told him to wait a moment and reported the request to his master.

'Did he say what he wanted?' asked Cicero, interrupting his work.

'No,' replied Tiro. 'I had the impression he was asking to see you alone. Perhaps the matter is confidential.'

Cicero seemed almost irritated by the request. He was

beginning to realize what a poor grip on reality the conspirators had. Along with a critical lack of organization and even of a coherent plan. This convinced him even further of the necessity of staying out of the plot, which risked being compromised at any time. But he couldn't refuse such an immediate request. He sighed. Perhaps it would give him the opportunity to offer some much-needed advice.

He replied, 'Tell him that he can come in and that I will receive him, but he must enter through the back door.'

Cassius. Always pale, gaunt, gloomy. His cold grey stare seemed to know no emotion. In reality, his character was no more stable than that of Brutus, his decision-making capacity rarely equal to the situations he faced. But he was a courageous man and a very good soldier, as he had proved in battle, during Crassus's unfortunate campaign in the East.

Cicero always tried to bring to mind everything he knew about a man when he was meeting him for an important reason, even if he'd seen that person shortly beforehand. Cicero knew well what went into a conspiracy. It was he, and not Cato, as Brutus had written, who had put down Catiline's attempt to overthrow the state twenty years earlier. Then it had been almost an even struggle between those intent on destroying the state and those intent on saving it, and it had ended at Pistoia, on the field of battle. But now the power was entirely in the hands of a single man. The plotters had a great advantage: being close to the intended victim. Some of them were even his most intimate friends.

When he finally arrived, Cassius entered and was accompanied to Cicero's study by Tiro. He was even paler than usual and the tension that was clawing at him was evident in his leaden complexion and a distinct tremor of his hands.

Cicero walked towards him and offered him a chair.

'The time has come,' said Cassius as he sat down, but Cicero interrupted him.

'It's better I do not know. No one, besides those taking part in the enterprise, must know. Apart from that, what did you want to tell me?'

'That we're ready and all the details have been decided. There's only one thing we're divided on and that's Antony. Some of us – quite a few, actually – believe that he's loyal to our cause and can be counted on, but I have my doubts about that. I think we have reason to fear him. He never leaves Caesar's side. And I'm afraid he knows something.'

Cicero pondered his words for a few moments, fingering the stylus he'd been using until his guest walked in.

'What he knows is not of great significance, since he hasn't made a move yet, and I don't imagine he will soon. Antony has his own plans and, remember this, he is anything but what he seems to be. He is extremely dangerous. If you don't remove him, this endeavour will end in failure. Mark my words . . .' He paused, letting his silence make an impact before concluding, like a judge reading a sentence, '. . . Antony must die!'

Cassius lowered his eyes and sighed. 'We know. I myself and others among us are convinced of the wisdom of your words, but Brutus won't hear reason. Listen to me, Marcus Tullius. You are the only person who can convince him. Allow me to arrange a meeting between you on neutral ground. There's an old abandoned building at the docks near the Tiber . . .'

Cicero stopped him with a gesture of his hand.

'I cannot. I'm sorry. I must not be involved, because my presence will be important afterwards. As far as Brutus is concerned, I hope, and I believe, that he will come to his senses in the end. You yourself are convinced and that should suffice to induce him to reconsider.'

Cassius understood. It was quite clear that they would not be able to count on Cicero until after the event. And it was for precisely this reason that a further precaution had to be taken, just in case something happened – something irreparable – before the fatal moment.

14

Romae, in insula Tiberis, a.d. III Id. Mart., hora decima

Rome, the Tiber Island, 13 March, three p.m.

MARCUS AEMILIUS LEPIDUS crossed the bridge on his horse and dismounted as soon as he reached the other side. The lictors were waiting for him, fasces in hand, to escort him to head-quarters. These were honours due the *magister equitum*, whose authority was second only to that of the dictator, appointed during a state of emergency. In reality, both were extraordinary offices, with powers that superseded those of the regular con-suls, who acted as the executive arm of the republic.

Antistius watched him from the window of his office. Lepi-dus was slender and agile, despite his years. He wore his hair combed forward to cover part of his forehead. This was more a habit than a hairstyle and had developed over long years of wearing a helmet during the military campaigns in which he had served alongside Caesar and won his esteem. His features were spare, almost hawk-like: a thin face, sunken cheeks, an aquiline nose. In a certain sense, although he was quite different from Caesar, the two men had something in common physi-cally, almost as if their long familiarity with the high command were contagious, somehow influencing their cast of features. He wore armour, with his red cloak belted over his embossed bronze breastplate. He briskly reviewed the honour guard, then entered headquarters. His duties as commander-in-chief awaited him, as well as his political commitments and the other business of the day.

Antistius closed the window and returned to his work. He had been going over the day's appointments for just a few minutes when a visitor was announced: Silius Salvidienus was asking to see him. He got up and went to greet him at the threshold.

'Come in,' he said, and invited him to take a seat.

He served his guest a cup of cool wine and took a diuretic potion for himself.

'How is Caesar?'

'He had a seizure last night but it didn't last long and so I didn't call for you. I've become quite the medical expert myself after assisting him for so long. Once the seizure had passed, he settled down and fell asleep.'

'You should have called me in any case. You mustn't take risks. This condition is treacherous. It's best that I spend the night at the Domus myself from now on. Any other news?'

'He's called for a meeting of his general staff this evening.'

'That's why Lepidus is back. He'll be there as well, I imagine.'

'Obviously. Lepidus is Caesar's right-hand man.'

'Of course. And Antony is quite resentful of that, if I'm to believe the rumours I hear. Who else?'

'Antony, naturally. He's still a fine soldier. Caius Trebonius, certainly. He was governor of Asia and has an excellent knowledge of logistics in the area. Decimus Brutus, who's had experience of commanding both infantry and cavalry and has always proved to be up to the challenge, even when commanding the fleet. He's still young, versatile and altogether reliable as an officer. Caesar holds him in high regard, and is quite fond of him as well. He contributed decisively to victory in Gaul, more than once. The commander never forgets such things and knows how to return a favour, but it's more than that. It's more than just recognizing a man's valour. Caesar believes deeply in friendship and in gratitude.'

'I know. He's already made him praetor and next year he'll be the governor of Cisalpine Gaul.'

'As far as I know, tonight there will be a preliminary meeting to assess the advisability of a campaign against the Parthians. Caesar is in possession of a map that Publius Sextius sent him some time ago which will serve to formulate a plan of invasion. But I've come to speak with you now for another reason. I was wondering whether you'd heard anything from your informer in Brutus's house.'

'No, unfortunately not,' replied Antistius. 'I'm hoping he'll show up soon. If he has detailed intelligence we can approach Caesar directly. Even in the absence of hard proof, he may be persuaded to act with prudence.'

'If we have names, the proof may come of itself. A number of unusual coincidences might be proof enough on their own.'

'There's Servilia as well. She may have succeeded in getting a warning through to him.'

'I hope so. I have reason to believe that she found a way to see him. You know that Caesar's no longer using his Hispanic guard?'

'What? That's impossible.'

'It's true. He told me he dismissed them because he doesn't want to be seen as a tyrant. Only tyrants need bodyguards.'

'Where's the sense in that? Does he want to die? All it takes is one fanatic – one lunatic – who would like to go down in the annals of history and he's gone.'

'You know what? I think it's a wager he's made with himself. He wants to prove that his clemency and the generosity he's shown, to friends and enemies alike, are sufficient to put him beyond risk. That he can walk the streets of Rome just like anyone else, without having to check his back all the time. He wants to believe that the people of Rome themselves are his garrison – his bodyguard. Along with the Senate, who have sworn to defend him with their own lives.'

'He can't be so naive.'

'It's not naivety. It's his faith in himself and in the people. He's the greatest man alive, Antistius. And only a great man can defy death so boldly.'

He didn't wait for an answer, but walked to the door.

'We'll stay in touch regarding all of this,' said Antistius. 'Let me know tomorrow who participated in the meeting Caesar has called for this evening and who, among those summoned, found an excuse not to attend.'

Silius nodded and left without another word.

Romae, in aedibus Bruti, a.d. III Id. Mart., hora duodecima

Rome, the home of Brutus, 13 March, five p.m.

ARTEMIDORUS had been attending to the library all day and had not yet managed to restore order to the chaos he'd found that morning. He was certain that the upheaval had been caused deliberately and the outright absurdity of the situation meant that he must obey without asking for any explanation. Perhaps this was just the start of a Sisyphean ordeal: once he'd reorganized the library, he'd come back the next day to find it turned upside down again and would have to start anew. What was the intention behind creating such a scene, if not to keep him busy, and distracted, and unable to deal with other activities? And if this were true, what activities was he being kept away from?

The mere thought that Brutus knew what he'd been up to terrified him, but he didn't dare make a move, demand an explanation or even give the impression that he was disturbed or frightened, because whatever he did would only worsen his plight. He tried to focus on the situation at hand with as much lucidity as possible and deduced that if someone had wanted to harm him, this was not the way to go about it. This ruse had been crafted to get across a clear message: 'Do as you're ordered and no harm will befall you.' There was no other explanation, as he'd left the library in perfect order just the day before. At this point, he was even hoping to find the same mess the next day, in order to confirm his hypothesis.

As he was painstakingly thinking all this through, the boy who sometimes assisted him came in. He looked around in bewilderment and asked, 'Do you need help, Artemidorus?'

'No,' he replied. 'I can manage on my own.'

'Fine. Then I'll be on my way. But if you need my help, just let me know and I'll come immediately. I've done this kind of work before.'

As he was speaking, the boy fingered the scrolls and their labels, picking them up and turning them over curiously. Then he took a little scroll nonchalantly from under his tunic and placed it on the catalogue table. He gave Artemidorus a sly grin and walked away without adding a word.

At first the Greek didn't even touch the scroll. It was as if he could feel invisible eyes watching him and he continued his work. But his gaze was increasingly drawn to that little roll of parchment and he finally gave in and opened it. It contained the other names!

He felt overwhelmed by a huge responsibility. How could he ever have agreed to do such a thing for Antistius? How could he have got himself into such a fix? And now how could he get out? He could choose to ignore the scroll, but it was too late now to feign ignorance. The boy knew that he knew and so did his friend. If he did not pass on the information and the plot was averted by some other means, what punishment would await him? And if he did pass on the message and things ended up badly, how would the people on that list see fit to deal with him?

He was floundering between Scylla and Charybdis, like Odysseus's fragile ship looking for a way through the straits. In either direction he saw monsters with gaping jaws ready to tear into him. In the end, he did nothing. He hid the scroll inside another bigger one and changed its label, and then set back to work, trying to appear busy. He was so worried about getting caught that he was even afraid of himself. As time passed, however, an idea began to form in his mind, a plan. If Brutus's faction won, the situation could only worsen for him, seeing that the man obviously suspected him of something if he was treating him in this way. If, on the other hand, the conspiracy were thwarted thanks to him, the most powerful man in the world would owe Artemidorus his life. A man who had shown thousands of times how generous he could be to those who had helped him. Antistius himself had guaranteed this and the doctor had always been true to his word.

Thrilling scenarios blossomed before his eyes. He could see himself in the house of the perpetual dictator, honoured and respected, dressed in the most sumptuous garments, delighting in the most refined delicacies. Served by young boys of beauty and grace who would respect him and indulge his every whim. He would have hairdressers, servants, secretaries. An opportunity like this came only once in a lifetime and he would be a fool to let it slip away. Therefore he would act.

His hands swiftly sorted through the scrolls now, one after another: Thucydides slipped easily into place, beneath him Callimachus and Apollonius Rhodius, one next to the other, neatly filling the slots allocated to them. Luxury editions of Homer and Hesiod occupied the top shelf at the centre of the library, earning this place both chronologically and because of their literary eminence. Every poet, historian, philosopher and geographer was returned to the spot he had always rightfully occupied and when, finally, sweaty and satisfied, Artemidorus studied the outcome of his labours, he could see that the library had been restored to its original glory.

He breathed a sigh of relief, more for having resolved his inner dilemma than for having completed the task assigned to him. But he did not leave the library. He preferred to remain there, reading and reflecting on how he could communicate the results of his investigation to Antistius.

He opened the door a crack and noticed one of Brutus's bodyguards leaning against the wall in the corridor. His arms were folded and he gave the impression of being there just for him. The first problem had been solved, but the one that remained was no less thorny.

Romae, in aedibus Bruti, a.d. III Id. Mart., prima vigilia

Rome, the home of Brutus, 13 March, first guard shift, seven p.m.

ARTEMIDORUS reasoned that, whatever happened, he would not be able to spend the rest of his life in the library and that it was time to move to the kitchen for the evening meal, where he joined several guests, none of whom was particularly important. Once in a while he was invited to join the master of the house at his table, but only on special occasions, when his erudition might contribute to enlivening the conversation.

He passed in front of the hulking guard acknowledging him with a slight nod of the head, which the guard did not return, and reached the kitchen safely. Even here the atmosphere seemed rather tense, although he couldn't have said why. He imagined that the openly worried demeanour of the master of the house had become contagious, influencing other members of the family as well.

After dinner he bade the others a good evening and retired to his quarters, exhausted after a day so full of work and emotions. But it wasn't over yet.

A short time later he heard knocking at the back door and

Caius Trebonius, were missing, since they were attending the meeting Caesar had called for that same evening.

Cassius Longinus spoke first, describing the stages of the attack, which would take place during the senatorial session on the Ides of March.

Since work was still being done on the Curia in the Forum, the Senate would be meeting at Pompey's Curia in the Campus Martius. Their first task would be to isolate Caesar from the rest of the senators and from any friends who might attempt to interfere, Antony, above all.

'I still feel that the best option would be to kill him,' he said impassively. 'But I know that Brutus does not agree with me.'

Brutus, having been singled out like this, spoke up at once. 'We've already discussed this and I've said what I think. We are killing Caesar to save the republic and that gives us the right to do so, but if we kill Antony, we are simply committing a crime. A murder.'

'Murder' was the first word the slave heard as he slipped into the broom closet and it made him shiver.

Cassius found Brutus's idealism unsettling, but tried to make him see reason: 'When safeguarding the state means taking up arms, it is evident that the violence will have to extend to those who protect the tyrant. It's the price that must be paid to recover the freedom of the Senate and the people of Rome. Antony cannot be held innocent. He has never strayed from Caesar's side and has reaped all possible benefits.'

'So have we reaped all possible benefits,' replied Brutus wryly.

A moment of heavy silence followed, during which Cassius realized that involving Brutus in the conspiracy had been rash. His fanaticism was a double-edged sword. It was becoming more and more difficult to control him.

'And it must be said that Antony has never sought to endanger the legitimacy of the state,' Brutus continued, 'or its institutions.'

'That can't be assumed,' protested Cassius. 'If he has designs on the state, he certainly wouldn't come running to tell us about them.'

'There's more,' Brutus said. 'All of you know that Caius Trebonius asked Antony to join with him and the others in Gaul, after they'd learned of the unhappy outcome of the Battle of Munda. He refused, but he kept that request secret. He was respectful of the choices of others and did not report anyone. Many of you owe him your lives. Trebonius will take care of Antony. He knows what to do.'

'I hope we shall not regret this. The responsibility you assume in taking this decision is enormous,' was Cassius's response.

Brutus dropped his head without saying a word.

'Now let me continue,' Cassius said. 'There have been various signs that lead us to believe that someone is aware of our plan, or is getting dangerously close to the truth.'

The men looked at each other in dismay.

Cassius went on in his flat voice, 'For this reason it is vital that we are ready to face any turn of events. We mean to prepare an ambush, but we may be falling into a trap instead.'

'What do you mean?' asked Petronius. 'Speak clearly.'

'We are men of moral strength and of noble lineage. We hold important military and political offices. We have enjoyed important privileges and, when necessary, have run great risks to defend our ideas. We are ready. What I am about to propose may seem terrible, but I feel it represents an honourable, necessary pact.'

'Speak,' said Brutus.

The others nodded.

'If our plan is uncovered while we are inside the Senate hall, there will be no way out for us.'

'No,' agreed Pontius Aquila. 'There will be no escape.'

'Well, then?' demanded Rubrius Ruga.

'Well, then, each one of us will have a dagger and I propose that we use them to kill each other rather than fall into the hands of the tyrant, rather than humiliate ourselves at his feet, rather than accept his loathsome pardon. We have done so once and the burning brand still stings, still marks us as if we were runaway slaves. My proposal is that each one of us should choose a companion, a friend, with whom to exchange this pact of blood. One will kill the other. We will all fall together and our lifeless bodies will be the symbol of our supreme sacrifice, made in the name of freedom.'

The murmuring that had met his proposal died down all at once and a profound silence fell over the room. The slave boy hiding in the closet held his breath so as not to be heard. If he so much as bumped into anything he would immediately be discovered and his life would not be worth living.

Cassius looked around, staring each of the conspirators directly in the eyes. He concluded, 'If any of you don't feel you can go ahead with this, you are free to leave. As long as you do so in time. No one will blame you and you will have nothing to fear from the rest of us. I'm certain none of us would ever betray another. I'm asking you to perform an act of heroism, but no one is obliged to make such an arduous choice. I'll say this again: if there is anyone who's not up to it, leave now.'

No one moved. Some because they believed that what Cassius proposed would be a fitting end for those who failed in an undertaking of this sort. Others because they feared what would happen if they were taken prisoner; death would be a liberation rather than suffering such pain. Others still because they thought it would never come to that, so sure were they that their plan would succeed. Even they preferred the risk of a disagreeable death to the shame of abandoning their companions and being branded as cowards.

After waiting long enough to allow anyone who so wished to desert the cause, and seeing that no one had decided to leave, Cassius took the initiative and walked towards Brutus.

He stopped directly in front of him and held out his dagger.

15

Romae, in Domo Publica, a.d. III Id. Mart., prima vigilia

Rome, the residence of the Pontifex Maximus, 13 March,
first guard shift, seven p.m.

CAESAR WAS getting ready to meet with his officers. He was
wearing a simple knee-length fatigue tunic, like the one he used
during his military campaigns, cinched at the waist by a leather
belt with an iron buckle. A servant was just lacing up his boots.
He gave him a quick look to make sure his clothing was in
order, then asked, 'Anything else, master?'

'See if you can do something to my hair,' replied Caesar,
looking at himself in the mirror.

The servant combed it slightly forward to partially hide the
early stages of baldness.

There was a knock at the door and Silius Salvidienus
appeared.

'Are they here?' asked Caesar.

'Yes, they're all downstairs. Calpurnia is offering them drinks.
Aemilius Lepidus, Decimus Brutus, Mark Antony, Caius Trebonius and the others. They appear to be in a jolly mood.'

'Have places been assigned at the table?'

'As you've requested. Decimus Brutus at your right, Mark
Antony at your left.'

Caesar seemed to ponder this for a few moments.

'Is something wrong, commander?'

'If Labienus were here, he would be sitting at my right.'

'Labienus is dead, commander, and you paid him the respects due to a faithful friend and a valiant enemy.'

'Fine, then. We can go downstairs.'

Caesar could see in Silius's face that he had something more to say, so he dismissed the servant.

'What is it?' he asked warily.

'It's not pleasant, I'm afraid. It's going to irritate you.'

'Well, let's have it, then.'

'There's someone who is passing around an interpretation of the Sibylline Books which claims that only a king can defeat and subjugate the Parthians.'

Caesar shook his head and sat down, crossing his arms. He sighed. 'So that's how far it's gone. This I would never have expected.'

'It's a serious matter, commander. Another bit of slander meant to alert the people to your presumed intention of establishing a monarchy in Rome and in the empire. Whoever it is is trying to isolate you and thus weaken you. A king would be loathed by the people and the Senate alike. Remember the Lupercalia festival. You told me yourself that most of the crowd were scandalized when you were offered the royal crown.'

'Do you know the source of this falsehood?'

'No.'

'Which means it will be attributed directly to me. I am the Pontifex Maximus and thus the custodian of the Sibylline Books, from where this oracle is said to come.'

'Commander, the intention of harming you is explicit. You must defend yourself.'

'What do you mean?'

'That your enemies are preparing something. Rumour has it that in one of the coming senatorial sessions a proposal will be put forward to proclaim you king.'

Caesar said nothing but his eyes were like those of a lion being stalked by hunters. From downstairs came the voices of the high commanders of his army, those men who were preparing to conquer the rest of the world.

Silius sensed that it was time to make his move. 'May I ask you a question?'

'Let's hear it,' said Caesar.

'Has anyone, in these last few days, attempted to put you on your guard against something?'

Caesar gave an involuntary shudder and Silius felt that he was about to share an important confidence that would allow him to ask more questions.

'I don't mean an explicit declaration,' he added. 'A veiled allusion, perhaps? Doesn't anything come to mind, commander?'

Caesar could see the raving expression of Spurinna, the augur, hissing at him, 'Beware the Ides of March!' but he turned calmly to Silius and said, 'We have to go downstairs. They're waiting for us.'

He took a scroll from the table entitled *The Anabasis of Cyrus* and started down the stairs.

Silius followed him and, before entering the meeting hall, stopped to listen to the enthusiastic welcome Caesar was receiving: military salutes, shouts of greeting, barracks banter. Then Caesar's voice, sharp as a sword: 'Commanders of the legions of Rome, magistrates, masters of the cavalry and auxiliaries!'

'Caesar!' they all replied in unison.

It felt as though the lion had leapt into the circle of hunters.

THE MEETING went on until late, a good two hours. Caesar began with the *Anabasis*. He summarized Xenophon's account of the expedition of the ten thousand Greek soldiers who, four centuries earlier, had made it nearly all the way to Babylon without striking a blow, but immediately pointed out that things had changed considerably since then, and that Crassus's army had been wiped out just ten years earlier by the Parthians at Carrhae. This was the main objective of the mission: to avenge the massacre of Carrhae. Rome had been humiliated, the triumvir defeated, thousands of her most valiant soldiers killed, her Eagles lost. But this would be only the beginning. The Parthians constituted a perennial threat, so the problem must be solved once and for all.

He went on to describe the tactical and strategic aspects of the expedition. He took, from a case already sitting on the table, the map that Publius Sextius had provided him with. A copy of the ancient Road of the King, it included all the other roads and caravan routes that crossed the vast territory of the Parthian empire, stretching all the way to Armenia, to Sarmatia, Media and Bactriana. He laid the map on the table and the members of the war council were awed by a masterpiece of geographical expertise the likes of which they had never seen.

Each one of them, leaning forward with his elbows on the table, eagerly regarded this vision of the eastern part of the world. Each one made his comments, with those who already knew something of the Orient tracing their fingers over the rivers, lakes, seas and mountains they recognized.

Then it was Caesar's turn. His officers followed the tip of his index finger as he drew out the lines of march and the attack routes on the parchment sheet painted in natural colours: brown for the mountains, bright green for the rivers, lakes and seas, light green for the plains, ochre for the deserts. The place names in Persian had been carefully transcribed in Latin in an even hand.

His plan was to attack on two different fronts, from Syria and from Armenia, converging his forces in a pincer on the capital, Ctesiphon.

The problems to consider, Caesar said, were the enemy cavalry and the double-curved bows the Parthians used, which could strike from a considerable distance. He pointed out that even if Crassus had won at Carrhae and had pushed on into enemy territory, his chances of succeeding would have been slight. Lost in the immensity of the Syrian and Mesopotamian deserts, deprived of his own cavalry, the army would have been easy prey for the continuous onslaughts of squads of enemy archers on horseback. Their tactics were to attack, strike and retreat, without ever engaging the infantry in hand-to-hand battle. This had been reported by a man who had miraculously survived the massacre, hidden under a pile of bodies.

As Caesar proceeded with his explanations, Silius noticed that some of those present were looking more at him than at the map. They were watching his expression rather than listening to his words. Why? What were they trying to read in their commander's face?

His strength, decided Silius; they were trying to gauge how much strength remained in that wrinkled brow, those eyes, that jaw, in his fisted hands leaning on the table.

Antony seemed the most attentive to Caesar's strategic plan, even interrupting him to ask for clarification. He seemed to be truly eager to leave on this Parthian expedition and play the role of subordinate commander in the vast theatre of operations. The others weren't showing real interest, as if they didn't believe it would happen. Decimus Brutus, for instance, was constantly talking under his breath to Caius Trebonius, making comments Silius would have liked to hear.

Perhaps Antony wanted to prove to Caesar – who had been treating him rather coldly since the Lupercalia incident, and who had seated him on his left at the table – that he was still his best officer, the only one among them capable of conducting wide-ranging, important operations. To let Caesar know he had been wrong to shut him out.

Silius himself was convinced of Antony's military worth, but still wondered about his behaviour at the festival. Had he been acting on his own initiative? Had he merely made a mistake, a glaring error of judgement? Could one believe that Antony had truly meant it as a sincere gesture of admiration? Offering Caesar the king's crown in order to say later that he had been the only one to openly acknowledge Caesar's true worth? Could it have been a calculated ploy to become Caesar's most trusted man, the most powerful in the empire after him?

Anything was possible, but nothing was convincing, because Antony was not a stupid man.

He could not have been unaware of the risks involved in making such a public gesture in front of such a large crowd. In the Senate it was a different matter, for here there was a relatively select group of aristocrats, most of whom owed everything to Caesar and bent over backwards to praise him. But not the people. Antony must have realized that suddenly forcing them to accept a choice that was universally felt to be scandalous, if not repugnant and even perfectly useless, was a huge risk. Not only because their reaction would be unpredictable, but even more so because the move had not been approved by Caesar himself. Silius believed Caesar when he said he had not been consulted. So what was the meaning behind the gesture, then? Had Antony acted on his own or was there someone behind him?

Although Silius had been over all this again and again, these thoughts kept crowding his mind and he was ashamed to realize he was not listening more closely to his commander as he illustrated his plans for universal conquest.

His generals were urging Caesar on now, enjoining him to conquer the whole world. They were raving about his plans, pressing him to undertake further exploits, to push past the boundaries of the inhabited world, to take on the desolate stretches of Sarmatia, the vast deserts of Persia and Bactriana, to follow the dreams of Alexander the Great. Now there was a model for you: larger than life, always victorious . . .

Silius Salvidienus was watching Caesar's face in the midst of this frenzy of excitement. His grey eyes were lit intermittently by a tired glow; otherwise they expressed mainly weariness and almost unbearable strain. These were the eyes of a man who could move only towards the impossible or towards death.

Both were undesirable outcomes.

The session ended in an atmosphere of general euphoria and Caesar announced he would convene the Senate for the morning of the Ides of March. There were various matters that would have to be finalized, some routine and others representing important new developments.

Caesar accompanied his guests to the door personally. As he was leaving, Marcus Aemilius Lepidus took his hand and said, 'I'm expecting you for dinner tomorrow night, then. I hope you haven't forgotten.'

'How could I forget?' replied Caesar. 'It wouldn't be wise to neglect the invitation of a man who has an entire legion in fighting order at his command!'

Lepidus laughed as the others slipped past one by one, meeting the escorts they had waiting outside.

Silius's glance happened to fall on Antony as he was exchanging a few words with his servants. That seemed odd to him, as did Antony's expression. He turned to Caesar and said, 'Commander, if you don't need me at the moment, there are a few things I have to look after.'

Caesar grinned. 'At this hour? How can I say no? What's she like? Blonde or brunette?'

'Brunette, commander,' replied Silius with the hint of a smile.

'Be sure to distinguish yourself in the line of duty, then.'

'You can count on that, commander,' replied Silius, trying to assume a rakish air. 'The Thirteenth never disappoints!'

He crossed the threshold, but before leaving turned around, serious again: 'Commander ... there may be another explanation.'

'For what?'

'For that rumour about the Sibylline Books. Maybe it's not someone who wants to isolate you or discredit you – or rather, maybe that's not all. Maybe someone is trying to force your hand ...'

Caesar said nothing.

Silius gave a nod and walked off into the dark.

SLIPPING BETWEEN the northern corner of the Domus and the House of the Vestals, Silius lingered in the shadows at the edge of the halo of light cast by a couple of tripods beside the entrance. He was keeping an eye on Antony's litter and the two armed bodyguards escorting him with lanterns in hand. The small convoy set off on the same road that Lepidus was taking towards the Tiber Island at first, but then turned left on the riverbank at the Sublicius Bridge, bound towards the portico of a small shipyard. Where was Mark Antony headed?

Silius followed at a safe distance, conveniently shielded by the big alders that lined the southern bank of the river. The darkness hid him, while Antony's litter was easily visible thanks to the lanterns his bodyguards held high to light their way and to frighten off muggers and thieves.

Silius saw the litter stopping and then a certain jostling about in the shadows. Something was happening. At that distance, he couldn't make out what it was, so he drew closer. He saw someone getting out of the litter dressed as a servant, though he could not be a servant, and someone getting into the litter who was dressed as Antony but was not him.

Silius followed the man dressed as a servant who was walking unaccompanied towards the Sublicius Bridge. It was Mark Antony. The men accompanying his litter were protecting a servant wearing Antony's clothing.

Silius crossed the bridge after him and continued shadowing him, although by this time he was fairly sure of where they were both headed: Caesar's villa on the other side of the Tiber, where Cleopatra lived. Antony was about to go in alone, at night and without an escort, wearing the clothes of a servant.

A chorus of dogs barking, then a door opening silently. Antony slipped in and the dogs quietened down. Just after that, a line of guards came around the western corner of the house, making their rounds of inspection at the garden's perimeter.

In a single moment, Silius saw many of his suspicions confirmed and the collapse of others that he might have defended vehemently if it had ever come to that.

He had to find his way in, but how? He could run back to the Domus, report to Caesar on what he'd seen and return with a group of men who would replace these guards and occupy the entrances. That would allow him to enter the villa and the queen's apartments, in order to spy on her and Antony. But all that would take much too long. Whatever was happening in that house had to be discovered without delay.

Silius entered the garden by climbing over the wall and carefully approached the villa. The dogs must have been busy greeting the newly arrived guest. Silius circled around the building cautiously, checking every corner. He'd been in that house before, with Caesar, and he'd know where to go once he got in. But the problem was getting in. Cleopatra's residence was a kind of fortress. Antony had let himself in the side door with a key, and the dogs had immediately stopped barking because they were obviously familiar with him.

The main entrances were guarded. And the patrol he'd already seen was encircling the perimeter.

He noticed a chimney at the end of the western corner of the house, where the servants' quarters were located. There were some square openings on the chimney wall where the wooden beams of a maintenance scaffold had been removed. He thought he could use them as toeholds, so he did just that. When the guards had passed he kicked off his shoes and climbed to the top. Part of the roof was covered with tiles; if he could cross without making any noise, he would find himself in the terraced area, which would make an easier surface to move on. Once on the terrace, he paused to get his bearings. To his right were the peristyle and the inner garden. He could hear the monotonous bubbling of the fountains. A little further on was the *atrium* with its pool at the centre, and in the middle was the master apartment. He remembered that there was a small thermal bath system on the other side of the house that probably wasn't being guarded.

He crossed the terrace and another section of tile-covered roof and easily reached the baths, which were covered in part by tiling and in part by fine plaster. He slipped down to the first terraced level and reached the dome of the *laconicum*, the steam bath, which was open at its centre to allow the smoke from the braziers to escape. He made the opening bigger by using his dagger to prise off the tiles, working in silence, and dropped in. He had the good luck to land on a pile of ashes that remained at the centre of the dead embers. And from there he slid to the floor without difficulty.

He was inside!

The queen must still be in her winter apartments, adjacent to the walls of the *calidarium*, to take advantage of the warmth created by the room's heating system. Accustomed as she was to the climate in Egypt, Cleopatra detested the cold, damp Roman winter.

Silius groped his way around in the almost complete darkness, attempting to recall the plan of the house. He was drawn like a moth to the dim glow cast by a lantern in one of the adjacent rooms. He had to try hard not to fumble or make any noise that would give him away. The house was immersed in silence and the slightest sound would bring on the dogs or worse.

He reached the *calidarium*, which was linked to the *laconicum* by a short corridor. He counted his paces and stopped at the place where, according to his calculations, the brick cavity wall that collected the heat produced by the baths met the queen's living quarters.

He put his ear to the wall and he thought he could make out voices having what seemed to be a conversation.

He used the tip of his dagger to chip away at the mortar

that joined one cavity segment to the next. He worked very carefully, well aware that if he could hear their voices, they'd be able to hear any noise he made. He was tense and sweating profusely, anxious to complete this mission he'd assigned himself. The sensation of being so close to making an extraordinary discovery made him feel strangely elated, almost inebriated.

As soon as he'd removed the layer of mortar between one heat collector and the next, he was able to stick the point of his blade into the brick and widen the hole he had made until it was half a palm wide. He drew close to listen.

The voices were clear and recognizable now, the voices of a man and a woman.

The man was Antony.

The woman spoke Latin with a strong Greek accent. She must be Cleopatra.

'I'll always be grateful to you for what you've done . . . but I'm afraid it was all for nothing.'

'I would have done anything for you, my queen. If Caesar had accepted the crown on the day of the Lupercalia festival, no one would have opposed him. The Senate would have ratified his title and you would have become the sovereign of the world. I would have served you with devotion, content just to be near you, protecting you. But Caesar didn't understand—'

'Caesar didn't want to understand. I've suggested it to him on numerous occasions, and each time he has refused to even talk about the possibility. He has recognized his son, but only in private form. However, I haven't given up yet. You must have heard the latest about the Sibylline prophecy.'

'I have.'

'Yes, my ministers have always had a certain hold over those simpletons, your priests. But he won't take the opportunity, I'm almost certain. It's clear that I don't count at all for him.'

'For me you are everything . . . everything, my queen.'

'You're saying that to console me.'

'I'm saying that because it's true. I see your image before my eyes day and night, everywhere I go. Your face, your body . . .'

'And my feelings? My hopes? My aspirations?'

'Yes, those as well. I want what you want.'

'Are you willing to swear to that?'

'I swear it, my queen. On the gods and on my own life.'

'Then listen to me. What I'm about to say is of the utmost importance. Our future, my son's future, the future of the entire world, depends on it.'

A long silence followed and Silius, with his ear glued to the hollow in the wall, feared that they had moved to another room where he would no longer be able to hear them. But then Cleopatra spoke up again. Although her voice was muted and distorted, its timbre and tone were laden with irresistible sensuality, made even more intriguing by that Greek lilt. Silius had seen her several times but had never heard her speak before. Now he could well understand how Caesar had fallen in love with her, how anyone who had the fortune to meet her, see her, listen to her, would find her entrancing.

'I've heard that Caesar's life is in danger.'

Antony didn't say a word.

'Do you know anything about this?'

Antony did not reply.

'I'm alone in this city. There's no one I can count on.'

Antony said something that Silius missed, then Cleopatra began to speak again.

'But I have met a few people here. I managed to find the ear of a man who is very close to Caesar, just before he was about to depart for a mission in the north of the peninsula. I asked him to find out whatever he could about this threat to Caesar's life. I told him what I knew and gave him some contacts . . .'

Silius thought of Publius Sextius and was startled.

'I made him swear that the matter would remain between the two of us. I wanted him to understand that it was Caesar's safety I was concerned about, immensely so, although Caesar himself seems to give it no thought. I should be hearing from this person by tomorrow. If it's any later than that it might be too late. Do you understand what I'm saying?'

Silius imagined that Antony had nodded or answered her with a look.

'Good,' continued Cleopatra. 'If anything should happen, you will be the only person I can trust in this city. Cicero despises me and there are many others who can't stand me. Antony, you must promise me you'll be careful. You must be prudent. Do it for me and for my son.'

Silius heard nothing more, but he'd heard enough. He was certain that Caesar would listen to him now and take immediate action. The problem now was getting out. He couldn't go back by the route he used to get in, because he had no way of getting up to the hole he'd dropped through at the centre of the *laconicum* dome. So he had to find a way out through the house. At least he was familiar with the layout and the darkness would cover him. He could get to the peristyle and from there to the servants' quarters. He could use the side door, slipping out between the guards' rounds.

A sudden gust of wind swept in from the hole in the dome and stirred up a cloud of ashes from the floor. Silius could not hold back a violent sneeze.

He froze, ears straining, heart in his throat. He heard nothing. After all, he thought, anyone in the house could have sneezed. A sneeze was no cause for alarm.

He started to move again, cautiously. He crossed the *tepidarium* and the *frigidarium*, reached the door and opened it on to the corridor that led to the peristyle. He looked round anxiously. There were only a few lanterns lit under the portico; no one was in sight. He made his way towards the *atrium*, staying close to the wall.

A voice rang out behind him as the light of several torches flooded the portico. 'Quite a bad cold you have there, Silius Salvidienus. What are you doing out at this time of night?'

It was Mark Antony.

16

In Monte Appennino, mansio ad Castaneam, a.d. III Id. Mart.,
prima vigilia

The Apennine Mountains, the Chestnut Tree station, 13 March,
first guard shift, six p.m.

SINCE PUBLIUS SEXTIUS had reached the Arno before daylight,
he decided to rest for a couple of hours until he could hear the
ferryman stirring. He led his horse on to the pontoon, which
was on a ferry rope, and soon found himself on the other side
of the river. He resumed his journey, keeping within sight of
the Via Cassia as he rode. He travelled the entire day, until
dusk, when he decided to head towards a light he could see in
the distance at the edge of a wood. The terrain was uneven and
rocky and the path he was using so rutted he couldn't wait to
get there. It was marked on the map he'd been given and looked
like a *mansio*, so he thought he'd be able to get something to
eat and perhaps even change his horse there.

As he got closer, he realized the light was actually reflecting
from a fire burning inside the building's enclosure wall. He
could see nothing else; the place did not seem to be guarded.

He stopped his horse, dismounted and began to approach
cautiously on foot. Realizing that the horse would draw attention, he tied the animal's reins to an oak sapling and went on
alone.

There was indeed a fire burning in the courtyard. Four

individuals had gathered around it, sitting on their travel bags. He thought he recognized one of them, a man wearing a grey cloak; his face was very pale and had a weaselly look. In the corner was a wagon with two horses still yoked to the shaft.

When the man in the grey cloak got to his feet, one of the other men followed suit. The other two remained sitting near the fire.

'I prefer working on my own, but seeing as you've caught up with me, at least keep your eyes open,' the man in grey said. 'Be wary of anyone who approaches. We'll relieve you in a couple of hours and then we'll be off. We'll take the same roads that he'll have to take, assuming, of course, that he's still behind us.'

'Have no fear, Mustela,' replied one of the two. 'No one gets by here without my permission.'

The man called Mustela answered, 'Decius, don't let your guard down. You know him. And beware of his cane. It's more deadly than a sword in his hands. He's very dangerous—'

'I know, I know, you've told me already. Just take it easy.'

Publius Sextius started at those words. Of all the roads that led to Rome, these four cut-throats had found the very one he had taken and were lying in wait for him no less. He had to act at once, without alerting them to his presence.

Mustela and his companion went in and Publius Sextius soon saw the light of a lamp behind a window on the second floor. It soon went out.

He slipped into the stables and sat down on the straw. A hound started barking, but Publius Sextius reached into his satchel for a chunk of salted meat, which he tossed over to the dog, who swallowed it whole. He came closer, wagging his tail, hoping for more food. It wasn't often that he enjoyed such generosity. Never, in fact. Publius Sextius petted him and gave him another bite. He'd made a friend who would not betray him.

Knowing he could rest easy from that point of view, he went

into the hayloft and then back outdoors again through a door that was slightly ajar. He was now on the opposite side of the *mansio*. The gigantic chestnut tree from which the station got its name extended its boughs towards the room that had been lit up a few moments before. The moon appeared in a wide gap between the clouds.

Publius Sextius began to climb the tree, pulling himself up on the lower branches, then using the forks in the trunk like a ladder. He soon arrived at the branch leaning closest to the window. It was easy work to open the unlocked shutters and prise the windowpanes apart with the knife he wore at his belt. He pulled it open cautiously and slipped inside without making a sound, but a beam of moonlight from the open window gave him away.

One of the two men jumped to his feet, shouting, 'What in Hades . . .'

Sextius, who already had his cane in hand, struck the man violently, knocking him to the floor.

Mustela, realizing that from being hunter he had become prey, was out of his room and in the hall in no time. He found a small balcony from which he could leap to the ground, stifling a cry of pain when he hit the hard earth below.

Publius Sextius was close behind and vaulted down after him. Decius Saurus had been left alone next to the fire, while his companion had gone off in search of wood. He tried to block the centurion's way, but Publius Sextius tackled him full on, sending him rolling into the flames.

Mustela jumped on to the first horse he could find and flew through the main gate at a gallop. Publius Sextius ran in the opposite direction until he found his own horse, untied him, leapt on to his back and urged him forward in pursuit of the fugitive.

Mustela had bolted off and was careering about madly, in the light of the moon, among the shadows cast by the trees that streaked the ground with eerie shapes. At every bend in the road, the gravel flew and scattered on to the embankment below.

All at once a bird, frightened by Mustela's passage, rose to the air directly in front of Sextius's horse, spooking him and causing him to rear up. The centurion, taken completely by surprise, fell and tumbled down the cliff that edged the road.

Mustela continued to race off at breakneck speed until he realized that he was no longer being followed. He pulled on the reins and his horse jerked to a halt. He turned back, sensing a trap. He moved slowly, looking in every direction, as tense and suspicious as the animal he resembled and whose nickname he bore.

When he spotted Publius Sextius's horse running wild, a self-satisfied grin curled his lips, deforming his features.

The centurion's horse was neighing and snorting, still obviously frightened by what had happened. Mustela dismounted and walked to the brink of the embankment. He saw broken branches and a scrap of the cloak his pursuer had been wearing stuck to a twig and waving in the wind.

'Farewell, Publius Sextius,' he murmured under his breath, still afraid that somehow the centurion might hear him. Then he remounted his horse and rode off.

Romae, in aedibus Bruti, a.d. III Id. Mart., secunda vigilia

Rome, the home of Brutus, 13 March, second guard shift,
eleven p.m.

ARTEMIDORUS was stretched out on his bed open-eyed, his lamp burning. He stared at the ceiling beams in a daze as he wondered what to do next. Every now and then he got up to spy on the two guards blocking the hallway. They were still there, unmoving and silent.

At times he would hear noises, footsteps along the corridor or crossing the *atrium*. He could tell where they were coming from by the noise they made. Brick, marble, stone: each material sounded different. He had grown used to distinguishing them in that house of ghosts, even in the dark: Brutus's nervous step, Porcia's pacing, even Servilia's light footfall when she came to visit her son and would stay for dinner or overnight.

Artemidorus poured himself another glass of water and looked glumly at the untouched tray of cakes that his young servant had brought to his room.

What the boy had reported had filled him with anguish. Thus far he'd said nothing, but what if they tortured him? What would happen then? Could he expect a slave to withstand torture and keep what he knew a secret?

Time must be running out. If Brutus was asking such questions, if the others had come back so soon, it must mean that action was imminent. Artemidorus was desperate to make plans, take precautions, protect himself . . . The boy had promised to come back, but that had been hours ago. Had his worst fears come to pass?

The silence and his anxiety had sharpened his senses to breaking point and he was sweating profusely, despite the fact that the temperature in his bedroom was always quite chilly. His tongue felt as dry as a piece of leather and stuck to his palate. He took another sip of water and tried to calm down.

He heard the dog whining in the rear courtyard, the creaking of the outside door, the scamper of feet on the gravel and then on the pavement of the *atrium*.

The sound was coming closer, turning into the footsteps of his young friend in the corridor leading to his room. At last!

He waited for the boy to knock.

'Come in,' he said.

'You know those two out there in the hallway are gone?' said the boy, entering.

'That's not possible!'

'Look for yourself.'

Artemidorus opened the door a crack and looked out into the corridor, which was lit by a single lamp. No one was there.

'I can't explain it. I'm afraid it's a trap.'

'They probably think you're sleeping. They've got other things to take care of. The master's guests are leaving.'

He picked up the tray with the uneaten cakes and made to leave, then turned at the touch of Artemidorus's hand on his arm.

'I'm afraid,' he blurted out. 'I heard terrible things downstairs. You must let me go.'

'No, wait,' said Artemidorus. 'I've been thinking about what you told me and I've come to a conclusion. You have to leave this house now, while you are still free to do so, before they start to suspect you. I'm saying this for your sake. I don't want them to hurt you.'

'I know, Artemidorus,' said the boy with a smile. 'But where can I go? Don't you know what they do with runaway slaves?'

'I would testify that I sent you out on an errand. I'm a free man and I have a good reputation. What's more, Decimus Brutus is the Praetor Peregrinus and deals with all foreign residents. He knows me well. Listen to me. As soon as day breaks, leave the house with an excuse. Say that you're going to buy me some medicine for my vitiligo; say the itching is driving me crazy. It's true. Here, take the money. Go to the Tiber Island and look for the hospital. Find Antistius, who is my doctor. Tell him that I've sent you and that you need to stay with him for a few days. You'll be safe, because he lives with Caesar, in the Domus Publica. No one will ever think of looking for you there. Do you understand?'

'Yes. I understand. Do you want me to tell him the names?'

'Shh! Are you mad? Whisper! No, don't tell him anything for any reason whatsoever. You stay out of this. I'll see to the matter myself.'

'Do you want to give me something to take to him?'

'Worse yet. If they catch you and search you, what will you say? They'll cut you into little pieces, one piece at a time, until they've got every scrap of information from you. I'll take care of this. I'm not sure how, but I'll take care of it. Sooner or later they'll have something better to do than keep me confined here. Do you understand what you're to do?'

'I do,' answered the boy.

Artemidorus opened a drawer and took out a little piece of parchment. 'This is a prescription Antistius gave me. It's a cure for constipation. He'll recognize it and be sure that I'm the one who has sent you. If you're stopped on your way, no one will have reason to scold you or suspect you of anything. If Antistius asks about me, tell him that I'm not free to move but that as soon as I can I will contact him personally.'

'I'll go first thing in the morning, then.'

'Go, and good luck. If everything turns out as I'm hoping, we'll see each other in a few days.'

The boy gazed into his eyes for a moment with a curious, enigmatic expression, halfway between affection and pity. He opened the door and walked away.

Artemidorus watched him for a while from the threshold and then, as no one seemed to be around, took a few steps down the hall to see if he could find out what was happening. But as he was about to turn left towards the peristyle, he found one of his guards in front of him.

'Out for a walk, maestro?' he said with a jeer. 'Where do you think you're going?'

Artemidorus felt a wave of fear and then one of powerless anger. 'To have a crap,' he replied.

In via Etrusca vetere, a.d. III Id. Mart., secunda vigilia

The Old Etruscan Trail, 13 March, second guard shift, eleven p.m.

PUBLIUS SEXTIUS, hanging one-handed from the branch of a thorn bush, was trying to grab on to a rocky outcrop and failing. He was bleeding from an extremely painful flesh wound and he could feel a warm trickle on his left side. All at once he heard his horse snorting.

'Here, boy, over this way . . . over here,' he said.

The horse seemed to understand his master's words. He drew close and pushed his whole head over the brink of the drop. In so doing his reins dangled forward, practically brushing against the hand gripping the thorn bush. Publius braced himself and swung back and forth until he had built up enough momentum to reach the reins with his free hand and grab them.

As soon as the horse felt the sharp tug he became frightened, dug in his rear hoofs and began to back up with all the strength he had. Once he had hauled his heavy load over the rim of the embankment, Publius let go, so that the terrified horse would not drag him off.

He tried to bandage his wound as best he could, then waited for the skittish animal to calm down sufficiently to approach his master again, helped along by the sound of Publius's voice and a handful of fresh grass in his fist. When the horse was finally within reach, Publius grabbed the reins and leapt on to his back, ready to resume his journey and make up for lost time.

As he was advancing at a good pace under the moonlight, he thought of the strange coincidence that could have cost him his life. How could those four be waiting for him, there in the *mansio*, as if he'd given them an appointment? He recognized the man in the grey cloak with the weasel's face from that station on the Via Aemilia where he'd changed his horse several days before. How could he have got ahead of him so easily? He had to have known exactly where he was going.

If someone had been there at that moment, they would have seen a grin forming on Publius Sextius's face. He was satisfied and triumphant at having solved the mystery. The arm that had so conveniently been used against him – Nebula's map – could be turned just as easily against them. So, in the same way that the enemy knew where to lie in wait, Publius Sextius knew where he'd be able to ambush his enemy.

The road was becoming wider and the vegetation less thick. More bare-boughed trees, rather than evergreens, let the moonlight filter through.

How much further did he have to go? Publius Sextius wished he could fly, even though his weariness was dragging him down considerably. He didn't remember when he had last had enough sleep, when he had consumed a normal meal sitting at a table with a jug of wine in front of him. He had been racing, racing against time itself, tiring one horse after another, but never giving up, never stopping to catch his breath. He would make it. He was Publius Sextius, senior front-line centurion, known as 'the Cane'.

The Eagle is in danger

The message he had to deliver rang through his mind a thousand times each day, each night.

He pulled up, exhausted, at the entrance to an inn on a road with a cluster of rather wretched-looking stone and brick houses encircled by pens full of sheep and goats. The inn doubled as a message station for those travelling on behalf of the state.

The innkeeper was a heavy-set man of about sixty, with thinning hair combed back from his brow. His shoulders were wider than his paunch, a rarity in his line of work.

'I'm a centurion,' said Publius, showing him the *titulus* he wore on his neck. 'I'm looking for a man who ran off from a *mansio* back there in the mountain, not only without paying his bill, but relieving a good number of customers of whatever they had in their pockets and the stableman of a good horse. A bloke with a face like a mouse or a weasel, take your pick, a straggly yellow moustache, hair like straw. He wears a grey cloak, day and night. Have you seen him, by any chance?'

The innkeeper nodded. 'Your man passed through here.'

'Where is he now?'

'He's gone.

'Gone where?'

The innkeeper hesitated. The information he had received didn't match what the centurion had just told him.

'What's wrong?' asked Publius Sextius.

'Seems strange to me that a pickpocket and horse thief like the one you've described would have access to a signalling station. That's where he's headed, but he'll be back. I gave him a better horse than the one he was riding and he left me all the money he had as surety.'

Publius Sextius scratched his chin. 'I know that place. It isn't far. Bring me a jug of wine, some bread and a piece of cheese. I have to eat something. And give some barley to my horse – he's earned it.'

The innkeeper served both man and horse promptly, relieved that he wasn't getting involved in this story, at least not for the time being.

In Monte Appennino, statio Vox in Silentio, a.d. III Id. Mart., secunda vigilia

The Apennine Mountains, the Voice in the Silence station, 13 March, second guard shift, eleven p.m.

THE STATION, perched high on the mountain ridge, was situated in such a way as to receive signals from both west and east. The second guard shift was ending and three men were on duty, two inside and one up in the watchtower. A gusty north wind was blowing and the man posted up there came inside, shivering and stamping his feet on the floor.

'There's a priority code coming in,' he said. 'The message regards the security of the republic.'

'What are you talking about?' asked one of his two comrades.

'We have to intercept any messengers directed south, especially two men fitted out as *speculatores*.'

'What do you mean by "intercept"?' asked the other.

'Stop them, I suppose,' replied the man who had just come in.

'What if they won't stop?'

The man drew his finger across his throat in an eloquent gesture and added, 'How else?'

Mansio ad Vicum, a.d. III Id. Mart., tertia vigilia

The Village station, 13 March, start of third guard shift, midnight

THE MILESTONE marked the sixth mile from Chiusi and Mustela turned to enter the courtyard of the *mansio*. He tethered his horse, walked up the stairs to his room, opened the door and closed it behind him. He was exhausted. He raised the wick on the oil lamp that was about to go out.

'Hello there,' said a voice in the dark.

Mustela drew his sword.

'I guess my time hadn't come yet,' said Publius Sextius. 'Surprised, my friend? Dead men don't show up out of nowhere, do they? But as you can see, I'm not. You thought you could take your time since I was out of the picture and so I made it here first.'

Mustela lunged forward, but Publius Sextius was ready for him. He parried the blow with his *gladius* and with a quick thrust sent the weapon flying from his attacker's hand. He then pounded his cane flat against Mustela's chest. The man collapsed to the ground.

Publius Sextius jerked him up and sat him down on the only chair in the room. Leaning back awkwardly, he seemed a disjointed puppet.

'Let's start by you telling me what signal you sent,' he hissed into his face.

'Forget it.'

Publius landed a stone-hard punch in the middle of his face and Mustela whimpered in pain.

'You'll kill me anyway, so why should I tell you anything?'

'You're wrong. If you talk I give you my word of honour I will not spill your blood.'

Mustela, still in pain from the wounds incurred during his long journey, was destroyed in body and spirit.

'They say that Publius Sextius always keeps his word,' he managed to get out.

'And so be it, in the name of the gods,' replied Publius Sextius. 'Well, then?' he said, raising his cane again.

'The message was to intercept two *speculatores* on the Via Flaminia or Cassia.'

'I see,' replied Publius Sextius, receiving the news with seeming indifference. He moved behind Mustela. 'Anything else?'

'Nothing else, I swear it. I'm a wreck. I can't take this. Leave me in peace.'

Publius grabbed his head and twisted it with a swift wrench, breaking the man's neck.

'There you go. You're at peace now and I've kept my word.'

He went down to the courtyard, mounted his horse and set off at a gallop.

17

In Monte Appennino, Lux Insomnis, pridie Id. Mart., tertia vigilia

The Apennine Mountains, Never-Sleeping Light, 14 March,
third guard shift, one a.m.

Publius Sextius had assumed control of the signalling station
manu militari. He had taken command of the squad of signal
corps auxiliaries by showing them his *titulus* and the persuasive,
knotty symbol of his rank. He went straight to the signalling
tower to transmit the counter-order and save the lives of
Rufus and Vibius, whom he didn't know but who, he was sure,
were two courageous young servants of the state. Lighting the
fire for the beacon was difficult enough in itself. The weather
had worsened considerably. Clouds covered the moon and
lightning bolts were discharging their flames on the mountain
peaks, swept by a raging wind. It had started raining again, on
and off. Publius Sextius was gripped by mounting distress,
obsessed by the realization that time was slipping away. His
mind continued to calculate the distance he might have been
covering if he had not been forced to interrupt his onward
journey. But how could he go on without trying to protect the
other messengers? The only way to stop them from being
killed was using the light, *Lux Insomnis*, like the code name of
the station. But when he was finally able to transmit the message, no one answered.

'Answer me, you drunk bastards, answer me,' growled

Publius Sextius, teeth clenched, but no light shone back over the Apennines, apart from the bluish flashes of lightning.

He left the signalling tower and went down to the room below, spreading the map that Nebula had given him out on the table. He placed a lamp on the map and ran his finger along the route to the point at which it intersected with the Via Cassia.

'Too far,' he murmured. 'Too far off my road. I would never make it in time. May fortune assist you, lads.'

He walked out to where his horse was waiting and rode off.

In truth they had received his signals up at the station, but could do nothing but remain inside the building because the storm was lashing the post with unnatural force. Clouds heavy with hail, edged in white, shot through with flashes and bolts of lightning, were unleashing a torrent of freezing rain on the signalling tower. Clumps of ice exploded upon impact with the stone paving slabs, shattering into thousands of pieces that glittered like diamonds in the sudden bursts of light. The whole building resounded with the incessant clatter, as if it were being targeted by a thousand catapults.

They could see the signals from the small splayed windows of the tower and the station master wondered what on earth could be happening in Rome, for such contradictory messages to be arriving in such quick succession. But the long wake of the civil wars had taught him not to ask too many questions and to follow orders as long as the accompanying code was exact. This new message was to annul instructions to intercept two *speculatores* and was to be put into effect immediately. The original message had been an order to kill, and the chief realized that he'd have to send a man out to stop it before it reached its destination. Hardly a man, in reality. The only person he could send was a boy – skinny, almost skeletal, with a perpetually bewildered expression. He had not the faintest hint of a beard, but a light downy fuzz like a chick's. That's why he was called Pullus.

He had neither father nor mother – or rather, he did, like anyone else, but no one knew who they were. He'd been raised by the army and was happy to do anything he could to make himself useful. He'd been a stable boy, baker, cook, dishwasher. But what he did really well was run. He could run for entire days and nights, light as a feather, animated by an energy that came out of nowhere. He couldn't run for as long as a horse, but when it came to getting around on steep, rocky terrain, Pullus was second to none, man or beast. He climbed like a goat, scaled mountain slopes like an antelope and leapt from one cliff to another with an agility and grace that contrasted greatly with his frail, ungainly appearance.

The station master handed him a ciphered document with his seal and ordered him never to stop until he succeeded in intercepting the original message. His chances were good, as he would be aided by the bad weather and by his unequalled familiarity with every nook and cranny of the territory, which would allow him to shorten and simplify each leg of the journey.

Pullus left at once, in the rain and hail, holding his shield over his head. The onslaught that was hammering away at his lid stopped before long and he was able to rid himself of the extra weight. Hiding the shield behind a bush, he ran on un-hindered at even a faster clip.

Pullus never hesitated or paused. He ran down rain-flooded paths, raising splashes of water that soaked him to the neck. He ran through the barren fields, under the leafless trees, through the sleepy villages. Dogs barked at the approach of his swift, light stride, taking him for the king of thieves, but they soon fell silent as his footfalls faded into the same nothingness they had materialized from.

He pondered his mission as he raced on, the young, tireless runner. Could he save both of them? If he had to choose, one would have to die so the other could be saved, but which one? He thought mostly about who the *speculatores* might actually be, and after discarding a few hypotheses, he was down to two names, the most probable. Two faces, two voices, two friends among the very few that he had. Including the dog at the station and the goat that he milked every morning.

Vibius and Rufus. He was willing to bet his goat on it. If he was right, there'd be no need to make a choice, because he knew how they moved. The flip of a coin decided who would go where and how. Knowing who they were made it easier to calculate. They had certainly left *Lux Fidelis* over five days ago, on two of which the weather had been bad. They would have begun along the high course of the Reno. The one heading east would have had it easy at first and then found things more difficult; the one who had taken the mountain route would have made slow progress at first and then been much quicker. Pullus decided to try to reach the former first, whichever of the two that was, and took off even more swiftly through fields and forests, following the briefest route possible thanks to his innate sense of direction in the dark, moving by instinct, like a blind man.

By morning he was on the street at a few miles from an important changing station. This was where he would wait. If his hunch proved to be right, one of the two would show up here before evening. He entered the *mansio* and handed over the coded message that annulled the first order. He gave instructions to refer the counter-order to all the remaining stations up to Rome. A messenger departed at once.

Having completed his mission, he would have been free to return to *Lux Insomnis*, but he wasn't ready for that. If by chance the two *speculatores* were his friends, he preferred to wait and be sure that his message had been delivered in time and that at least one of them had been saved.

It had stopped raining, but Pullus was soaked through and shivering with the cold. Every now and then he would run around in a circle to keep warm. He kept scanning the horizon, the rain-damp street that came from the north. A mule-drawn cart passed and its driver cast a curious glance at the odd bloke running around a milestone. A shepherd passed as well, with a flock of sheep, and then a peasant pushing a heifer forward along the loose earth on the left-hand side of the road. The traffic increased as the day wore on, but no one that fitted the description of either of his friends put in an appearance. It was late in the afternoon when he saw a horseman followed by another man on horseback as well, lagging behind him. The second seemed to be advancing with some difficulty.

The first stopped to let the second catch up and Pullus recognized him: Rufus!

'Rufus!' he yelled as loudly as he could. 'Rufus!'

The horseman jumped to the ground and ran up to him. '*Pulle*! I knew we'd run into you!' He hugged the boy, realizing he could count every rib and vertebra, scrawny as he was.

The second horseman rode up as well: Vibius. He showed signs of a violent altercation and his horse seemed exhausted. He must have kept up a gallop for a very long stretch indeed.

'Why are the two of you together?' asked Pullus.

'Yesterday morning,' replied Vibius, 'as I was approaching the fifth *mansio*, two armed men tried to stop me. I fought back but the two of them together were too much for me. I got away and raced off as fast as I could until I lost them. At that point, I decided to find Rufus. We always have a contingency plan and a second meeting point. But let me tell you, you look terrible, boy! Cover up or you'll catch your death!'

He took a dry blanket from his bag and tossed it over the boy's shoulders. Pullus regained a little colour, and a little voice.

'We received two messages up at the station. The first was to intercept two *speculatores* at any cost. I wondered whether it might be the two of you. But then we got a second message, last night, which began with the army code and cancelled the first order. We couldn't answer because of the bad weather, but I took off right away and didn't stop until I got here. A messenger set off with the counter-order this morning, so you shouldn't have any problems.'

'I always knew we could count on you,' said Rufus. 'But who do you think gave the counter-order?'

'I don't know. The commander didn't give me time to ask.' Then he added, 'What will you do now?'

Vibius turned to his comrade. 'You go on. I'll leave you my horse. He'll recover quickly if he's not carrying a rider. You can alternate the two and cover a greater distance.'

Rufus tied the second horse to the harness of his own as Vibius took the provisions satchel and the flask. They said goodbye.

'Who knows, maybe none of this will have been necessary,' said Vibius.

'That's what I'm hoping,' replied Rufus.

'Good luck, my friend.'

'Good luck to the two of you! Be careful.'

'No one will notice a couple of men on foot,' replied Pullus with a tired smile.

Rufus jumped on to his horse and took off, pulling along the riderless horse of his comrade. Meanwhile, Vibius and Pullus set off down another road.

Caupona Fabulli ad flumen Tiberim, pridie Id. Mart., hora nona

Fabullus's Inn at the Tiber River, 14 March, two p.m.

PUBLIUS SEXTIUS recognized the inn from a distance and he stopped. The weather had got better but was not stable and from the way the sky was looking he guessed it would worsen again that night. He had to get as close as possible to his destination so as not to lose another day. But would it make a difference, one day more or less? His long experience on the battlefields and roads of the empire had taught him that very often a mere hour gained or lost could indeed decide the outcome of a battle or even of a war. In any case, it was best to arrive early to whatever event destiny had prepared for you. If the event was favourable, nothing would change. If it was unfavourable – or catastrophic – there might be time to prevent it from happening, or at least limit the damage.

What he desired most keenly was to stretch out on a bed and relax limbs tormented by the strain of endless riding. Then to eat something and drink a cup of strong red wine. But he decided to lie down on the ground under the shelter of an ancient olive tree, to eat a piece of cheese and soften a chunk of dry bread with water. Better this than risk another unpleasant encounter after everything that had already happened to him.

He slept as he was used to sleeping in these circumstances, without ever drifting into unconsciousness and without losing the sense of time passing. He had left his horse free to graze, certain it would not wander off. When he felt a little stronger, he called the horse with a whistle and started off again.

He headed in the same direction for a long while, avoiding places where too many people were to be found, until he was forced to return to the Via Cassia so as to be sure to find a way to cross the water. One could always count on a bridge of stone, at least; they never collapsed.

The terrain was very rough and he couldn't stray too far from the road, although he mostly stayed on the loose-surfaced track at the side of the stone pavement. It was much faster that way and he felt that he was making up for lost time. Fortune seemed to be smiling on him now, he thought, as he managed to change his horse at a farm near Sutri without drawing attention to himself. The breeder accepted the difference in price between the horse Publius Sextius was leaving and the one he was buying, and he was free to set off once again at a fast pace. He was bound for the banks of the Tiber, beyond the Via Cassia, where he'd be able to board a ship at last.

He could feel that his mission was drawing to an end. He

would soon be able to relay his message and to report directly to Caesar.

But all at once, as the sun was about to sink behind the hills, a horseman appeared in the middle of the road, barring his way. In his hand he held a drawn sword.

At first he thought of turning around, but two things stopped him. One, he'd never done such a thing in his whole life; he'd never turned tail. And two, he was curious. Curious to see who dared to take on Publius Sextius alone. Traitor or foe, whichever he was, perhaps he deserved this confrontation.

He slowed his horse to a walk, drew his own sword and advanced down the middle of the road. The other man did the same. When he was about fifty feet away, Publius halted his horse and spoke first.

'Who are you? What do you want?'

'What do you care who I am when you are about to die?'

'Pure curiosity.'

His adversary had stopped as well. 'My name is Sergius Quintilianus. Does that tell you anything?'

His left hand pulled firmly at the bit, as his horse was snorting and stamping at the sight of the other stallion opposing him. The horseman rode forward until he was very close.

'Pharsalus,' he added. 'Do you remember now?'

Publius recognized him. 'Yes,' he replied, 'I do. I spared your life on the battlefield.'

'After having killed my son, who stood before you defending his wounded father.'

'You know what it's like in the heat of the battle, man. There's no time to make distinctions. When I realized what had happened, I held back. Let me go on my way now. We all have our own nightmares.'

'You should have killed me as well. You don't heal from a wound like that. By sparing my life you doubly humiliated me.'

'You could have killed yourself. You had a weapon.'

'I was about to do just that, Publius Sextius, but in the brief time I took to reflect, my hatred welled up over all else. I decided to live so I could find you and kill you. After such a long time, fortune has made the wait worth my while.'

He pointed westward at the sun, which was nearly touching the line of the hills. 'Before it drops below the horizon, your blood will have placated the *manes* of my dead boy.'

'I must reach Rome. If you try to prevent me, I'll have to kill you.'

'Then use that sword you hold in your hand!' shouted Sergius Quintilianus, urging his horse forward.

Publius had anticipated the attack and was not taken by surprise. He rushed forward himself and met his opponent's blows with unfaltering skill and strength. The blades crossed high and low with deafening crashes, sending sparks flying as one screeched along the edge of the other. Sergius lunged once, twice, three times, seeking his adversary's heart. Unable to reach it, he disengaged, turned around and charged forward again with savage determination. Publius dodged him at the last moment but managed to strike him at the waist with the cane he held in his left hand, something Sergius had not expected.

Sergius Quintilianus was showing signs of weakening. He pulled his horse up short, panting, hunched over in pain. He would have been easy prey just then. But the centurion stopped his horse and dealt him no blow. Sergius was quick to return to the attack. He feinted a slash to his opponent's groin, thrusting up at the last minute, towards his sternum. The blade missed Publius Sextius's chest by a hair's breadth, but tore into the still-gaping wound caused by his fall over the cliff.

Sextius felt a piercing, searing pain that reawakened the blind fury of the battlefield. His sword and cane struck out alternately with devastating force. Sergius Quintilianus fought back with all the rage and hate that burned in his blood. He attempted another assault, moving back to give himself the room to charge, but Publius Sextius could see the sword heading for his neck and he ducked, then swiftly spun around and drove his blade deep into the other man's side before he could ride away. Sergius Quintilianus tumbled to the ground and the horse ran off, out of control. Publius Sextius dismounted and drew close. His adversary was gasping for breath and pressing his hand against the wound, blood welling up between his fingers.

'Kill me this time,' he said. 'I'm a soldier like you are. Don't let me rot here in my own blood.'

Publius Sextius bent down. He was bleeding as well and breathing hard. 'You don't have to die,' he said. 'I'll send someone to get you. It's possible to live without hate, bitterness, spite. We have to rise above the past, or we're all dead . . .'

But his adversary had already decided differently. He jerked up, wielding a dagger in his left hand. But Publius had seen the intent in his eyes and he sank his sword into the other man's heart.

Sergius Quintilianus fell back, lifeless. He who had so often been defeated by his enemies and by destiny had been defeated once again and for ever this time. But his eyes shone for a moment with the look of a soul finally at peace.

The sun slipped below the mountains and was covered by the night.

Romae, in Domo Publica, pridie Id. Mart., hora undecima

Rome, the residence of the Pontifex Maximus, 14 March, four p.m.

THE COMMANDER of the third cohort of guards entered the Domus scowling and was immediately taken to Caesar.

'Nothing,' he said. 'There's no trace of him anywhere.'

Caesar gave a long sigh. 'It seems strange to me that he hasn't managed to get word to me, one way or another . . .'

'You said that as he was leaving last night he mentioned an encounter with a lady.'

'That's correct, tribune.'

'I wouldn't worry too much, then. You said that he'd gone off at other times and that you have always left him free to go where he pleased.'

'That's true, but I've become accustomed to having him always at my side. If I don't see him I feel . . .'

'I understand. But I'm sure he'll show up. Tomorrow, maybe, or the next day. Maybe it's precisely because he is always at your side that he felt the need for a bit of distraction, and if it's a pretty lady he's with, it's not difficult to imagine why he's lingering. If anything serious had happened, we'd have heard about it by now.'

'Yes, you're right, of course,' replied Caesar. 'But keep looking. I don't feel right about this. I need him here.'

'There's no need to ask, Caesar. We'll keep looking until we've found him.'

'Good. And keep me informed. Whether it's good news or bad, I want to know.'

The tribune took his leave and returned to his task. Caesar remained alone in his study to ponder Silius Salvidienus's strange behaviour. A thousand thoughts came to his mind. It just wasn't like him to disappear in that way without sending a message of any sort. His parting words the night before had made Caesar think that he'd be gone for a few hours, perhaps the night. No longer than that.

Might he have been surprised by the husband of this lady he was seeing in a compromising situation? That didn't seem like him. Besides, everyone knew who he was. Who would have dared hurt a hair of his head?

He turned his thoughts to Antony, who had sent him a message that he would come by presently to collect him and take him to dinner at Marcus Aemilius Lepidus's on the island. At least going out would distract him from his thoughts. The fact that he hadn't heard from Publius Sextius in days, and now the disappearance of Silius Salvidienus, troubled him. It was as if someone had decided to deprive him of his most trusted men, the only ones he knew he could count on.

When a servant came to announce that Mark Antony was waiting in the *atrium*, Caesar rose to his feet.

They walked side by side, proceeding at a good pace and chatting about this and that, and about the next day's senatorial session.

At a certain point, as they were walking down the Vicus Jugarius in the direction of the Temple of Portunus, Caesar said, 'We have a challenging session awaiting us tomorrow, so let's not make this a late evening. Lepidus's dinners are always lavish affairs. At least there are no mosquitoes at this time of year. That's something, anyway.'

Antony smiled. 'You just make a sign and I'll find an excuse for us to go,' he replied.

Mansio ad Tiberim, pridie Id. Mart., hora duodecima

The Tiber station, 14 March, five p.m.

CENTURION Publius Sextius reached the *mansio* after travelling east for about three miles. He entered through the main gate and slipped off his horse with some difficulty. He felt rather unsteady on his feet, but it lasted only a moment and then he rallied. As he was nearing Rome, the stations were more heavily guarded and staffed by army officers as well.

Publius approached a guard and showed him his *titulus*. 'Call your commander. I'm on an official mission and I have to take the ferry, but I don't have a penny to my name. And I need something to eat. I'm about to collapse.'

'Take a look in that cupboard there. The innkeeper is still sleeping off last night's drink. I don't think he'll be cooking anything soon.'

As Publius Sextius was rummaging among chunks of dry bread and some cheese rinds, the guard walked off to report to the officer in charge of the post.

'There's a centurion from the Twelfth in there who's in a big hurry and needs change for the ferry. Sounds like he's the one we're waiting for, doesn't it?'

'Yes, it's him for sure. Tell him I'll receive him. Have him come here.'

The guard found Publius Sextius nibbling at a piece of bread with some cheese, swallowing the hard crusts with a little water.

'The officer in charge will see you at once, centurion. Follow me.'

The man's expression, stance and tone of voice made a simple invitation sound more like an order, and Publius smelt a trap.

'The commander wants to see you right now,' repeated the guard. 'It's important.'

Publius was certain that there was someone in the other room ready to arrest him, if not kill him. He turned to the trough where the horses were feeding, spotted one with a bit, bridle and harness, jumped on to his back and spurred him on.

The guard shouted, 'Hey, what do you think you're doing?' Then, turning to his comrades, he cried, 'Close the gate, fast!'

Alerted by the shouting, the officer rushed to the door of the command post. He too started yelling: 'No! Don't let him go! Stop him!'

The two servants nearest the gate tried to close it, but it was evident they wouldn't be fast enough.

The officer called again, 'Wait, I have to talk to you!'

Publius Sextius didn't even hear him. The pounding of the horse's hoofs on the pavement was much louder than any voice could be.

An archer on the guard tower that loomed over the entry gate took the man galloping off down the road for a horse thief, so he swiftly nocked his arrow and took aim. When the commanding officer saw this, he shouted out, but the arrow was already in flight and it struck deep into Publius's shoulder. The centurion looked as though he would fall, but he somehow straightened himself and rode off.

The *mansio* officer cursed his over-eager subordinate. He had wounded one of Julius Caesar's men in person! He immediately sent out a squad to intercept him and bring him back so he could be treated. But Publius Sextius took advantage of the darkening sky and took off down a side path. He entered the forest and hid in a dense thicket of yews, brambles and pines, trying to keep his horse as still and silent as possible. He could hear his pursuers galloping by in the rain but the sound soon faded into the distance.

The pain was intense.

The arrow had torn clean through the muscle. He took out his dagger and sawed away at the shaft until he cut it through and could snap off the tip end. Then he drew his sword, laid the flat of his blade against the jagged shaft, clenched his teeth and, using a big stone, knocked against the blade until he had pushed the arrow shaft through his flesh. He pulled it free, bandaged his shoulder tightly with a piece of his cloak and grimly resumed his journey, trying to make his way towards the river.

He walked on cautiously, listening out for the sound of anyone following. He emerged into the open at last and found himself in a grassy clearing that ended at the riverbank. There was an inlet not far away, to his right. A rope ferry was rocking on the water, along with several other moored boats, one of which would be big enough to carry him and his horse. He approached the boatman.

'Friend,' he said, 'I need you to take me to Rome right away, but I don't have a penny to pay you with. I'm a centurion of the Twelfth and I swear to you, on my word, that upon our arrival you'll be paid double what you usually charge for a crossing. If I'm lying you can keep my horse. What do you say?'

The boatman unhooked the lantern from the head of the boat and held it up to his face. 'I say that it looks like you've been to Hades and back and that someone had better take care of you or you're a goner.'

'Take me to Rome, my friend, and you won't be sorry.'

'A centurion from the Twelfth, you say? I'd take you for nothing if I didn't have a family to support . . . Get in and let's go.'

Publius Sextius didn't wait to be asked twice. He walked his horse up the gangplank and settled him on board, securing his harness to the mast and the railing. The boatman pulled in the plank, loosened the moorings and set off, following the current. Publius Sextius staggered down to the hold, dead tired and feverish. He stretched out on a pile of fishing nets, pulled his cloak over his head and fell into a deep sleep.

The commanding officer at the *mansio* saw his men come back empty-handed and flew into a rage. 'Do you realize what you've done? That was one of Julius Caesar's most trusted men. Not only did you nearly kill him, you couldn't even catch up with him! A man who hasn't slept in days with an arrow in his shoulder! So now what do we do? Can you tell me what we do now?'

His men stood there mute and confused.

'It's dark out there, commander . . . It's not easy to find someone in the forest.'

'You idiots! He said he needed money for the ferry. That's where you should be looking for him. Find him, or otherwise we're all up to our necks in trouble. Do you understand that? If you see him, talk to him from a distance. Make sure he knows that there was a mistake, that we have an important message to give him. Now move, damn you!'

They sped off, bound for the riverbank, but they still found no trace of the man they were searching for. All they could do was return to the station and report their failure. Black clouds were masking the moon and thunder boomed over distant seas.

Romae, in insula Tiberis, pridie Id. Mart., prima vigilia

Rome, the Tiber Island, 14 March, first guard shift, seven p.m.

AT THE ISLAND Caesar was welcomed by eight drum beats and the honour guard presented arms. Lepidus's quartermaster received him and accompanied him to the room in which the other guests were waiting, chatting among themselves. Lepidus greeted Caesar with a cup of wine and took him to the dining room, which had been prepared for the thirty or so guests. Caesar was relieved that there weren't too many of them; that meant he should be able to get away early.

The dinner turned out to be quite pleasant. There was no eccentric or extravagant behaviour on the part of his fellow diners and the conversation actually strayed to interesting topics, philosophy, mainly. Did the gods exist and were they the same all over the world? Were they different aspects of a single god or distinct beings, expressing the various aspects of nature? Was there another world where good actions were rewarded and bad ones punished, as some held, or was the human mind destined to simply go out, like the light of a lantern – with no revelation, no glimpse of eternal truth, only a cruel descent into infinite darkness and silence?

Little by little, the conversation turned to an even more disturbing topic: death itself. Each of the guests found something light and even elegant to say about such a serious subject.

Lepidus turned to Caesar at a certain point and asked, 'What do you think would be the best way to die?'

Caesar glimpsed an expression in his eyes that he couldn't interpret. He turned to the other dinner guests, who were awaiting his answer in silence. Then he looked back at Lepidus and said, 'The best death? Rapid. And sudden.'

18

Viae Cassiae ad X lapidem ab Ocriculo, Idibus Martiis, tertia vigilia

The Via Cassia, ten miles from Ocriculum, 15 March, start of the third guard shift, midnight

THE VIA CASSIA, lashed by the storm, was quite deserted, but Rufus continued his mad gallop under the pouring rain. He was soaked through and his hair was plastered to his forehead. His horse's laboured breathing, the obsessive pounding of his hoofs on the ground, the lightning bolts themselves, all charged him with a mounting excitement and a flood of powerful energy. All of a sudden he felt the rhythm change and the animal's breath turned short and wheezing. He tugged at the reins and drew to a stop.

A flash of lightning illuminated the milestone that indicated the distance from Rome. Rufus jumped to the ground and stood there for a while under the angry sky, stroking the horse's steaming muzzle. He was frothing at the mouth and Rufus was moved at the thought of how much strain he had withstood. He decided to release him and to finish his journey with his other mount.

'Farewell, my friend. Good luck,' he said, then he mounted the second horse and dug in his heels, diving into the wall of water pouring down from on high.

The freed animal gave a loud whinny and kicked once at the sky, then stopped, head hung low in the middle of the storm.

Romae, in Domo Publica, Id. Mart., tertia vigilia

Rome, the residence of the Pontifex Maximus, 15 March,
third guard shift, one a.m.

CAESAR WAS returning home, accompanied by Antony. He
seemed despondent and withdrawn.

'Did something upset you, Caesar?' asked Antony.

'No, but I don't feel well. I'm tired and I haven't been
sleeping well. My mind is troubled and my responsibilities weigh
on me as never before. I worry I won't be able to fulfil the task
I've set for myself and fear my dignity may be at stake.'

'I've felt the same way at times. Since I've been consul I've
found myself in the situation you're describing more than once.
I've made mistakes that later I couldn't believe . . . Maybe we're
not meant for politics. Our place is on the battlefield. Once
you're back at the head of your legions you'll find strength and
faith in yourself. And so will I.'

'That may be,' replied Caesar. 'But the fact is this is how I'm
feeling now and I don't think things will get much better as
long as I'm here in Rome. And this prolonged absence of Silius
doesn't help matters.'

'I didn't know that Silius was absent. What happened?'

'Last night, after all of you had gone, he asked if he could
leave the house and he led me to believe he was seeing a lady
friend. A perfectly natural request. The problem is that he hasn't
come back and I don't know what to think.'

'Oh, he'll be back soon. I wouldn't worry about him, Caesar.
He's a man who can take care of himself. Anyway, we're here
for you. We're at your side and you know you can always count
on us. I'll see you in the Senate tomorrow.'

Caesar looked at him and for a moment the scene at the
Lupercalia festival flashed so vividly before his eyes that it
seemed real, and he thought he saw a crown in Antony's hands,

stretching towards his head. They'd already spoken about the matter, on the same day it happened. Caesar had been furious, but Antony merely apologized, claiming he hadn't realized what was going on.

Caesar said nothing and went in.

Antistius was waiting for him with his potion. Calpurnia had had a bath prepared for him, thinking it would relax him before he went to sleep.

Thunder rumbled over the city.

Calpurnia sat next to the tub, the lamp light casting a golden glow on her cheeks. She was tender at such moments, a gentle companion. Caesar touched her hand.

'Have you noticed that Antistius has a boy here with him tonight?' she asked.

'A boy? That's curious. Do you know who he is?'

'No. He said that he'd taken him in because his master was beating him.'

'If Antistius has allowed him to stay he must have good reason to do so. Surely he'll contact the man and tell him not to treat the boy so harshly.'

Calpurnia shrugged. 'Maybe. To me it seems strange. I think he should be interrogated.'

Caesar abruptly changed the topic. 'Do you know Spurinna the augur?'

His wife seemed surprised. 'I know who he is, but I've never spoken to him.'

Calpurnia bit her tongue. The man had a reputation for strangeness and was part of the circle of another woman, her rival. She would have preferred to end the discussion there, but she could tell that Caesar wanted to talk.

'They say he's a seer. I know people who have consulted him. Why do you ask?'

Caesar hesitated, holding back. 'The other day,' he said finally, 'I saw him.'

The scene reappeared sharp and clear before his eyes. It had to be his disease that was having this terrible effect on him, these sudden, violent apparitions from the past. The event filled his head and his own voice seemed to be coming from far away, as if another person was describing what he was seeing at that instant.

'He is really frightening-looking. Deep, dark circles around his eyes, that emaciated face with such hollow cheeks—'

Then he heard nothing. All he could see was Spurinna's lips, moving without making any sound.

He shook his head, as if to cast off the vision, but all at once he heard Calpurnia's voice, speaking in an anguished tone: 'The Ides of March are today.'

Caesar replied without emotion, 'Yes, they are.'

Neither of them said any more. The only sound to be heard was the water burbling from the marble mouth of a satyr into the bathtub.

Calpurnia broke the unbearable silence. 'Seers and oracles are always very ambiguous. It's their nature. That way, no matter what happens they can always say they foresaw it.'

'You're right,' said Caesar. 'But why the Ides of March?'

'Why not?' replied Calpurnia. 'He might have said any date at all.' But her voice betrayed her concern.

'I don't think so,' said Caesar. 'He was thinking of something specific. I could read it in his eyes. I can see things in men's eyes. I've had a lot of practice: the eyes of my soldiers, of my officers. Tension, resentment, fear, resignation. A commander has to know what's going on in his men's minds.'

Calpurnia tried to sustain her hypothesis. 'Maybe he saw illness, or the loss of a loved one, or . . .'

'Or the loss of everything,' concluded Caesar darkly.

Calpurnia's eyes filled with tears. 'You know I can't stand to hear you talk this way. I'm not strong enough. I've put up with a lot, you know I have, without ever losing my dignity. It hasn't been easy being the wife of Caesar. I've even accepted not having a child, not giving you an heir. But this I can't bear.'

She burst into tears.

Caesar got out of his bath and wrapped himself in a linen cloth. He brushed Calpurnia's hand with his fingers.

'Don't cry, please don't. We're both very tired and I feel alone. Silius hasn't come back. I haven't heard from Publius Sextius in days. Come now. Let's try to get some rest.'

A peal of thunder crashed over the Domus Publica and the floodgates of heaven opened. A downpour of rain mixed with hail rattled on the roof of the building and pelted over the eaves. Each antefix on the roof vomited a spray of dirty water on to the pavement below, while the flashes of lightning illuminated the leering satyr masks with a ghostly light.

Calpurnia reached over to her husband in their bed and curled her arm over his chest, rested her head on his shoulder. She held him thus until she could hear his breathing becoming deep and regular. Julius Caesar slept. Then Calpurnia abandoned herself to sleep as well, lulled by the sound of water on the roof.

Romae, in Domo Publica, Id. Mart., tertia vigilia

Rome, the residence of the Pontifex Maximus, 15 March,
third guard shift, two a.m.

THE MARBLE STATUE of Julius Caesar at the entrance to the Domus Publica shone under the beating rain. The right arm of the perpetual dictator was raised in an oratorical pose and the breastplate he wore, sculpted in grey marble, gleamed like real metal. A sudden flash lit up the statue, then a bolt of lightning struck it full on and exploded Caesar's likeness into a million pieces, which flew in every direction, then clattered down the stairway. On the pedestal only the legs remained, truncated below the knees, and the statue's feet, still strapped into their military sandals.

Jolted awake in the dead of night by the crash of thunder, Calpurnia sat up in bed and saw that the window shutters had become unhooked and were banging noisily against the outside wall. The statue flashed into her mind and she screamed. A shrill, prolonged shriek that Caesar stopped by pulling her close in bed.

'Calm down! It's only the window!'

'No!' cried Calpurnia. 'Your statue was struck by lightning – it has smashed to pieces! What a terrible omen . . .'

She got out of bed and ran towards the window, followed by Caesar, who had tried in vain to hold her back.

Caesar got there first and looked below. The statue was in its place.

'It was only a dream,' he said. 'Nothing has happened. The statue is intact.'

Calpurnia approached hesitantly, as if she were afraid to look. Caesar was right: the statue stood upright on its pedestal, glittering with rain at every flash of lightning.

'Go back to sleep now,' Caesar told her. 'Try to calm down.' But as he said those words he felt his own terror mounting and knew that an attack was coming on. Cold sweat beaded his forehead. He went to the ground floor on the excuse of needing a glass of water and made for Antistius's room to wake him, but then he paused.

The feeling had passed. Perhaps it had been a nightmare, like Calpurnia's.

Instead he went to his study, where the oil lamps hanging from the big bronze candelabrum still burned. His glance fell on the table and the scroll of his *Commentarii de bello Gallico*, open on a rest. He laid his hand on the scroll and ran his fingers along the text, unrolling it on one side and rolling it up on the other. As if by chance, he stopped at the chapter which described the great battle against the Nervii. The scene opened before his eyes, so intense and so physical that he could hear the shouts and smell the acrid stench of blood.

He was fighting on the front line. A gigantic Gaul struck him with his axe and snapped his shield in two. He tried to defend himself with his sword, but he felt himself slipping on the blood-slick ground. He fell to his knees and was about to be killed when Publius Sextius, wounded himself, lunged at the enemy and ran him through from front to back with his sword. Publius was holding out his hand, helping him to get to his feet.

'We'll see this through, commander!'

'We'll see this through, centurion!'

A voice rang out from behind him: 'Caesar? What are you doing here? I heard noises . . . Why don't you try to get some rest? Shall I prepare another potion for you?'

'Antistius . . . No, I just wanted a glass of water and I came in here to . . . put out the lights.'

'How are you feeling?'

'I thought I was about to have a seizure, but no . . . I feel fine.'

'Any news of Silius?'

'Unfortunately not.'

'Or Publius Sextius?'

'No. I thought I'd send a message to the changing station, in case they see him . . .'

'Silius has already taken care of that. He told me so himself. If he passes through, they'll stop him and let him know he should report to you at once.'

'Good . . . good.' Caesar nodded meditatively. 'Then I'll go back to bed.'

He put out the lamps, one after the other, murmuring to himself, 'Where are you? Where have you gone, Publius Sextius?'

Romae, in Domo Publica, Id. Mart., ad finem quartae vigiliae

Rome, the residence of the Pontifex Maximus, 15 March,
end of the fourth guard shift, before six a.m.

CAESAR WAS already up. Disturbed by Calpurnia's nightmare,
he hadn't slept more than a few hours. Antistius heard him, put
on a dressing gown and went into the kitchen to prepare a hot
potion of aromatic herbs. He took the drink to Caesar's study.
A trumpet sounded from the west, announcing the last watch.

'The guards are going off duty.'

'Yes. Today will be a long, tiring day. First you have a
session with the Senate, then a private meeting with your chiefs
of staff, followed by the ceremony on the Capitol in the late
afternoon. And you have an invitation to dinner as well . . .'

'Bring me a cloak,' said Caesar. 'I'm cold.'

'Don't you feel well?'

'I've got a chill and my head hurts.'

Antistius attempted to make light of this. 'Lepidus's wine
doesn't have a reputation for being the best.'

'I don't think it's the fault of the wine. I haven't been able
to sleep well for ages now.'

Antistius touched Caesar's forehead. 'You have a fever. Lie
down and try to relax. I'll fix you something that will help you
sweat it off.'

Caesar lay back on a couch and lifted a hand to his forehead.
He would have liked to ask for news of Silius or Publius Sextius,
but he knew there was no point.

19

Romae, in aedibus Ciceronis, Id. Mart., hora secunda

Rome, the home of Cicero, 15 March, seven a.m.

CICERO HAD already had breakfast and had dressed for the day, which was starting out chilly, in his woollen winter tunic. He was reading and taking notes on a waxed tablet. Another invention of Tiro's. Two layers of wax were spread, the one underneath being dark and the one on top a natural white colour. The stylus scratched away the top layer and what he had written appeared dark on the white surface, as if he were using ink on parchment.

The discreet knock at the door was surely him.

Cicero answered, 'Come in.'

Tiro entered, holding a letter. 'It's from Titus Pomponius,' he said. 'His servant brought it a few moments ago. It's urgent.'

Cicero opened it.

Ides of March

Titus Pomponius Atticus to his Marcus Tullius, hail!

Yesterday I was not well. A strong headache tormented me all day and prevented me from attending to my daily activities. The usual potion of malva and rosemary didn't help and my condition is no better today. Hence I'm afraid I won't be able to visit as I had planned and I'm sorry about that. The storm kept me up most of the night and I'm sure that if I went out the wind and damp would only worsen my headache. I would advise you to stay at home as well today and to take care, because a strong north wind is blowing. May you stay in good health.

Cicero folded the letter. 'Malva and Rosemary' was the code that indicated an encrypted message. The serious nature of the letter was evident in the extremely ordinary content, which contrasted with the urgency declared by the messenger.

So the time had come; today was the day chosen for the enactment of their plan. The Ides of March!

'I've had your litter prepared, master,' said Tiro. 'The session today is at Pompey's Curia.'

Cicero stood and placed the letter on the shelf behind him.

'I don't feel very well,' he said without turning. 'It's best I do not leave the house today.'

Romae, in Domo Publica, Id. Mart., hora secunda

Rome, the residence of the Pontifex Maximus, 15 March, seven a.m.

THE STORM of the night before had filled the city with debris: dry, broken branches, some with dead leaves still attached, were scattered everywhere, along with tiles which had fallen from the rooftops and been smashed to pieces and shutters torn from their hinges and carried off by the wind, now lying abandoned against the walls or on the pavements. Little clumps of unmelted hail remained in the corners of gardens and porticoes. The air was cold and crisp now.

The weather had cleared as the sun rose, so that now only a few ragged clouds skipped over the intense blue sky. In the distance, towards the east, the mountain tops were white with snow.

Caesar had eaten and was preparing to go out. He was standing in the middle of the *atrium*, wearing a pure-white, full-length tunic. He observed the servants as they helped him to finish dressing. One of them fastened a belt at his waist, another was lacing up a pair of elegant boots, while two more draped the purple-rimmed toga on his shoulders and around his left arm.

Calpurnia stood aside with a worried expression. As soon as the servants had left she continued what she had been saying before they arrived.

'I had terrible dreams, awful premonitions. First, there was your statue exploding into pieces, but then I dreamt that I was holding you in my arms. You were wounded, dying . . . Caesar, don't go, I beg of you. Don't leave the house.'

'Listen to me, Calpurnia. You are a learned, intelligent woman. You can't believe in dreams. They are nothing more than the consequences of our daytime anxieties, our fears or our desires. Dreams show us what we've already lived, not what we're going to experience. Do you know why you dreamt those things? Because you've been listening to too many rumours and because I myself had the foolish idea of telling you about Spurinna and his ranting. That's why.'

Calpurnia looked at him wide-eyed as the tears began to form. Her mind was full of nightmares and Caesar's words could not dissipate them.

'What do you think I should do, then? Send a messenger to tell the Senate I can't participate in the session that I myself convened because my wife has had a bad dream?'

'You're ill,' insisted Calpurnia. 'You have a temperature and you didn't sleep enough. You don't look well.'

'I won't hear of it. What would they think of me? I want them to approve the allocation of a sizeable amount of money for my veterans and I don't show up because I'm complaining of ill-health?'

Calpurnia was twisting her hands, then trying to dry the tears that were now coursing down her cheeks.

'What can I do to keep you from leaving this house? Do I have to remind you what you owe me? That I never said a word or changed my behaviour in any way when I knew, when everyone knew, that you were betraying me? Must I remind you that I have always cared for you with devotion, even when the Queen of Egypt bore your child, even now that – I'm certain of this – she continues to send you ardent messages of love?'

Caesar wheeled around to look at her, anger rising in his face, but Calpurnia did not stop her tirade.

'Go ahead. Curse me, swear at me, disparage me. But do one thing for me, one thing alone! Do not leave these sacred walls on such an ill-omened day. I've never asked you to do anything before and I never will again. I will let you go dry-eyed when the moment comes. Just do this one thing for your legitimate wife. I ask you for nothing else.'

She couldn't help but burst into tears.

Caesar stood watching her in silence, dumbfounded. In the end he gave in.

'So be it. I'll try to find a pretext that won't make me seem ridiculous. But now, please, leave me alone.'

Calpurnia left in tears and Caesar called his doctor.

'I'm here, Caesar,' Antistius replied, rushing in.

'Send a courier to the Senate. Have him announce that I won't be able to attend the session. You invent a plausible excuse.'

'You're not well, Caesar. Isn't that enough?'

'No. But it won't be a problem for you to think of something more serious.'

'Naturally. And I won't have to make anything up.'

'Go then. I can't have the senators waiting for me.'

Antistius threw a cloak over his shoulders and set off for the Campus Martius. As he was crossing the Forum he saw Cassius Longinus, Tillius Cimber, Publius Servilius Casca and a few others he did not know on the north side of the square.

They were walking purposefully, in groups. Cassius had a young lad with him, no doubt his son, who that day would publicly assume the *toga virilis*, formally becoming a man.

A cold northerly wind was blowing but the sky was quite clear and the sun was shining on the city. As they got closer to Pompey's Curia, where the session was scheduled to be held, Antistius saw the litters of several noble senators whom he had come to recognize. Others, the traditionalists, were briskly making their way on foot, while others still, wearied by age, were using a cane or leaning on their sons' arms.

He saw Licinius Celer, Aurelius Cotta, Publius Cornelius Dolabella, and recognized an elderly senator who was a friend of Cicero's, Popilius Lenate, then Caius Trebonius and others. He quickened his step so he would get to the Senate before everyone else did. When he arrived at his destination, he looked around and realized that nearly all the senators were present. He couldn't see Cicero anywhere, but he saw Decimus Brutus and, a little further on, Marcus Junius Brutus, who was looking surly.

He approached the table of the chancellor, the senator in charge of drawing up the minutes of the session, and communicated his message.

'Caesar won't be able to come today. He is indisposed and feverish and did not rest all night. I beg you to make his apologies to the assembly.'

He was still speaking when Decimus Brutus leaned close and asked, 'What has happened, Antistius?'

'Caesar is ill. He won't be joining the Senate this morning.'

'What? That's impossible.'

'No, it's true. He had a sleepless night and is running a temperature. He requests that the session be adjourned.'

Decimus Brutus turned to the chancellor and said, 'Make no announcement before I come back.'

Antistius was struck by how coldly Decimus Brutus had reacted to the news, not even asking what the problem was with his friend and commander. He decided to return to the Domus to see what would happen.

A murmur ran through the assembled senators, who were perhaps already consulting on the matters of the day. Now they had something else to talk about. Many of them looked worried. Some left the group they were with to join another, while others whispered into the ear of a companion, who nodded gravely or showed surprise, concern, uneasiness.

Antistius left through the large portico and hurried back, taking care to avoid Decimus Brutus, who preceded him by about ten paces. He entered the Domus just a few moments after Brutus. He could already hear his voice and Caesar's.

'Caesar, the Senate is waiting for you. What's wrong?'

Antistius entered just then. Caesar was lying on the couch, looking grim.

Antistius spoke up: 'Haven't I answered that one already? Can't you see he's ill?'

Decimus Brutus didn't even turn in his direction. He got closer to Caesar and peered at him, before announcing, 'He doesn't look so bad.'

'I'll decide how serious this is,' replied Antistius. 'He has even had an asthma attack,' he lied. 'He must rest.'

Decimus Brutus struggled to hold his temper against the insolent little doctor who dared to contradict him. He ignored him and turned to Caesar instead.

'You convened the Senate. Your absence will be interpreted as an insult, a lack of respect. In the name of the gods, don't do this. We have enough difficulties as it is.'

Calpurnia entered the room as well and said, 'He's ill. Go back and tell the Senate that Caesar is unable to preside over the session. Even a blind man could see how sick he is.'

'Not going at all would be much worse than making this small effort. He can go in his litter. All he has to do is put in an appearance: greet the Senate, express his respect, apologize for his poor state of health and return home. In an hour he'll be back. Not showing up would be a huge political mistake. It would fuel rumours, gossip, slander and nastiness of every type.'

Caesar sat up and turned to Calpurnia. 'Decimus is right. I'll open the session and then I'll leave. I'll just stay long enough to be seen and exchange a few words with some of the senators, then I'll come back here. We'll soon be having lunch together, Calpurnia, you'll see.'

He drew close and, in an affectionate tone, said, 'There's no need to worry. Trust me.'

Calpurnia looked back with dismay and resignation. She knew she'd lost. Her eyes filled with tears nonetheless. Antistius did not move. He stood at the threshold, watching as Caesar's litter went off, accompanied by Decimus Brutus, bound for the Theatre of Pompey.

Romae, in aedibus Bruti, Id. Mart, hora tertia

Rome, the home of Brutus, 15 March, eight a.m.

THE BOY slipped up to Artemidorus's quarters, after making sure that he was no longer under surveillance.

'Master,' he said, 'what are you doing here?'

'What are you doing here?' replied Artemidorus.

'Antistius sent me. I came to tell you that Caesar has left the Domus Publica. He had decided not to go, because his wife wanted him to stay, but then an important person – a man with the same name as your master – came to call.'

'Brutus?'

'Yes, that's right. He convinced him, forced him really, to go and meet with the Senate. They'll be arriving about now. Antistius is worried. He wants to know if you have any news for him.'

'Gods!' exclaimed Artemidorus. 'Quickly, take me to an un-guarded exit.'

As the boy went out into the hall, Artemidorus put a scroll into his pocket and rapidly wrote out a few words on another:

> *The day of the conspiracy is almost certainly today.*
> *I will provide a list of the conspirators later.*

He then followed the boy to one of the rear doors.

'Take this,' he said, pressing the note into his hand. 'Run as fast as you can and give it to Caesar before he gets to the Curia. I'll try as well to get to the entrance of the theatre before he does. One of us has to succeed. If you can't find Caesar, go to Antistius at the Domus and give the scroll to him. Give it to no one but him! Tell him that I'm going directly to the Senate to bring Caesar the same message.'

The boy cut down a side road and started running as swiftly as he could, eager to reach Caesar before he arrived at his destination. Artemidorus set off for the Curia by another route. The boy caught up with Caesar's entourage as they were about to enter the Campus Martius. He tried to get close, but there was an enormous crowd thronging around Caesar. Everyone wanted to talk to him; everyone had a petition they wanted him to hear. Although he tried as best he could to push his way through, the boy was shoved rudely out of the way and nearly trampled on. He tried again, but found himself blocked by an impenetrable wall of human bodies. Out of breath and disheart-ened, he ran back to the Domus. When he arrived he asked one of the servants where Antistius was, only to be told that he had left. The boy curled into a corner of the kitchen. 'I'll wait here until he comes back,' he said. 'I have to give him a personal message.'

Artemidorus was still pushing his way through the crowds that were milling around the streets and squares, not even sure why he'd taken on such a daunting task. Perhaps he'd realized that destiny had given him the chance to change the course of events and he couldn't miss the opportunity.

Romae, ad Pontem Sublicium, Id. Mart., hora tertia

Rome, the Sublicius Bridge, 15 March, eight a.m.

THE BOAT drew up at the dock on the far side of the bridge and the boatman descended below deck.

'We're here, commander!' he exclaimed. 'You've had a good rest.'

Publius Sextius opened his eyes and covered them at once with his hand to protect them from the glaring light of the sun. He slowly made his way to the deck as the boatman finished mooring the vessel and lowered the gangplank. The centurion untied the horse and led him carefully to dry land.

'Wait here,' he told the man. 'I'll send someone to pay you. I need the horse.'

'Don't worry,' replied the boatman. 'I can recognize a man of his word at first glance. I'll wait.'

Publius Sextius mounted his horse and headed towards Caesar's gardens.

Romae, in Curia Pompeii, Id. Mart., hora quarta

Rome, Pompey's Curia, 15 March, nine a.m.

CAESAR stepped down from the litter shortly before it arrived at the Senate, preferring to arrive on foot as he always had. But there was yet another crowd of people awaiting him at the entrance to the Curia. Antony, who had been standing on the stairway, spotted Caesar and went towards him to guide him in. Decimus Brutus never left his side, determined to protect him from the pressing throng. One man reached out to grab him by his tunic, a second tried to hand him an appeal, another a petition. Others merely wanted to touch him because he was everything they would have liked to be.

Caesar stopped suddenly in his tracks because he had spied, among the crowd, a face he knew well.

The soothsayer.

He called out, 'Spurinna!'

The man turned and the throng parted, somehow aware that nothing could come between their locked eyes.

'Spurinna,' said Caesar then with an ironic smile. 'Well? The Ides of March have come and nothing has happened.'

The seer stared at him intensely as if to say, 'Don't you understand?'

He spoke aloud. 'Yes, Caesar, but they are not yet gone.' Then he turned and disappeared among the crowd.

Artemidorus ran up at that moment, panting, feeling as if his heart would burst. He calculated the spot that Caesar would reach within a few steps and was there waiting for him, having pushed and shoved his way to the front of the mob. As soon as Caesar was close enough, he thrust the scroll into his hand, saying, 'Read this now!' He ran off as quickly as he could, frightened by his own boldness.

At this point Caesar was practically being carried along by the ebb and flow of the populace towards the entrance to the Curia. He tried several times to open the scroll, but the press of the petitioners prevented him from doing so. Some of the senators came forth and created a kind of corridor through which Caesar could calmly make his entrance. Antony had kept up with Caesar all this time and Decimus Brutus looked over and made eye contact with him. Caius Trebonius had just stepped up and he took Antony aside, apparently to tell him something important.

Caesar passed the two men, so closely they could have touched him, and entered.

Romae, in aedibus Bruti, Id. Mart., hora quarta

Rome, the home of Brutus, 15 March, nine a.m.

PORCIA WAS consumed by anxiety. She tortured herself by continuing to calculate the timing of the act that she knew must be commencing, counting the steps of her husband and the others as they took their places and readied themselves for what was to be. She couldn't bear the mounting agony of the wait. When one of the maids returned from the Forum, where she'd gone to do the shopping, Porcia demanded news of Brutus. Not receiving an answer that satisfied her in any way, she summoned a servant and ordered him to run to the Curia to see what was happening. When he didn't return, she sent another.

Time seemed to stand still; no, to stretch out endlessly. She was sure that the lack of news meant that the plan had come to nothing, the enterprise had failed, Brutus and his friends had been captured and would be subjected to public scorn and derision.

In fact, the servants had not returned because they hadn't even yet arrived.

The tension had become intolerable. She paced back and forth, up and down the *atrium*, twisting her hands. She felt terribly light-headed and her heart was racing. She thought she would go to her room, to stretch out on her bed for a moment, but her heartbeat had become so irregular that she couldn't catch her breath. Her lovely lips turned pale, her face became ashen, her legs folded beneath her and she collapsed to the floor.

Her maidservants ran over, screaming in fright. They did all they could to revive her, but nothing worked. Their shrieks alerted the neighbours, who found Porcia in that state, pale and still, showing no signs of life. The word spread that she had died and someone took it upon themselves to run to the Curia and tell Brutus what had happened.

Porcia regained consciousness soon after and was helped to her feet. But none of those present was aware that the news of her death was already travelling towards the Curia, where Brutus was ready, dagger in hand, to strike.

Romae, in hortis Caesaris, Id. Mart., hora quarta

Rome, Caesar's gardens, 15 March, nine a.m.

PUBLIUS SEXTIUS stopped his horse in front of the entrance to the villa and showed his *titulus* to the doorkeeper.

'Announce me to the Queen. I am centurion Publius Sextius. She's expecting me. Then send someone to pay the boatman waiting at the docks at the Sublicius Bridge.'

The doorkeeper had recognized him and motioned for him to follow. He led him inside the villa towards Cleopatra's apartment, where the Queen received him at once.

'You're wounded!' she said as he swayed on his feet before her, deathly pale. 'I'll have my doctors take care of you.'

'No,' replied Publius Sextius. 'Not now. There's no time. My lady, you must listen to me. I have completed the task you assigned me and I have good reason to believe that there is a conspiracy under way to murder Caesar. The fact that someone has been trying at every turn to prevent me from reaching the city – even by attempting to take my life – makes me think that the act is imminent. Please, allow me to go to him and warn him in person.'

Cleopatra seemed to hesitate. 'Are you certain?'

'No, my lady. I'm not certain, but I believe it's very probable. Where is he now? He needs me.'

'He's meeting with the Senate,' replied Cleopatra.

'Take every precaution you can for your own safety. I must go. I'll explain what I've learned later.'

'Wait,' said the Queen, but Publius Sextius had already gone. She called her child's tutor at once.

'Prepare the prince,' she ordered. 'And have my ship readied for departure. We must be ready to leave at any time.'

The tutor, a dark-skinned eunuch, set off immediately to do as he had been told.

Romae, in Curia Pompeii, Id. Mart., hora quinta

Rome, Pompey's Curia, 15 March, ten a.m.

MARCUS JUNIUS BRUTUS was trying to quell the pounding of his heart as he sought a glance of reassurance from Cassius. The other conspirators were in no better state. Every movement, any unexpected word, made them jump.

Publius Servilius Casca started when one of the senators took him by the arm, and felt even worse when the man grasped his hand and murmured, 'You know? Brutus has told me about your little secret . . .'

Casca felt that all was lost. He was on the verge of losing control and he began to stutter, 'No, that's not possible. He can't—'

But the man gave a little chuckle and went on, 'I know you're planning to stand for aedile. Not an easy affair, is it, to raise the kind of money you'll need for your electoral campaign. But Brutus told me how you're going to do it.'

Casca breathed a sigh of relief and regained sufficient control to send the senator on his way with some sharp words: 'I won't accept such insinuations. My behaviour has always been beyond reproach.'

Brutus had approached Cassius and was quietly conversing with him when Popilius Laenas, one of the oldest of the venerable assembly, came up to them with a cordial expression. He took them aside and said in a rather loud whisper, 'I wish you luck in completing your plan. But act quickly. Something of this sort won't stay a secret long.'

Having said this, he walked away quickly, leaving Brutus and Cassius stunned.

Did Popilius know? And, if he did, how many others? In the meantime, Caesar was already crossing the threshold and walking into the room. Popilius walked up to him as Brutus watched in horror.

'Look!' he said to Cassius. 'He's approaching Caesar . . . It's over, my friend. We must ready ourselves to die an honourable death. May our blood be on the head of the tyrant! Pass word on to the others.'

With that, he grasped the hilt of the dagger under his cloak. Cassius then spoke quietly to Pontius Aquila, who was standing nearby, and he turned to Rubrius Ruga and to Caius Casca.

Popilius Laenas began to chat with Caesar in a free and easy way, and the two men conversed for a while without paying attention to anyone else. No one could hear what they were saying.

The conspirators, who had all been alerted by word of mouth, seized their daggers and moved towards the companion with whom they'd exchanged the death oath.

But nothing happened.

Popilius had the air of requesting, rather than revealing, something. He kissed Caesar's hand and was answered with what seemed to be reassuring words.

Brutus cast a soothing look around the room and gave a nod as if to say that their panic had been unnecessary. They all calmed down.

Just then an out-of-breath messenger came asking for Brutus. He caught a glimpse of him, ran over and bent close, still panting, trying to control his emotions.

'Your wife, master, lady Porcia . . .'

'Speak up, what's wrong?'

'She's fallen ill, or perhaps . . .'

'What?' insisted Brutus, grabbing him by the tunic.

'Perhaps she's dead,' replied the servant, and took to his heels.

Brutus dropped his head in confusion and anguish. He knew he should go to Porcia, but he couldn't desert his friends at this moment. No matter how events unfolded, this would be a tragic day for him. Cassius laid a hand on his shoulder.

Caesar went then to his golden chair.

A brief exchange of glances between Cassius and Tillius Cimber was their cue. The plan could go ahead.

Cimber approached Caesar.

'What is it, Cimber?' he asked with a touch of impatience. 'It's not about recalling your brother from exile again, is it? You know what I think about that and I haven't changed my mind.'

'But Caesar,' began Cimber, 'I beg of you . . .' In saying this, he grasped Caesar's toga, which slipped off his shoulders.

This was the second and final signal. Casca stood behind Caesar and dealt the first blow.

Caesar bellowed out in pain and surprise.

The roar of the wounded lion thundered in the hall and outside of it.

He shouted, 'This is violence!' and before the dagger could strike him again he twisted around, stylus in fist, ready to plunge it into his assailant's arm. Casca's hand trembled and the second cut was only skin deep. But there was no escaping the daggers that surrounded Caesar now, everywhere he turned.

The entire Senate was afire with shouts and cries. Someone called out Cicero's name.

Absent.

Outside, Antony turned instinctively towards the door, but Caius Trebonius's hand nailed him to the wall.

'Don't. It's all over by now.'

Antony pulled away from him and fled.

Caius Trebonius took his own dagger in hand and entered.

Caesar was still trying to defend himself, but they were all upon him. He was struck by Pontius Aquila, then Cassius Longinus, Casca again and Cimber, Ruga and Trebonius himself . . .

Each of them wanted to sink his dagger into Caesar's flesh and they ended up hindering – even wounding – each other. Caesar was writhing about furiously, still roaring and spouting blood from his wounds. His garments had turned red and a vermilion pool was widening at his feet. With each move he made, the conspirators closed in further, slashing at him as at an animal caught in a trap. The more their victim became incapable of defending himself or even moving, the more their ferocity grew.

A last stab from Marcus Junius Brutus.

To the groin.

Caesar whispered something, looked him in the eye and gave up.

He pulled his toga over his head then, like a shroud, in a final attempt to save his dignity, and collapsed at the feet of Pompey's statue.

The conspirators raised their bloody daggers high, shouting, 'The tyrant is dead! You are free!'

But the senators were scrambling to get out, overturning their chairs and seeking a way to escape.

The few who remained, most of them part of the conspiracy, followed Cassius and Brutus through the city streets towards the Capitol, shouting to the odd frightened bystander, 'You're free! Romans, we have set you free!'

No one dared join them. Doors and window were bolted shut and shops were closed. Shock and panic spread.

An old beggar glanced up with rheumy eyes, his skin pink with scabies. It made no difference to him.

Romae, in Curia Pompeii, Id. Mart., hora sexta

Rome, Pompey's Curia, 15 March, eleven a.m.

PUBLIUS SEXTIUS rode up at a gallop and leapt to the ground in front of the Curia stair. A trickle of blood came from the hall.

His heart contracted in his chest.

He walked up the steps one by one, certain of what had already happened, overwhelmed by a sense of infinite despair.

All his efforts had been in vain.

He took in the scene at once: Caesar's disfigured body, his garments heavy with blood; the impassive expression of Pompey's statue.

Silence. A bloody silence.

From behind the pedestal appeared Antistius, who had recognized him. His eyes were full of terror and tears.

'Help me,' he said.

Three of the four litter-bearers entered then, carrying the folding stretcher that was always kept inside the litter, in keeping with Antistius's instructions. They set it on the floor.

Publius Sextius lifted the corpse by the shoulders and eased it on to the stretcher, as Antistius took the feet. They covered it as best they could with Caesar's blood-soaked toga.

The litter-bearers then raised the makeshift bier and walked towards the exit.

Publius Sextius unsheathed his sword and thrust it into the air. He stiffened in a final salute to his commander as he was taken out of the Senate hall. At that same moment Caesar's arm slipped from the stretcher and dangled in the air, swaying with every movement the bearers made. And that was the last image

impressed on the mind of Publius Sextius, known as 'the Cane':
the arm that had conquered the Celts and the Germans, the
Hispanics and the Pontians, the Africans and the Egyptians,
hanging limply from a lifeless body.

Viae Cassiae, ad VIII lapidem, Id. Mart., hora decima

The Via Cassia, eight miles from Rome, 15 March, three p.m.

RUFUS careered into the station at the eighth milestone, having
pushed his steed to the limit. His destination, finally, after such
a long struggle. He jumped to the ground and rushed past the
two sentries, displaying his *speculator* badge.

'Where is the commanding officer?' he asked as he raced
past.

'Inside,' replied one of the two.

Rufus entered and reported to the young decurion on duty.
'Message from the service. Top priority and maximum
urgency . . .'

The decurion rose to his feet.

'The message is: "The Eagle is in danger."'

The decurion regarded him darkly.

'The Eagle is dead,' he replied.

20

Romae, in insula Tiberis, Id. Mart, hora undecima

Rome, the Tiber Island, 15 March, four p.m.

LEPIDUS, barricaded inside army headquarters, was meeting with his chiefs of staff to decide on the best way to proceed when Mark Antony was announced.

Filthy and sweating, dressed in a ragged cloak and looking like a beggar, the only remaining Roman consul was brought before Lepidus.

'We know everything,' said Lepidus. 'I had hoped you would come here. Where have you been until now?'

'Around. I was hiding. I saw what happened afterwards. Those idiots thought that if they went around shouting, "Freedom!" the people would run to their sides and applaud them as tyrant-killers. Instead, they came close to being murdered themselves when they started ranting against Caesar. They had to turn tail and run back to the Capitol, and as far as I know they're still there, with the crowd outside calling for their blood. In any case, I've understood something important: they don't know what to do. They don't have a clue. None of them even started to think of what would happen afterwards. It's incredible but it's true.'

'Fine,' was Lepidus's response. 'The Ninth is camped just outside the city, in full combat order and in a state of alert. All it takes is one order from me and they'll descend on Rome. We'll rout them out one by one and—'

Antony raised his hand. 'We need none of that, Marcus Aemilius Lepidus. It would be a grave mistake to use the army. The people would be terrified and the Senate even more so. We'd find ourselves directly in a state of civil war, which is exactly what he strove to end once and for all. We'll negotiate.'

'Negotiate? Are you mad?'

'I'm perfectly lucid and I'm telling you it's the only sensible way to proceed. The people are completely disoriented and the Senate is panicking. The situation is on the verge of mayhem. We have to take the time to turn things around, in our favour, to fight the spread of terror, blood, despair. We must make Rome understand that Caesar's legacy is still alive and will be perpetuated. Sending the army into the city would signal that the institutions are no longer capable of governing the state, and that would be a very bad message indeed. I say that tomorrow you have dinner with Brutus and I with Cassius.'

Lepidus listened incredulously as Antony explained exactly what he would ask from Brutus and what he could concede. He continued in a resolute tone, 'We have to put them at ease, make them believe that we respect their ideals of liberty. More, that we share their ideals. Only when we are sure that the city is on our side will we go ahead with the counter-attack.'

Lepidus thought over Antony's words in silence as his officers – six military tribunes in full battledress – looked on. At last, he said, 'How am I to greet my guest, then? "Hail, Brutus, how did it go in the Senate this morning? Lively session, I hear. Do you want to wash your hands?"'

'This is no joke. If we make it known that the heads of the two opposing political factions are at dinner together, negotiating for the good of the people and the state, the situation will return to normal. Caesar's legislation will be passed by the Senate – his allocations for the veterans and all the rest. And when the moment comes, we will make our moves. Don't worry. Our time will come. You tell Brutus that we can share their point of view, at least in part, but that Caesar was our friend and that we have duties that must be performed, duties towards the army and the people. I'll take care of the rest. Tomorrow I'll be back and we can start planning our strategy.'

Lepidus nodded. 'You are the consul. Your authority stands. We'll do as you say, but if it were up to me—'

'Fine.' Antony cut his words short. 'Send a maniple of legionaries immediately to garrison the Domus Publica. No one who is not a member of the family will be allowed access to Caesar's body before the funeral. Now, give me some decent clothes and a mounted escort, of at least ten men.'

Lepidus had him accompanied to the officers' quarters and provided him with what he needed.

Antony left with his escort and headed for the other side of the Tiber, where Caesar's private villa was located.

He found it abandoned. Even the servants had fled. He crossed the *atrium*, then the peristyle and entered the servants' quarters. He stopped in front of an iron door locked from the outside. He took a key from the hook above the door and opened it. Silius Salvidienus stepped out, looking uncertain and suspicious.

'Caesar is dead,' said Antony. 'Nothing else matters any more.'

'What?' asked Silius incredulously, his eyes wide.

'He was murdered, this morning at Pompey's Curia. A plot hatched by Brutus and Cassius. They thought up a pretext to keep me outside. There was nothing I could do.'

Silius dropped his head without managing to say a word. His eyes filled with tears.

'I loved him too,' said Antony, 'regardless of what you may think. Those who killed him will pay, I guarantee that. Go to him now. The time has come to say farewell.'

Silius gave him a bewildered look, his eyes glistening, and made his way slowly towards the door.

Antony left a couple of men from his escort to guard the

villa and returned with the rest of the entourage to the other side of the Tiber, bound for home.

Romae, in Colle Capitolio, Id. Mart, hora duodecima

Rome, the Capitoline Hill, 15 March, five p.m.

CAIUS CASCA, on guard with several other armed men on the north side of the Capitol, could not believe his eyes when he saw the surviving consul, Mark Antony, walking up the Sacred Way with his sons, preceded by the flag of truce.

Casca ran back uphill to find his brother Publius.

'Antony is willing to negotiate. He's at the end of the street and he has his sons with him.'

'What's happening?' asked Brutus as he saw them speaking.

'Antony is willing to negotiate and has his sons with him,' repeated Caius Casca. 'Strange, wouldn't you say?'

'Go and see what he wants.'

The two brothers exited on to the north landing and began to make their way down, preceded by a flag of truce as well and by two armed men. They soon found themselves face to face with Antony. He was the first to speak.

'Each one of us imagined that we were right to do what we did, but we must acknowledge that Rome is now in a state of utter confusion. The city could easily slide back into civil war, a disaster that must be avoided at any cost. The full powers of the republic must be restored, but in order for this to happen, we all have to return to the Senate, call a regular session and discuss how these matters can be dealt with.

'I hereby propose that the Senate be convened to discuss the future order of the state. We have an entire legion camped outside the walls. We could use military force to decide the issue, but we prefer a rapid return to normality and an end to bloodshed. This very evening, I am expecting Cassius to join me for dinner at my house, and Brutus has been invited by Marcus Aemilius Lepidus. As a token and pledge of my good will, I will leave my sons with you.'

Publius turned to his brother. 'Go and report to the others. I'll wait for you here.'

Caius Casca nodded and returned to the top of the hill. Every now and then he turned to take in the two little groups halfway up the ramp who faced each other without moving, in total silence. The two boys sat on a little wall to the side and chatted with one another.

Cassius, Marcus and Decimus Brutus, Trebonius and the others accepted the conditions and Caius ran back down to where his brother was waiting to report that the proposal was acceptable. Antony bade his young sons farewell, embracing them and instructing them to behave well in his absence. He then mounted a horse and rode off.

Romae, in Domo Publica, Id. Mart., prima vigilia

Rome, the residence of the Pontifex Maximus, 15 March, first guard shift, seven p.m.

SILIUS ENTERED with a hesitant step, as if he were crossing into the other world. The door jambs were veiled in black. Cries and laments rose from inside. He walked through the *atrium* and reached the audience chamber, where Caesar was lying in state. Antistius had had his body washed and laid out, and his features had been composed by the undertakers to convey the solemnity of death.

Calpurnia, dressed in black, was weeping softly in a corner. Her eyes were swollen and her cheeks were pallid. She too had been defeated by a death that she had felt coming, that she had practically announced – unheeded, like Cassandra, by gods and men.

Antistius looked up but said nothing, because the stony expression on Silius's face allowed no words. He walked away and went to sit on a bench leaning against the wall, his head low. Every attempt to stop this from happening, he thought, had been thwarted. He turned over the small, bloodied parchment scroll he held in his hands. It was Artemidorus's warning, along with the complete list of the conspirators: the message that had never been opened, that had not saved Caesar's life, due to a cruel trick of fate. Had Caesar found an instant to read it, the destiny of the world would have changed.

On the bench beside Antistius was a tablet with his notes, along with another message, the one that Artemidorus's young friend had carried. In vain. On the tablet the doctor had diligently noted, as was his habit, a description of every wound. Caesar had suffered many of them, but the cuts that had penetrated his flesh, those that had drained him of the last drop of blood, were twenty-three in number.

Only one of which was mortal.

A wound to his heart.

Who had it been? Who had cleaved the heart of Caius Julius Caesar?

Thoughts flitted through his mind continuously. Elusive, indefinable, useless thoughts. 'If only I had realized . . . if only I had told . . .'

At least he was used to seeing Caesar dead, to considering him gone. But not Silius. Silius was seeing him for the first time in that state. The composure of his features lent a total absurdity to his silence and immobility. He, Silius Salvidienus, could neither accept nor believe that Caesar's arm might not rise, that his eye might not open, bright with that imperious expression. He could not believe that Caesar's face, so intact, so recognizable, could not suffice to call his limbs back to life.

In the end, he surrendered to the extreme, inescapable

violence of death, this death, and then the tears fell from his dull, dazed eyes and scalded his ashen face.

He remained on his feet, still and silent, for a long time in front of the bier, then, with a distressed expression, he stiffened into a military salute, his voice ringing metallic from behind clenched teeth: 'Front-line centurion Silius Salvidienus, second century, third maniple, Tenth Legion. Hail and farewell, commander!'

He turned then and walked out.

He wished he had a horse on which to gallop far away, to another world, over endless plains; to be carried off by the wind like a leaf dried up by the long winter. He stopped, instead, after a few steps, incapable of going on. He sat down on the Domus stair that opened up on to the Sacred Way. Not much later, he saw two people leaving the House of the Vestals on his right. People he knew well: Mark Antony and Calpurnius Piso, Caesar's father-in-law. What were they doing at this time of day, in such a situation, at the House of the Vestals?

They stood in front of the entrance and appeared to be waiting for someone. A servant soon came up with an ass-drawn cart holding a box. They set off again all together and he lost sight of them in the darkness.

Silius realized that Antistius had come out of the Domus as well and had witnessed the scene.

Antistius said, 'They went to get Caesar's will, without a doubt. The Vestalis Maxima herself is responsible for holding his will and testament, and can release it only to the executor, Piso.'

'What about Antony, then? What does Antony have to do with Caesar's will?'

Antistius reflected a few moments before answering. 'It's not inheriting his worldly goods he's interested in. It's his political inheritance. Brutus and Cassius were deceived. Caesar demonstrated that it is possible for a single man to rule the world. No one had ever wielded such unlimited power. Others will want what he had. Many will try to take his place. The republic, in any case, is dead.'

Romae, in aedibus M. Antonii, Id. Mart., secunda vigilia

Rome, the home of Mark Antony, 15 March, second guard shift, after nine p.m.

ANTONY RECEIVED Cassius as promised, while his sons were being held hostage on the Capitol. At the same moment Brutus was dining on the Tiber Island, at the headquarters of Marcus Aemilius Lepidus. Everything had been planned, down to the last detail.

Cassius, the victor, was even paler than usual. His gaunt face spoke of nothing but sleepless nights and dark thoughts.

The two men reclined on dining couches facing each other. Only two tables separated the *triclinia*, set with a simple meal: bread, eggs, cheese and beans. Antony had chosen a dense, blood-red wine and he mixed it personally in front of his guest, lingering deliberately at the task, taking care not to spill a single drop.

Antony began to speak: 'Caesar dared too greatly and was punished. I . . . understand the significance of your gesture. You did not mean to strike the friend, the benefactor, the man whose magnanimity spared your lives, but the tyrant, the man who broke the law, who reduced the republic to an insubstantial ghost. I understand you, then, and recognize that you are men of honour.'

Cassius gave a deep nod and a fleeting, enigmatic smile crossed his lips.

Antony continued, 'But I am incapable of separating the friend from the tyrant. I'm a simple man and you must try to understand me. For me, Caesar was first and foremost a friend.

Actually, now that he's dead, lying cold and white as marble on his bier, only a friend.'

'Each man is what he is,' replied Cassius coldly. 'Go on.'

'Tomorrow the Senate will meet at the Temple of Tellus. Pompey's Curia is still . . . a bit of a mess.'

'Go on,' insisted Cassius, fighting his irritation.

'Order must be restored. Everything must return to normal. I will propose an amnesty for all of you and you will be given governmental appointments in the provinces. If the Senate wishes to honour you they may do so. What do you say?'

'These seem like reasonable proposals,' replied Cassius.

'I want only one thing for myself.'

Cassius stared at him suspiciously.

'Allow me to celebrate his funeral. Allow me to bury him with honour. He made mistakes, it's true, but he expanded the dominion of the Roman people enormously. He extended the confines of Rome to the shores of the Ocean and he was the Pontifex Maximus. What's more . . . he loved Brutus. Now he's dead. Fine. His punishment was commensurate with his error. Let us deliver him to his final rest.'

Cassius bit his lower lip and remained silent for a considerable length of time. Antony gazed at him serenely with a questioning expression.

'It's not in my power to grant your request.'

'I know, but you can convince the others. I'm sure you'll succeed. I have done my duty and I've given proof of my good faith. Now you do your part. I won't ask for anything else.'

Cassius stood, nodded in leaving and walked out of the room. The food was still on the table. He hadn't touched a thing.

Portus Ostiae, Id. Mart., ad finem secundae vigiliae

The port of Ostia, 15 March, end of the second guard shift, midnight

ANTONY ARRIVED at the port accompanied by a couple of gladiators, who remained at a distance.

A plank was lowered from the ship and he began to walk up it. The still water in the basin gave off a putrid stench and made Antony feel nauseous. The ship was about to set sail, the Queen on board, about to make her escape. The whole world was breaking up.

Cleopatra suddenly emerged from the aft cabin.

Regal even in this situation, she stood haughty, garbed in a pleated, transparent linen gown, her forehead crossed by a fine gold-leaf diadem, her arms bare, her lips red, her eyes lengthened with shadow nearly all the way to her temples.

'Thank you for coming to bid me farewell,' she said. She spoke softly, but in the silence of the night her voice rang out clearly nonetheless.

They were alone. There was no one else to be seen on the deck. And yet the ship was ready to set sail.

'Where is he now?'

'At home,' replied Antony. 'Watched over by his friends.'

'Friends? Caesar had no friends.'

'We were taken by surprise. No one could have imagined it would happen that day, in that way.'

'But you were prudent, as I had asked.' The Queen's voice was calm but ironic, like that of any powerful person satisfied at having corrupted a man, or brought him to his knees. 'What will happen now?'

'They are in trouble already. They have no plan, no design. They are dreamers and fools. I am the surviving consul. I've convened the Senate for tomorrow and I've urged them all to show up. Before his ashes are placed in the urn, they'll be reduced to impotence. There will be a new Caesar, my queen.'

'When that happens, come to me, Antony, and you will have everything you've always desired.'

Light as a dream, Cleopatra turned and vanished.

Antony went back to the shore.

The ship pulled away from the harbour and was soon swallowed up by the night. All that could be seen, for a short time, was the sail being raised at the helm, fluttering in the dark air like a ghost.

21

THE ATMOSPHERE at the beginning of the session, which was presided over by Mark Antony, consul in office, was tense and decidedly cold. There were plenty of drawn faces and hostile looks. Caesar's supporters were still shaken, indignant and seething with resentment. The conspirators and their friends could not mask a certain arrogance. Cicero was among the first to take the floor. He had been absent the day of the plot but someone, in the confusion of the attack, had called out his name.

He was proud of having put down Catiline's conspiracy in the past, so although he was not technically one of these conspirators he didn't want to miss out on the opportunity of playing a leading role this time as well.

He spoke as the consummate orator he was. He who not so long ago had proposed that the senators shield Caesar with their very bodies should he be threatened, and had even had his proposal approved with a *senatus consultum*, was now singing the praises of those who had stabbed him to death with their daggers. He celebrated the courage of the tyrant-killers who had restored the liberty of the republic and the dignity of its highest assembly.

They had had every right to murder him; the despot had been justly punished according to the laws of the state. They should thus be immediately absolved of any criminal charges, since they had acted – at their own risk and peril – for the common good. He proposed, therefore, an amnesty for all those involved, and despite some disappointed grumbling, a vote was taken and this was approved.

But it was not enough to satisfy him. After exchanging a few words in an undertone with Cassius, Cicero said, 'This unhappy time, this dark age of the republic, must be forgotten as soon as possible. The body of the tyrant must be buried as soon as possible, in private and at night. Such a burial should be considered an act of piety towards a dead man and nothing more.'

A murmur of protest rippled around the room.

It was the turn of Caesar's supporters to speak now and Munatius Plancus took the floor.

'We shall allow posterity to judge whether what happened at Pompey's Curia was an act of justice. Those of us who were friends of Caesar are grieving and living a moment of bitter sorrow, but we are prepared to disregard these emotions so as not to fuel an endless round of hatred and revenge.

'I would like to draw attention to the courage and generosity of consul Mark Antony. Distressed and saddened as he is over the death of a friend he loved deeply, he has refrained from taking revenge and has even offered his own sons as hostages, so that all quarrels and conflicts may come to an end, so that no more Roman lives are taken, so that the menace of a disastrous new civil war may be averted. I move that he be paid public tribute and that he be invited to make his thoughts known, here and now, within these sacred walls.'

Plancus's proposal won a large majority of votes. Everyone was terrified at the prospect of a new civil war. Antony thus took the floor and began to speak.

'Conscript fathers! I thank you for having recognized my

efforts and my commitment. I myself voted in favour of your request that amnesty be granted to Brutus, Cassius, Trebonius and their companions. But I cannot accept that Caesar be buried at night and in secret, as if he were a criminal. He did make mistakes, although his hand was forced at times. He sought to solve Rome's problems through negotiations and dialogue on innumerable occasions and he did all he could to prevent Roman blood from being spilled.'

A burst of indignant protest rose from the group that supported Brutus, Cassius and Cicero, and Antony swiftly changed his tactics.

'If you don't want to believe this, how can you not believe in what the man accomplished? He expanded the borders of the Roman Empire all the way to the waves of the Ocean. He subjugated the Celts and Germans, and he dared to raise the Eagle on ground never before trodden by Roman feet: the remote land of Britannia. He defeated Pharnaces and added the kingdom of Pontus to our dominions. He approved a great number of laws to help and sustain the populace. He filled our coffers with immense treasures pillaged in the territories he conquered. He promulgated measures to defend the provinces but also to punish local governors who were incapable or corrupt. Do you believe that the tomb of the man who will be forever remembered for having carried out such glorious enterprises should be hidden in some obscure site, his funeral kept a secret?

'No, conscript fathers! You must grant me this. Allow me to celebrate his funeral and to read his will in public. His testament, at least, will help us to understand if we have acted justly or if the last honours I wish to attribute to him are undeserved.'

Upon hearing these words, Cicero hissed at Cassius, 'What did I tell you? If you allow him to celebrate Caesar's funeral and read his will, your undertaking will have been in vain! You must absolutely prevent him from doing so.'

But Brutus disagreed. As Antony continued with his fervent

plea, he replied, 'No, you're wrong, Marcus Tullius. Antony has always been a man of his word. He left his sons in our hands, he dispersed the hostile crowd that had formed on the Capitol and he voted in favour of our amnesty. We are men of honour and we must behave as such. Antony is brave and valiant. We must not turn him into our enemy. We shall convince him to join us, in order to restore the authority of the republic and the liberty of the Roman people. Trust me. If he were not well meaning, he would already have unleashed the legion camped outside the walls on us. It would have been easy for him to do away with us in no time. But he didn't. All he's asking for is a funeral and we have to allow it.'

Brutus was adamant, and if Brutus voted in favour of the motion, the others could not vote against it.

Cicero, outraged and impotent, snapped at Brutus, 'You will see! This will be no ordinary funeral!'

But the proposal was approved and the session ended.

Romae, a.d. XVII Kal. Apr.–a.d. XIV Kal. Apr.

Rome, 16–19 March

ANTONY HAD Caesar's body transported to the Campus Martius, where it lay on an ivory bier draped in purple and gold, near the tomb of his daughter Julia, born of his second wife, Cornelia. Behind the bier he had raised a shrine in gilded wood that perfectly reproduced the Temple of Venus Genetrix. Inside the shrine he hung the robes that Caesar had been wearing on the Ides of March, arranged so that the dagger slashes and the bloodstains were in plain view for all to see.

He had the shrine surrounded by a maniple of surly legionaries of the Ninth in full combat order, so that no one dared to approach.

The procession of people bringing gifts to be burned on his funeral pyre began. A long, long line of men and women of the Roman populace, of veterans, of friends. There were even some senators and knights. Some threw in precious objects, others a simple, early-spring flower. Many wept, others regarded in silence the lifeless body of the greatest Roman ever to have lived.

The body lay in state for three days and then the funeral began. The coffin was hoisted on to the shoulders of the magistrates in office and escorted by hundreds of legionaries in parade dress, led by officers wearing their red cloaks and crested helmets, to the sound of bugles and trumpets, and to the sombre, rhythmic beating of drums. Two soldiers at the fore held up the hanger with Caesar's bloody tunic as a kind of trophy. His wife, Calpurnia, trailed behind, weeping, helped along by her maidservants.

Tension mounted with every step, reaching a peak when a theatrical machine was drawn up alongside the coffin. Gears were set in motion and a likeness of Caesar's naked body was raised up high: a wax statue with twenty-three wounds reproduced in gory detail, dripping with a vermilion stain that looked just like blood. In this way, even those who had not seen his corpse could witness the devastation wreaked on Caesar's body.

In the Forum, in a clearing quite close to the Domus Publica, wood had been piled for the pyre. The bier was placed upon it. A leaden silence fell on the crowded square.

An actor recited the verses of a great poet:

> I spared their lives
> So they could kill me!

This gave rise to an explosion of indignant shouting that grew even louder when a crier read out the words of the *senatus consultum* in which the senators had sworn to defend Caesar with their own lives. Curses and insults rang from every corner of the square.

Then two centurions appeared, armed to the teeth: Publius Sextius, known as 'the Cane', and Silius Salvidienus. Each held a torch and took up position beside the pyre.

Antony mounted the Rostra and raised a hand to request silence from the already agitated crowd, which was seething with violent emotions that threatened to spill over at any moment.

Brutus, hidden at the far end of the square, behind the trees of the Iuturna fountain, could see even at this distance the grotesque wax image of Caesar stabbed. He could hear in his mind the words that Caesar had said to him with his last breath, as Brutus had thrust his dagger into Caesar's groin. 'Even you . . .'

He instantly understood what Cicero had meant to say at the session at the Temple of Tellus. All was lost. Nothing could stop a new, bloody civil war from breaking out.

All at once, in the sudden, mortal silence, Antony's voice rang out.

'Friends, Romans, countrymen! I have come to bury Caesar!'

Epilogue

Decius Scaurus and his companions, thwarted by the fury of Publius Sextius and deprived of the leadership of Mustela, had continued on their mission, but they never succeeded in closing in on the centurion, who had escaped down the parallel paths of the Apennines. Too late, however, for meeting his appointment with destiny.

Three days later they found the body of their commander, Sergius Quintilianus, at the side of the Via Cassia. His life had ended in combat.

They paid their last respects to him, simply, then burned his body on a pyre of woody vines. They threw their weapons into the fire as a final homage to his memory.

They brought his ashes back to the villa and buried them together with those of his son, at the foot of an old cypress, so they could rest, finally united, in the kingdom of shadows.

Author's Note

This novel tells a true story, a story which is at once familiar and shocking, by focusing on the date of its tragic conclusion: the Ides of March, that is, 15 March, 44 BC.

On that day, Julius Caesar, the greatest Roman, was assassinated.

Much has been said about his death and the enigmatic, difficult-to-explain events that accompanied it. The true motives of the conspirators have long been debated as well. The central question is the same one we ask ourselves today: is civil liberty preferable to security and the promise of peace?

Caesar's assassination was preceded by a long, bloody period of civil war, rife with political and institutional chaos. Caesar stepped forward as the person who could re-establish concord, peace, a stable government. But in exchange, the people of Rome would have to accept restrictions of their civil rights. The conspirators thus believed that they had good reason to kill Caesar. They considered the act virtuous in that it would serve to bring down a tyrant, or even nip a return to monarchy in the bud.

The fact is that Caesar's assassination was futile. The ruling classes of the time effectively deprived themselves of the best of their leaders without succeeding in offsetting a new era of ferocious civil wars and without stopping the ascent of a monocratic imperial system of power.

To take on such a complex historical moment in a novel may seem facile, and in part it certainly is.

But an emotional reading of such dramatic events allows us to step inside a crucial time in western history, to relive the passions

261

that animated the era and the conflicts that tore it apart, to meet the characters who were the leading players and the forces behind them. It allows us to imagine the nuances of their personalities, the contradicting urges that moved them.

History is, in fact, always moulded by passions such as hate, love, greed, frustration, disappointment, fanaticism, the desire for power and the thirst for revenge, rather than by rational reflection, philosophical meditation and ethical motivations.

This event, which inspired Shakespeare in one of his most masterful plays, reeks with violence and pathos at every turn. A maelstrom of contrasting forces come together to turn a murder into an epoch-making event. The Ides of March was one of those times when the river of history overflows its narrow banks, rushing, seething, carrying off any obstacle that lies in its way, like that chaotic force which the Greeks called αναγκη meaning 'necessity' or 'ineluctability' that nothing and no one can govern until it finds enough room to spread out freely again and flow forward in peace.

Caesar's story mirrors the greatness and the meanness of power and its illusions. In the end a man's body lies lifeless, pierced by twenty-three dagger wounds, while the 'victors' have already lost and even been condemned. And this because history follows a path that neglects to consider the plans, dreams and desires of men, a path that is, finally, in great part a mystery.

THE NARRATIVE STRUCTURE of this novel concentrates on the eight days preceding the Ides of March, associating figures who actually existed with fictional characters.

The race from Cisalpine Gaul to Rome of Publius Sextius and his pursuers visits places, including some stations and inns, which are actually mentioned in ancient itineraries (notably the *Tabula Peutingeriana*), a thirteenth-century copy of an ancient Roman map that showed all the military routes of the Empire, currently conserved at the Hofbibliothek of Vienna) along with others that are fictitious. The *cursus publicus*, that is, the Roman Empire's postal system, was established by Augustus. Thus in Caesar's time it did not yet exist, but we can assume that basic structures like the inns (*cauponae*), way stations (*mansiones*) and horse-changing stations (*mutationes*) were already in use.

As far as the correspondence between Cicero and Atticus is concerned, although a number of their letters have been preserved and published, the ones appearing here are wholly imaginary.

V.M.M.

Characters

ANTISTIUS – Caesar's doctor. The character is inspired by the doctor of the same name who, according to Suetonius (*Caesar* 82) autopsied the murdered dictator's body. He concluded that only one of all twenty-three stab wounds was fatal – the second.

ARTEMIDORUS of Cnidus – The character is inspired by a Greek teacher who actually existed. He frequented the home of Brutus and was familiar with some of the other conspirators. On the Ides of March he handed Caesar a scroll with a list of the conspirators, but Caesar, pressed by the throng, never opened it. He was holding it in his hand when he was murdered.

BAEBIUS CARBO – Fictional character. Legionary stationed at an inn and postal-exchange station. Naive and a bit presumptuous, he takes his responsibilities to legendary front-line centurion Publius Sextius, known as 'the Cane', so seriously that he is over-zealous in his reaction to Rufus and impedes him from carrying out his mission.

CAIUS CASSIUS LONGINUS – Conspirator. Representative of the most extremist elements of the conspiracy and organizer of the same, along with Brutus. Quaestor under Crassus in the East during the Parthian War (53 BC), he survived the rout of the Battle of Carrhae. He later became a supporter of Pompey but, like many others, reconciled with Caesar and was nominated *praetor peregrinus* (magistrate for foreign residents) in 44 BC. After the Ides, the Senate made him governor of Syria. In 42 BC, certain that his side had lost at Philippi, he committed suicide. He was a devotee of Epicurean philosophy.

CAIUS SERVILIUS CASCA – Conspirator. Brother of Publius, he killed himself after the battle of Philippi in 42 BC.

CAIUS TREBONIUS – Conspirator. A general and veteran of the Gallic War, he commanded the siege of Marseilles (Massilia) and was responsible for the repression of Pompey's supporters in Spain. The year before the conspiracy, at Narbonne (Narbo), he had informed Antony of the plot to murder Caesar, putting both men in an embarrassing position, since Antony apparently kept the plot secret. On the Ides of March it was he – according to Cicero and Plutarch – who chatted with Antony to prevent him from entering the Senate. The governor of Asia, he was killed at Smyrna on the orders of P. Cornelius Dolabella, proconsul of Syria and sympathizer of Mark Antony.

CALPURNIA – Caesar's wife, daughter of Lucius Calpurnius Piso Caesoninus. According to Plutarch (*Caesar* 63) she was an honourable, intelligent woman. The day before the Ides of March, she had a premonition of her husband's murder and tried in vain to stop Caesar from going to the Senate. She is said to have always remained faithful to his memory.

CANIDIUS – Fictional character. Brutus's head servant, distinguished by his blind obedience and his perfidious ransacking of Artemidorus's library.

CASSIUS PARMENSIS – Played a secondary role in the conspiracy. After fighting at Philippi in 42 BC at Brutus's side, he joined up first with Sextus Pompey and later with Antony. In 31 BC, after Actium, he fled to Athens where he was murdered by a hired killer probably working for Octavian. He was probably the last of the conspirators to die. A respected man of letters, he was mentioned by Horace in his Epistles (I, 4).

CLEOPATRA VII – The last queen of Egypt. Universally acknowledged to be a woman of great charm and beauty, she probably had considerable political skills as well. Daughter of Ptolemy XII Auletes, she was meant to govern Egypt with her younger brother and husband Ptolemy XIII, who was a minor at the time. Achillas, the royal prefect and army commander (responsible for Pompey's murder), was keen to safeguard his own claim to power and forced Cleopatra to flee to Alexandria, where she became Caesar's lover. She gave birth to Ptolemy Caesar, known as Caesarion ('little Caesar'), and had grand designs for the child's future. The queen's immense ambitions were frustrated by Caesar's assassination. She returned to Egypt and found a new, powerful protector in Antony, whom she married in 37 BC. The ill-fated naval battle against Octavian in 31 BC at Actium forced first Antony, and then Cleopatra, to commit suicide. She dramatically poisoned herself by inducing an asp to bite her.

DECIMUS JUNIUS BRUTUS ALBINUS – Conspirator. Caesar's trusted friend, listed among the heirs in his will. A general, he was one of Caesar's most valiant officers and distinguished himself in several campaigns, playing a key role in the siege of Marseilles (Massilia) as commander of the fleet. Praetor in 45 and 44 BC; Caesar had designated him consul in 42 BC. He was instrumental in the success of the conspiracy, personally persuading a reluctant Caesar to go to the Senate on the Ides of March. After the War of Modena (Mutina) the following year against Antony, his position became untenable and he tried to reach Brutus and Cassius in Macedonia, but was assassinated on his way there.

DECIUS SCAURUS – Fictional character. Veteran of the Tenth, he originally served under Caesar but later sided with Pompey's supporters and took a position with Sergius Quintilianus, for whom he attempted, unsuccessfully, to stop Publius Sextius.

LUCIUS CALPURNIUS PISO CAESONINUS – Caesar's father-in-law. A man of consular rank and a refined intellectual, he was responsible for having Caesar's will opened and read in Antony's home.

LUCIUS MUNATIUS PLANCUS – A consummate opportunist, Plancus managed to survive all the civil wars unscathed. Consul in 42 BC, the year in which he founded Lyon (Lugdunum), he was Caesar's friend. Immediately after the assassination he did everything he could to avert the risk of a new civil war. In the years that followed, he sided at times with Octavian, at times with Antony. It was he who proposed in the Senate in 27 BC that Octavian be awarded the title *Augustus*. He was also a man of letters.

LUCIUS PONTIUS AQUILA – Conspirator. Tribune of the plebs in 45 BC, he was the sole person who refused to stand at Caesar's passage while celebrating his triumph in Spain. Caesar was furious, and mocked him at length for this act. After the Ides, he became Decimus Brutus's second-in-command. In 43 BC he was killed during the siege of Modena (Mutina).

LUCIUS TILLIUS CIMBER – Conspirator. Initially one of Caesar's supporters, he was the propraetor for Bithynia and Pontus in 44 BC. He played an active role in the conspiracy. On the Ides of March, he signalled to the others by tugging at Caesar's toga with the excuse of asking that his brother be recalled from exile. He eventually joined up with Cassius at Philippi, where he died.

MARCUS AEMILIUS LEPIDUS – Born into an illustrious family, he was praetor in 49 BC and proposed the law which named Caesar dictator. He was consul in 46 BC and acted as *magister equitum* ('commander of the cavalry') in 45–44 BC. Caesar was invited to dinner at his home the night before the Ides of March, and when the question of what was the best death was raised (perhaps agreed upon beforehand by some of the guests) Caesar replied, in a curiously prophetic way, 'sudden and unexpected'. After the dictator's death, at Antony's suggestion, Lepidus dined with Brutus in an attempt to reach an agreement. After the War of Modena (Mutina) he sided with Antony, joining him and Octavian in the second triumvirate. Octavian's irresistible rise to power relegated Lepidus to the prestigious but secondary role of *Pontifex Maximus* (High Pontiff), the position he assumed after Caesar's death.

MARCUS ANTONIUS (Mark Antony) – Caesar's fellow consul in 44 BC. He was born on 14 January, 84 BC, and after a reckless youth he sided with Caesar, to whom he was related, participated in the Gallic War and joined Caesar after he had crossed the Rubicon. After the Battle of Munda in March 45 BC, he was approached by Caius Trebonius and asked to participate in a plot to take Caesar's life. He refused but never revealed this conversation. During the Lupercalia festival in February 44 BC, all sources agree that he offered Caesar the king's crown, which was refused. His behaviour remained ambiguous during the Ides of March conspiracy in 44 BC. It was Trebonius who delayed him outside the Senate while the conspirators were murdering Caesar, thus effectively saving Antony's life. Considered an impulsive, violent and dissolute man, he showed extraordinary political acumen in the hours following Caesar's death which allowed him to turn the situation around and force the conspirators into a defensive position within days. One year later (April 43 BC) he initiated the War of Modena (Mutina) against Decimus Brutus who was governing Cisalpine Gaul. Defeated, he joined Lepidus in Gaul and from there organized the summit with Octavian that led to the second triumvirate, the elimination of Cicero, his arch enemy, and ultimately the defeat of Brutus and Cassius at Philippi. Once Lepidus was out of the picture, he shared dominion of the empire with Octavian, keeping the East for himself and marrying Cleopatra, queen of Egypt. Defeated at the Battle of Actium, in Greece, in September 31 BC, he attempted in vain to hold off against Octavian at Alexandria and ended up committing suicide.

MARCUS JUNIUS BRUTUS – Conspirator. Born into the illustrious *jens Junia* he was thus a direct descendant of Lucius Junius Brutus, who had driven out the last king of Rome and founded the Republic nearly 500 years earlier. Servilia, his mother, was Caesar's mistress for many years, fostering the rumour that Brutus was Caesar's natural son. Brutus grew up under the influence of Marcus Porcius Cato Uticensis who embodied the most conservative current of

Roman society. Cato was his uncle and became his father-in-law when he married Cato's daughter Porcia. In keeping with his Stoic education, Brutus sided with Pompey at Pharsalus. Although he was later pardoned by Caesar and enjoyed a close personal relationship with him, he became the ideological hub of the conspiracy. After the Ides of March, he was forced to flee to the East. In 42 BC he fought at Philippi where he was defeated by the triumvirs and committed suicide. Plutarch says (*Brutus* 36) that before the battle he was visited by a frightful ghost who announced his defeat.

MARCUS TULLIUS CICERO – One of the great cultural figures of ancient Rome, famous as an orator. In 63 BC, as consul, he had a central role in the harsh repression of Catiline's conspiracy. Robbed of a primary role in politics by the first triumvirate, he supported Pompey, albeit without great conviction, and was later pardoned by Caesar. At the time of the plot against Caesar, he maintained an attitude of great prudence, perhaps convinced, at least in part, that the conspirators were unlikely to be capable of restoring the traditional Republican institutions. This fundamental indecisiveness came to the fore again later when he tried to obtain Octavian's protection. The open hostility he showed towards Antony (who he attacked violently in his *Philippics*) would ultimately prove fatal. In 43 BC he was killed by Antony's soldiers, and his head and hands were put on public display on the Rostra.

MARCUS TULLIUS TIRO – Cicero's secretary. Once a slave, he had been freed and became one of the orator's closest associates. A renowned man of letters himself, he published some of Cicero's works. He is also remembered for having invented a stenography system, the Tironian notes. He outlived the man who had once been his master, dying when he was nearly one hundred years old on a farm that he owned near Pozzuoli (Puteoli).

MUSTELA – Fictional character. Spy and hit-man for the forces opposing Caesar. An unattractive, dangerous individual, well fitting his nickname '*mustela*' or weasel. Fearless and determined, he races against time in a duel to the death with centurion Publius Sextius 'the Cane'.

NEBULA – Fictional character. Spy and informer. The most elusive figure in the novel, he can seemingly melt away into the countryside at will. A man of no face; only his voice identifies him. Yet he plays a central role, because the information he provides is wholly accurate and could save Caesar's life if it reaches Rome in time.

PETRONIUS – Played such a secondary role in the conspiracy (it is said that he provided the weapons) that he is remembered by historians by his *nomen* only. Perhaps killed at Ephesus by Antony in 41 BC.

POPILIUS LAENAS – Elderly senator, friend and confidant of Cicero as evidenced in the letters they exchanged. Both Plutarch and Appian report that on the Ides of March, he approached Brutus and Cassius, urging them to carry out their plan without wasting time, citing the risk that news of the plot might leak.

PORCIA – Wife of Marcus Junius Brutus and daughter of Marcus Porcius Cato Uticensis. Loyal to conservative Republican ideals, according to Plutarch (*Brutus* 13), she was a passionate, proud, intelligent woman who loved her husband. She was aware of the conspiracy.

PTOLEMY CAESAR – Son of Caesar and Cleopatra. When his mother returned to Egypt after Caesar's death, she had him recognized as king. After the Battle of Actium and the suicides of Antony and Cleopatra, he was murdered on Octavian's orders.

PTOLEMY XIII – Son of Ptolemy XII Auletes, he was nominally King of Egypt from 51 to 47 BC. Tradition has it that he was married to Cleopatra, his older sister, and was meant to rule with her. The members of Cleopatra's court, in particular Achillas, who commanded the Egyptian army and was behind Pompey's treacherous murder, plotted to bring about the 'Alexandrian War' in which Ptolemy took on Caesar and his newly acquired mistress, Cleopatra.

He drowned in the Nile during a battle, leaving Cleopatra the sole sovereign of Egypt.

PUBLIUS SERVILIUS CASCA – Conspirator. Present at the Lupercalia festival where he acted in an ambiguous way. He was the first to strike Caesar, near the neck. After being defeated at Philippi in 42 BC he committed suicide.

PUBLIUS SEXTIUS, known as 'THE CANE' (BACULUS) – Front-line centurion, fiercely loyal to Caesar. The character is freely inspired by a centurion who actually existed, Publius Sextius Baculus, whose endeavours were so heroic as to be mentioned three times by Caesar in his *De Bello Gallico*. The first passage (II, 25) recounts a severely wounded Baculus standing off against the Nervii tribe who are overwhelming the Twelfth Legion. In the second, Baculus, acting as the senior centurion of the entire legion, is taking part in a war council, consulting with Galba, the legate of the Twelfth, and with military tribune Volusenus, on how to repel an attack on the winter camp (III, 5). Finally (VI, 38), while recovering from his battle wounds, he is fighting off the enemy as they threaten to penetrate the camp. He demonstrates almost super-human will-power and loyalty to his general, willing to face any trial in order to save him, without a moment's hesitation.

PULLUS ('Chick') – Fictional character. He has no mother or father, but was brought up by the army and taught to carry out any number of tasks and services, although there is only one thing he is really good at: running. His inexhaustible energy allows him to run for entire days and nights, light as a feather, even on the roughest, most hostile terrain. This ability proves precious in saving the lives of Vibius and Rufus.

QUINTUS LIGARIUS – Conspirator. Famous for Cicero's eloquent defence of him in the *Pro Quinto Ligario* after he had been accused of treason. How he died is not known, as is true for several of the minor conspirators, but Suetonius (*Caesar* 89) claims that none of those who stabbed Caesar lived more than three years after that day, and that none of them died of natural causes.

RUBRIUS RUGA – Conspirator. A lesser figure in the conspiracy about whom not much is known. The circumstances of his death are also unknown.

RUFUS – Fictional character. A young man belonging to the reconnaissance corps (*speculatores*). All of his features give away his Celtic origins: he is tall, blond, his eyes are an iridescent blue. His heart is still torn between the legacy of his ancestors and his Roman soul. Together with his friend Vibius, he races against time to make sure that the precious information he has about the conspiracy makes it to Rome.

SERGIUS QUINTILIANUS – Fictional character. Supporter of Pompey and veteran of Pharsalus, where he lost his son. A man of principle, he is obsessed by the desire for revenge, and plays an important role in preventing the messengers from getting their information through to Rome. His fate is decided in a dramatic final encounter with centurion Publius Sextius.

SERVILIA – Half-sister of Marcio Porcius Cato Uticensis. A woman of extraordinary personality, she was Caesar's mistress for many years. Suetonius (*Caesar* 50) claims that Caesar loved her more than any other woman, to the extent that he gave her, on the occasion of his first consulship (59 BC), the gift of a pearl worth six million *sesturtii*, an enormous amount. From her first marriage with Marcus Brutus, Marcus Junius Brutus was born. She had three daughters with her second husband, Decimus Junius Silanus; as fate would have it, one married Marcus Aemilius Lepidus, another Cassius Longinus, one of the conspirators.

SILIUS SALVIDIENUS – Fictional character. Centurion of the Twelfth Legion, Caesar's adjutant. Utterly loyal to his commander, he is concerned that Caesar is putting himself at risk and circumspectly collects information with the help of Antistius, hoping to put Caesar on his guard. He begins to suspect Antony, and discovers by chance that he is seeing Cleopatra unbeknownst to Caesar. He and Publius Sextius render Caesar last honours during the funeral ceremony at the *Campus Martius*.

SURA – Fictional character. Taciturn mountain guide, he leads Sextius through the sinister Apennine forests one long, snowy night.

TITUS POMPONIUS ATTICUS – One of Cicero's closest friends, his nickname – 'Atticus' – referred to the twenty years he spent in Athens when Marius and Sulla were warring. He never entered politics; his dedication to his studies shielded him from the violence of the civil conflict that followed. His sympathies lay with Pompey's supporters and the Republicans, but only on a personal level. He thus survived the wars between the triumvirs and Caesar's assassins and the later clash between Antony and Octavian, unscathed. He was a great scholar, expert in a number of disciplines and keeper of one of the most important private libraries of Rome. He wrote a work celebrating his friend Cicero's consulate and his victory over Catiline. He kept up an intense correspondence with Cicero, which has been preserved. When he fell gravely ill in 32 BC, he refused to take any nourishment and starved himself to death at the age of seventy-eight.

TITUS SPURINNA – Etruscan augur. Suetonius remembers him as the man who warned Caesar against an imminent threat on the Ides of March. On the fatal day, mocked by Caesar who reminded him of his dire prophecy, Spurinna replied that the Ides of March had come but were not yet gone.

VIBIUS – Fictional character. A scout (*speculator*) like Rufus, he is the exact opposite of his friend, physically: his dark hair and black eyes are typical of his Apulian origins. The bond between Vibius and Rufus comes through in their easy camaraderie, seeming to incarnate the simplicity and courage of the Italic peoples.

'THE WRESTLER' – Fictional character. Works for Caesar's supporters. He knows the territory like the back of his hand, and his brutish appearance belies his skilfulness and intelligence. He struggles against all odds in the attempt to get the message that could save Caesar to Rome.

Places of Ancient Rome

(mid first century BC)

CAESAR'S VILLA BEYOND THE TIBER – It is not known exactly where the villa stood; presumably in the modern Trastevere district, in the direction of Ostia. The villa which housed Cleopatra was surrounded by extensive gardens, rich with trees, statues and water-lilied ponds. Antony's villa was probably not far away, perhaps on the Janiculum.

CAMPUS MARTIUS – An area north-west of the city and outside the metropolitan territory dedicated, since the age of the kings, to Mars, the god of war. The 'Field of Mars' was once used for growing crops, but became urbanized during the Republican and Imperial ages. Pompey had a theatre built there, along with the Curia where Julius Caesar was assassinated.

DOMUS PUBLICA – The residence of the Pontifex Maximus, located near the *Regia* (meaning 'royal residence') where the kings of Rome were said to have lived. Religious rites were celebrated at the *Regia* in Caesar's day.

FORUM – The forum was the political, economic and religious heart of the city, the place that preserved the most ancient memories of the origin of Rome. The area was once a marsh before it was drained by the Tarquinian kings who built the city's first sewer, the *Cloaca Maxima*, which made it possible to pave the area and transform it into a public meeting place. The forum was surrounded by the great basilicas, the Senate Curia, the *Regia*, the

House of the Vestals and the Rostra, the great tribune from which orators spoke.

HOUSE OF THE VESTALS – Residence of the vestal virgins and the Vestalis Maxima, the chief vestal, whose duty it was to ensure that the sacred fire burning in the circular Temple of Vesta never went out. It was located at the point where the Via Sacra joined the Via Nova, which led to the Palatine.

POMPEY'S CURIA – The temporary seat of the Senate. Pompey's Curia was one of the great monumental structures raised in the *Campus Martius*. It was part of an enormous complex built in 55 BC that included a temple, a theatre and a gigantic four-sided portico that ended with the Curia where the Senate held its session on the Ides of March, 44 BC. Opposite it were four Republican temples whose ruins are still visible today at the Largo di Torre Argentina square.

PONS FABRICIUS – Built in 62 BC, the oldest masonry bridge in Rome. It still connects the left bank of the Tiber with the Tiber Island.

PORT OF OSTIA – The settlement, which probably dates back to the fourth century BC, was founded, according to tradition, by none other than Ancus Marcius, the fourth king of Rome. It was the harbour and emporium of Rome. Ships arrived from all over the Mediterranean laden with goods that were redistributed on to smaller boats that sailed up the Tiber to the city, where they were then unloaded into the warehouses lining the riverbanks.

TEMPLE OF DIANA – There were several temples dedicated to Diana in Rome; the most famous stood on the Aventine hill. The one where Caesar and Servilia meet in the novel is found in the area of the Flaminius Circus in the *Campus Martius*.

TEMPLE OF JUPITER OPTIMUS MAXIMUS (Capitolinus) – Perhaps the most ancient sanctuary of Rome. Standing on the Capitoline hill, it was built during the age of the Tarquinian kings and dedicated to the Capitoline Triad (Jupiter, Juno and Minerva). It was burned down, restructured and restored numerous times. Its original architecture must have closely resembled an Etruscan temple, with a tufa podium, masonry walls and a wooden roof, decorated with multi-hued terracotta ornaments.

TEMPLE OF SATURN – The oldest temple in Rome, along with the Temple of Jupiter Capitolinus. Construction was begun during the age of the kings and the temple was inaugurated in the fifth century BC. Completely rebuilt by Munatius Plancus three years after Caesar's death.

TEMPLE OF VENUS GENETRIX – Built by Julius Caesar in his forum. The sanctuary was dedicated to the legendary forebear of the *gens Julia* who was believed to have descended from Julus, the son of Aeneas, who was the son of Venus herself. The propagandistic intent was evident: Caesar was the new father of his homeland, following in the steps of Aeneas.

TIBER ISLAND – An alluvial island in the Tiber river, connected to the mainland by two bridges, the Pons Fabricius and the Pons Cestius. In the first century BC, it was given the shape of a ship, achieving an extraordinary monumental and scenic effect. The Temple of Aesculapius, god of medicine, was built on the island in 290 BC, after a great plague broke out in Rome. The island may have been one of the reasons Rome was originally chosen as a settlement site, acting as a natural ford between the north and south banks of the Tiber, thus connecting the north and south of the Italian peninsula.

TULLIANUM PRISON (later Mamertine Prison) – The oldest prison in Rome, excavated in the south-eastern slopes of the Capitoline hill. Notable prisoners included Tiberius Gracchus, Lentulus and Cethegus – Catiline's fellow conspirators – Vercingetorix, Jugurtha the King of Numidia and, according to an early Christian tradition, the apostle Peter.

VIA SACRA – The street that went from the *Velia*, where the *rex sacrorum* lived, to the *Regia*. From here, it continued to the Temple of Saturn where it turned into the *Clivus Capitolinus*.

VICUS JUGARIUS – The street which began at the Tiber river and led to the Forum, passing between the Temple of Saturn and the Basilica Julia.